What o~~

"Sometimes I read four or five books a week. *The Wemberly Warehouse Files* novel is one of the better reads of the season. It kept me riveted as it moved fast through the story. Kevin Henry isn't sure who his friends are and whom he can trust. Bill W. Smith is a good story teller and this is his best yet."

—Jim Craft retired from furniture management of large furniture stores in Memphis, Tennessee

My best to an old friend, David Veara!

Bill W. Smith

the WEMBERLY
warehouse files

BILL W. SMITH
the
WEMBERLY
warehouse files

TATE PUBLISHING
AND ENTERPRISES, LLC

The Wemberly Warehouse Files
Copyright © 2014 by Bill W. Smith. All rights reserved.

No part of this publication may be reproduced, stored in a retrieval system or transmitted in any way by any means, electronic, mechanical, photocopy, recording or otherwise without the prior permission of the author except as provided by USA copyright law.

The opinions expressed by the author are not necessarily those of Tate Publishing, LLC.

Published by Tate Publishing & Enterprises, LLC
127 E. Trade Center Terrace | Mustang, Oklahoma 73064 USA
1.888.361.9473 | www.tatepublishing.com

Tate Publishing is committed to excellence in the publishing industry. The company reflects the philosophy established by the founders, based on Psalm 68:11,
"*The Lord gave the word and great was the company of those who published it.*"

Book design copyright © 2014 by Tate Publishing, LLC. All rights reserved.
Cover design by Jan Sunday Quilaquil
Interior design by Caypeeline Casas

Published in the United States of America

ISBN: 978-1-63122-086-9
Fiction / Mystery & Detective / General
14.02.24

DEDICATION

To my sister, Peggy Bigham, whose constant support and help has encouraged me to continue to write and to Charles Buckner, a long time real estate appraiser who mentored me in many ways through the early years and later years of my appraisal career.

CHAPTER 1

Prominent Real Estate Banker Found Dead, the newspaper headline stated. "Kennon Foster was found late Saturday morning, lying in his own blood, and an autopsy was ordered to determine if the cause of death was suicide or if it was murder," the article read.

Kevin Henry had some thoughts but was hesitant to voice them. He had started his private business in real estate appraisals a couple years ago. In the past, he had been a staff appraiser and loan officer involved in real estate loans. This business of financing real estate nowadays was handled a far cry differently from the principles of finance he had known.

The savings and loan industry had turned sour. The S&L, where he had worked, Central Arkansas Workers Savings and Loan Association, had gone belly-up. His job was gone. His old boss, James Carpenter, was in trouble. The Office of Thrift Supervision had put the fear into many in their organization. The Feds were still snooping around. Congress was breathing down the necks of top officials in the state. Kevin had slipped out, just in time—he hoped.

New federal laws were being changed to try to prevent the next fiasco. New real estate appraisal laws were now in effect in some states. All states were being required to stiffen their appraisal laws. Stricter appraisals were to be required, and more appraisers would be needed. All appraisers, old and new, would be required to have a license to do business and be required to pass minimum tests before getting the license. A certification by an appraiser organization had previously been the determining qualification of an appraiser and a measure of the appraiser's education and knowledge. It was hoped the new licensing laws would help clean up the real estate appraisal industry.

Kevin had worked in real estate sales for a couple years before his time at the S&L where he had achieved his appraising skills and lender knowledge. After his savings and loan association had started going under, his boss had suggested he start his personal real estate appraisal business. He had a degree in real estate finance and banking and knew real estate well. He had achieved a master's degree in the finance business and was considered a brilliant loan officer who was sometimes called upon for consulting work.

Kevin had hands-on experience in real estate finance after ten years as a loan officer and as a staff appraiser. He had worked as a salaried person, and loans were approved on the basis of the principles of good finance, but things were different now. Everyone in each part of the industry was paid a commission on his or her production. Every bank officer's income was based on profits, and of course, bonuses depended on the bottom line.

It was 1992, and Kevin was now self-employed, and if he didn't have assignments, there was no pay, but he felt okay with that because he didn't mind hustling. He had worked his way through college and appreciated the dollar. He and his wife, Marylyn, had worked hard, and they had saved for a home and were planning to start their family when she developed the brain tumor. They were thankful she wasn't pregnant yet. They fought the brain tumor for two years, and besides their insurance, they had spent everything they had saved, trying to stop the tumor but to no avail. She had suffered terribly, and he wished he could have had more to spend for her if it would have helped. He was still paying some of the debts.

Marylyn had loved to watch Kevin play baseball for the S&L's company team in the summer. He could maneuver his six foot two frame so easily at second base, and she was always his biggest cheerleader. The summer she died, he carried her emaciated body to the stands and sat her in the cushioned chair so she could watch. Oftentimes he would make a run into home plate and see her struggling to applaud and yell. He missed her. Two years had passed.

CHAPTER

2

Kennon Foster had come to Little Rock from Texas and had been hired to head the local mortgage branch office, New Home Mortgage Company, which was owned by New Bank of Pulaski. He was a wiry man, about five feet, eight inches tall with thinning hair. His energy level was always high, and he was very productive and very demanding of everyone he dealt with. His desk was filled with cases he was working on.

Kennon was busy, and he insisted his staff be busy. They had to generate revenue or leave. He pushed them hard at times, and stress permeated the office staff. He irritated some of the loan originators and made some fearful of him. He didn't hesitate to chew someone out in front of others in the office. They were successful by force, for a little while, at least. His office had risen to first place ranking among the bank's six branches, and he intended to keep it there.

Loan applications had to be approved. Credit checks had to be good. Appraisals had to be sufficient. He needed appraisers who could hit the numbers. That was a term used for making the value sufficient for the loan, which usually had to be as much as the sale. When real estate sales agents brought loan prospects to his office, they expected Kennon's people to make things work.

The appraisal had to come in with a high enough number to make the loan work.

If an appraiser couldn't hit the number, he or she would be removed from the approved list of appraisers—plain and simple! The appraised value was not just to be what the appraiser found it to be according to what was the approved method of finding the value but what the sale price was on the contract. It didn't matter if the buyers were paying too much for the property or if the borrowers were borrowing more than the property was worth, everyone wanted the appraisal report to show enough. That's what everyone wanted! And the Feds were coming down hard on the appraisers. "This entire financial downfall was the appraisers' fault," the finance people said. "They misled us."

Kevin Henry had received the assignment to appraise a nice property in west Little Rock and had applied himself to the task and brought it to the mortgage company promptly. He knew there would be some unhappy people, but he could not find the value to be sufficient for the purchase price. He handed the envelope, with the three copies of the report, to the processor. "I'm sorry, but the value is short," he told her. I have pushed the value as high as I could possibly justify. Maybe they can adjust the sale price."

"Uh-oh!" she said. "We'll have a problem now."

Jenny Lafferty was a top real estate agent with Bristol Real Estate Inc. She was a ten-million-dollar producer, the top producer in her company, and one of the leading producers in Pulaski County. She had an outstanding personality, and sales seemed to come easy to this petite blonde. On the beauty scale of 1–10, she was a 9. Eyes turned when she walked by. But she took no foolishness when her business was on the line. She could be tough as nails.

People in related industries seemed to jump when Jenny barked. You know? She brought lots of business to the table.

Jenny had walked into Kennon Foster's office with steam running out of her nostrils. The buyer's loan application was being denied. Jenny had been told the appraised value was less than the amount of the sale contract. And this sale…it was for 659,000 dollars. Jenny's company would receive half of the 6 percent commission. Jenny would receive 80 percent of that which would amount to $15,816. She had worked hard for that…she said.

Jenny's broker had called Kennon also. He was going to miss out on $3,954. He wanted that. He had to pay some bills. The employees could hear Jenny's screams coming from behind the closed doors. "I'll think twice before I bring you anymore business," she screamed. "You apparently don't know how to run a mortgage company." She was fuming mad.

Kennon was summoning all his diplomatic skills as he listened to Jenny. *Listen, listen,* he was reminding himself. *That damned appraiser,* he was thinking. *It's his fault.* When Jenny was finally worn out from her tirade and had left, he picked up the phone and called that new appraiser. "How dare you come in here with a low appraisal? I don't know how you got this assignment anyway," he yelled. "This is one of our top customers, and now you have messed her up and could cost us her business. Where did you learn to appraise anyway? You have cost this office $13,000 fees on this deal with the servicing business for the bank!" He slammed the phone down and went to his processor's office and chewed her out. He was mad! "That's the second appraiser in the past three months we've had to scratch off the list. Get back to old Jim Hammons. Maybe he's learned his lesson and won't fail to give us our numbers now."

"What a mess. No one knows how to appraise anymore," Kennon grumbled as he sat down at his desk again and took the call from Frank Harley, the president of New Bank of Pulaski.

"Kennon, what's going on? I just got a call from Jenny Lafferty's broker. I want you to call that appraiser and talk some sense into him. Bristol Real Estate brings a lot of business to this bank." He was really up in the air. "I want that loan made. Real estate values will probably be going up sufficiently to make up for any over evaluation. We've got to have an adequate appraisal. You know we can't order another one because we can't afford to have two appraisals in the file for the same property, so get that appraiser to raise his figures," instructed the president of the bank that owned the mortgage company.

Frank Harley had been a star football player at the university and was a large man with broad shoulders. He was popular in the state and had lots of connections. He was still the chief executive officer and was building his bank with a large number of depositors. He hoped to attract a buyer for his bank someday. He had been a cigar-smoking executive until smoking in public buildings was becoming more unpopular. He had suddenly and totally quit smoking, and it was still difficult for him to hold his temper. Besides, he was accustomed to having people respond favorably to his orders.

Joe Munchero, the listing broker of the subject property, had called Jenny, yelling at her because the sale was now falling through. Joe was the broker-owner of Arkansas River Valley Real Estate and a good salesman also. He had listed the subject property. Jenny had been forced to tell Joe that her buyer didn't want that house now since it did not appraise for what he had offered to pay for it.

Somehow the buyer had found out about the low appraisal. In most cases, they tried to keep that quiet until they tried to get the figures up satisfactorily. Joe's seller was mad at him because the sale had fallen through. "I had thought we had this place sold," the seller had said. "You know we went ahead and bought that larger house contingent on our's selling. Now we'll have to start all over again. Some agent," the seller had muttered to Joe in disgust.

Joe was losing big money. His commission on Jenny's sale would be $19,770. All of it was his. Plus, he had sold his seller a newly constructed house in west Little Rock in a new subdivision. That sale would have paid 5 percent commission. Nine hundred thousand dollars was the price. The commission was $45,000. Altogether, he was losing $64,770. He was livid. He and his wife were planning a trip to Greece along with his financial broker. Talk about messed up plans!

"You let us down, Jenny," Joe said in parting. "I thought you could handle things, you of all people," he dug her a little in parting.

"That darned appraiser," Jenny said as she hung up the phone. *What does he know? Kennon Foster should have known better than to assign one of my sales to an untested appraiser*, Jenny thought. "The buyer was willing and able to pay that price for it," she had told the appraiser. She had called Kevin and tried her best to coerce him to change his appraisal value. She even threatened him some. "I'll put out the word that you are too conservative, and you know that'll kill your business," she threatened. She had effectively done that before with other appraisers. At that time, Realtors could request certain appraisers or request that certain appraisers be avoided.

"But the comparable sales history won't support that price. The cost of land and construction, less depreciation, won't support that price," Kevin Henry had explained. "I have followed the approved approach to value and pushed the number as high as I could find support. That's the top of the range," Kevin had explained. "Yes, the old rule of a real estate value being: what a willing and able buyer would pay is no longer the rule. Now the rule in part is what a willing, able, and *knowledgeable* buyer, *not under duress*, would pay. The *cost approach* will not support a higher value and the *comparable sales* will not support any more. I cannot find support for a higher value. I have given the value at the top of the range, and I do not want to provide a phony appraisal report. These buyers were coming to Little Rock from California, and I understand why it looked like a good deal to them. California prices are far above ours in Arkansas," he explained.

"I don't care what your screwed up methods are. I know what the value of that property is, and you are too ignorant or stubborn to know how to handle this," Jenny had declared.

Joe Munchero had also called his friend, Frank Harley, the CEO. "Frank, you know I have been a depositor of yours since you came to that bank. If you don't do something about this sale that Jenny Lafferty and I have together, I'll consider another bank in the future. I can't tolerate this kind of treatment," Joe had told his friend, the banker.

Kennon Foster had tried one more time. He called Kevin and told him he should be able to raise the value on that appraisal if he wanted to. He tried persuasion. Kevin kept telling him that there was no way he could find proper support for the higher numbers they wanted. "I would just have to flat out produce a lie," Kevin had insisted. "I don't want to do that. I hope you can respect that."

"Well, you handle your business the way you want, Kevin…I'll handle mine the way I want," Kennon Foster said in parting.

Kevin knew what he meant. "I have lost his business," he told himself.

Everyone was mad. They were really mad!

CHAPTER 3

Kevin sat at his breakfast table reading the follow-up article in the newspaper. "Police have not yet revealed the cause of death for Kennon Foster. It is an ongoing investigation," the spokesman had said. *That's curious*, he was thinking. *There is more to this than meets the eye.* Kennon had been in Little Rock only a couple years or so. How many enemies would he have developed that soon, but if it were not a health issue, then it would have been suicide or murder. It has been over a month now."

Kevin thought about the banking industry, and the savings and loan associations. There is a lot going on now in that business. Could his death have anything to do with clients? Had he developed enemies this soon? He was known for the pressure on his employees. Could one hate him enough? If police were thinking it is suicide for sure, they would probably say so. Are they thinking there is foul play? If so, Kevin reasoned, who would be behind it?

He knew the savings and loan crisis was major. It had threatened to throw the country into a major recession. Texas was already in a recession because of the oil industry and the S&L crisis. A major S&L was known to be involved in land flips and other criminal activities. There were major schemes discovered. As bad land investments were auctioned off, real estate prices collapsed, office vacancy in Texas rose 30 percent, according to some records. The world oil glut had hit in the early eighties, and crude oil prices fell over 50 percent, which further exacerbated the recession. In Tulsa, Oklahoma, oil exploration almost ceased, a major engineering and geology firm terminated 250 high-paying jobs—geologists and engineers. Real estate values had dropped rapidly. Some people were desperate.

The Federal Savings and Loan Insurance Corporation (FSLIC) was bankrupted—to the cost of $20 billion. Five US senators, known as the Keating Five, were investigated by the Senate Ethics Committee for improper conduct. They had accepted major contributions from Charles Keating, head of Lincoln Savings and Loan Association. It was rumored the senators had put pressure on the Federal Home Loan Banking Board, who was investigating possible criminal activities at Lincoln.

The Federal Home Loan Banking Board regulatory staff was reduced, thanks to budget cuts. By 1989, congress and the president knew they needed to bail out the industry. They agreed on a bailout measure known as FIRREA and provided $50 billion to close failed banks and stop further losses.

It was rumored Shelton McKinley and Franklin S&L of Texarkana were knee-deep in questionable activities. Kevin remembered Kennon Foster had been an employee at Franklin, but that had been two years ago.

There was nothing in the newspaper yet about his previous connection to other places. Maybe it was irrelevant.

—☙—

Tuesday's paper had news update about the Kennon Foster death: "The coroner's report is not yet complete, and authorities are still investigating the death. Kennon Foster, a newcomer who had gained prominence quickly, the paper said, was a rising star in the Little Rock mortgage industry and was slated for a promotion. He was expected to move into the New Bank of Pulaski soon.

"His experience in major financing was needed," Frank Harley had stated. "We will definitely miss his knowledge and experience in the finance industry."

CHAPTER 4

Cheryl Inmon called from New Bank of Pulaski. New Bank of Pulaski was not new anymore because it was chartered in 1926 and had been fairly prominent for many years. Cheryl said Mr. Frank Harley, president of the bank, had asked her to have him come by to look at a commercial appraisal assignment.

Cheryl had been Mr. Harley's personal secretary for only six months, but she was known for her quick understanding of the task at hand. She was a single parent with two children, ages six and eight. Her husband had died shortly after the youngest was born. In her early thirties, Cheryl was very professional and was the epitome of a sharp and efficient executive secretary. In addition to that, she was very attractive and added a certain amount of prestige to Mr. Harley's office. He was now relying on her more and more in his personal cases. "Come by at two o'clock, and we'll review the case," she said.

Kevin had never done any appraisal work for New Bank of Pulaski and was glad to be considered, especially, in view of the recent blowup of the appraisal for New Home Mortgage Company. "Sure," Kevin said quickly. He wasn't sure he wanted the commercial assignment but thought he may as well take a look at it.

Precisely at two o'clock, he walked into the offices of Mr. Frank Harley's bank and handed his business card to the receptionist. "I am here to see Ms. Inmon," he said.

"Yes, Mr. Henry, she is expecting you. Would you like some coffee or something else to drink?" She spoke in a courteous and efficient manner.

Professional, Kevin thought. He had heard that was par for that office.

Kevin was shown in and was greeted warmly with an outstretched hand of Cheryl Inmon. The office was immaculately decorated. "Please have a seat," she said. I have the papers ready to review." Kevin couldn't help but observe her posture and smell the slight aroma of perfume. She wore a blouse with a skirt that complimented her slim, shapely body.

They exchanged some courtesies, and she asked him how long he had been doing real estate appraisals. Kevin handed her his resumé, and she looked over it carefully. "Very interesting," she stated. "I see you have a background in the S&L banking. Mr. Harley told me he thought you were familiar somewhat with banking.

"I'll get right to the task at hand. We have a lien on this warehouse property, and the owner needs some refinancing and wants to take some cash out. We will need a generous appraised value and will need this report within the next two weeks. Can you get it back to us by then?" Cheryl said and showed Kevin the picture of the large Wemberly Warehouse Property with sixty acres of land on Riverside Drive Extended. "The owner needs cash that will bring the lien up to $13,250,000." She sat back and watched his expression. His face showed nothing. She was thinking that he had an interesting face; in fact, she thought he was rather handsome and was glad Mr. Harley had requested this appraiser. She noticed there was no ring on his finger.

Mr. Harley walked into the office, just then, and Cheryl introduced them. "Welcome to New Bank of Pulaski, Mr. Henry. We are looking for a good appraiser to handle some of our work. I hope you can find a good value in the warehouse property. Our client needs a generous value."

A little chill went over Kevin, and he hesitated a moment. "Mr. Harley, I'll do my best to find the highest value for the highest and best use of the property. I follow all the rules of the principles of appraisal practice. The number will be whatever it works out to be," he said.

Mr. Harley was a tall man with moderately graying hair and stood about two inches above Kevin. His eyes squinted a little as he looked closely at the appraiser. Kevin thought he could see a little disdain in his expression. *He probably thinks I'm a little independent for a newcomer to the business*, Kevin thought.

"We'll have more work for a good man," Harley advised.

"Mr. Harley," Kevin said, "I have room for more work. I try to do a good job, and I try to be efficient. Let me assure you the report will be professional, carefully done, and one that will stand up under all scrutiny," Kevin said and looked Harley straight in the eye.

"Yes, yes," Harley said. "That is what we would expect. We are looking to add at least one more appraiser to our panel. Ms. Inmon will be in touch with you." He held his hand out toward Kevin and gave a quick handshake and walked out.

Cheryl Inmon had an expression of surprise but made no remark at the moment. "Thank you for coming in, Mr. Henry, I'll be in touch with you shortly." She stood and extended her hand. For some reason, Kevin thought he would like to hold that hand a little longer. She smiled, as though she had read his thoughts. He had not had that feeling since his wife, Marylyn, had died two years ago.

Wednesday morning he had finished both of the Cabot appraisals by ten o'clock and was about to leave the office when the phone rang. "Good Morning…Henry Appraisals," he said with his most professional voice. "Kevin Henry speaking."

"Good Morning to you!" the voice said. It was Cheryl Inmon. He had not expected to hear from that office again. He felt they were not planning to use him after the interview. "Mr. Henry, this is Cheryl Inmon, Mr. Harley's assistant. I hope you're having a pleasant day. The day looks beautiful outside, and it makes it hard to stay in, doesn't it?" They talked a little while. Then she added, "Mr. Harley asked me to discuss the warehouse case with you again and asked me to invite you to a lunch at the Top of the Arlington. That is always such a nice view of Little Rock when the weather is nice like today. Would twelve o'clock sharp be good? I'll meet you there or I can pick you up."

Kevin was familiar with the Top of the Arlington. It was a restaurant located on a revolving floor of the Arlington Executive Suites Building. Usually, important business deals were transacted during a fine meal, while the floor slowly revolved and gave a view of Little Rock. One was able to see all of Little Rock during a meal. He knew that was an expensive lunch. He had eaten there a few times when he was an assistant at the Central Arkansas Workers S&L.

"Sure," Kevin said. "That sounds good. I just finished some work and would like a break. I'll meet you there." *This is interesting*, Kevin thought. *I haven't ever gotten an assignment this way.* He hurried to his bedroom and changed into a pair of slacks with a blazer and put on a straight tie he had just bought. He dashed a little cologne on his arm and left. Eating at the Top of the Arlington was not like Woody's Cafeteria. He left soon because he knew the lunchtime traffic would be thick.

Kevin pulled into the Arlington parking lot and left his Chevrolet Blazer with the valet. He walked inside and took the elevator to the fifty-second floor. As they rose to the top, the outside bubble car he rode in provided a wonderfully revealing view of Little Rock. It was always breathtaking when they neared the top. He got off at the fifty-second floor and stepped onto the still mat before entering the revolving cafeteria.

She was sitting in the waiting area of the restaurant and rose when she saw him. Immediately, Kevin felt this was going to be a pleasant treat. She looked gorgeous. He hoped she couldn't see his heart beating through his jacket; it was thumping.

"You smell good," she said and extended her hand with the long, slender fingers. "Isn't this place fantastic? Mr. Harley said he wanted us to discuss this important appraisal in an important setting. Do you like this place?" she said. Her even teeth showed as she smiled.

Kevin couldn't help but notice her hair that fell softly to her shoulders and just a little cleavage that showed. She had class. "This place is out of the book. I have always been amazed when I come here. Little Rock has arrived, restaurant wise," Kevin said.

A white-gloved waiter showed them to a table and took their orders. Cheryl shifted in her seat and smiled. "Mr. Henry, may we get down to business?" He nodded yes, and she pulled out the rolled up photo of the warehouse situated on the sixty acres on the Arkansas River.

"This warehouse belongs to a very important client of the bank. The client needs to borrow additional $2,250,000 cash with an increased lien on the warehouse property. It appraised for $11,000,000 the last time, which was about two years ago when Kennon Foster had just started to work in the New Home Mortgage Company office. He was handling the loan, as a special assignment from Mr. Harley. You may or may not be aware of the possibility of a major factory locating on the sixty acres in the near future. That would greatly enhance the value of the property," she concluded. "Now…the property needs to appraise for an amount in excess of $13,250,000 for us to make this loan—more like $15,000,000 would be good. If it should fail to appraise for enough, that would kill our deal and would affect other deals we have working with this client."

Kevin was listening and looking at her as she talked. *Gosh, she is gorgeous*, he thought. But a strange feeling had come over him. He liked this woman, but now she was being used, he felt, to set up a sure thing appraisal. This was what the teacher in the appraisal ethics and law had warned against recently. These were warning signs sticking out a country mile. He wished they had met under different circumstances. This man Harley was using this attractive assistant to try to sway the appraiser.

"Mr. Harley said your fee might be as much as $15,000," Cheryl added. He knows there will be a lot of work," Cheryl Inmon stated. She smiled again and watched him carefully.

Kevin didn't react, but he knew a typical fee might not be more than $7,500. He sat back in his chair a little and looked at her beautiful face solemnly. May I call you Cheryl?" he asked.

"Of course…if you must," she said but smiled.

Kevin winced at that but said, "Ms. Inmon then, I am not sure you are aware of the severity of your apparent assignment," he said as he leaned forward, keeping his voice low. "We had a recent continuing education class, which had examples given that showed assignments being made, subject to certain results. The appraisal industry has been turned upside down the last few years. Investigations are being made on a large scale, including some in Little Rock. An appraiser is supposed to turn an assignment back when this type request is made. "I could use the fee associated with this assignment, but no, I can't accept this."

Kevin looked into her eyes and saw small tears well up in them. "Ms. Inmon, I'm afraid Mr. Harley has sent you to try this assignment on me because I am fairly new with my business. But I'm not new in the finance business or that new in the appraisal business. That property appraised for $11,000,000 the last time, and it is pretty common knowledge that there is greater excess warehouse space in Little Rock now, and the value of warehouse property has declined steadily in the past five years. It should be expected the value of this property should be less, if that last appraisal was correct when it was made. We can assume that, before working it. Now…with regard to the possibility of a major factory locating on the sixty acres, that does not yet add value. There is no evidence of a contract. Anyway, we cannot give value to the maybes. Even if the value were given subject to the factory, I cannot take an assignment with the value predetermined. I'm sure Mr. Harley knows that…I cannot accept the assignment. I'm sorry!"

After they ate in silence a while, Cheryl pulled out the bank credit card and motioned for the check. "Thank you for coming. I have enjoyed having lunch with you today, and I had hoped there might be more such occasions. Please don't disrespect me too much for doing my job." She walked slowly to the elevator. Kevin stood but waited at the table until she disappeared.

He too had hoped to see her at lunch more.

CHAPTER 5

A month after his lunch appointment with Cheryl Inmon, Kevin pulled into the Walmart parking lot Friday evening and noticed the black Expedition SUV parked with the hood up. He took notice because there was a woman bent over with her head and shoulders hidden under the hood. He stopped, backed up, and asked if she needed help. She stood and immediately covered her face. "No!" she stated firmly. It was Cheryl! She bent down under the hood again. "No thanks!" she said again. Steam was still rising from under the hood. She pulled back again and saw he was still there.

"I think I have a problem," she said with exasperation. "I think a water hose is burst." And she held her hands in front of her as she looked at the engine smudge on them.

Kevin reached down to the door pocket of his Blazer and pulled the shop towel out that he always kept for such occasions with his own vehicle. He opened his door and offered the towel to her. She smiled and accepted the towel, which she used to wipe her hands. "Thank you, Mr. Henry," she said. "I guess I'll call my insurance company for roadside assistance. I can handle it now. Thank you again. You are very kind," she said in a dismissive tone and handed the towel back to Kevin. She turned to get into her vehicle, and he laughed.

Cheryl turned toward him, put hands on her hips, and asked, "What's so funny, Mr. Henry." Kevin looked at her and felt a little chemical reaction course through his veins. Her hair was a little out of place from the steam. She was even more attractive, at that point, as she looked a little more helpless. She looked back at her Expedition and started laughing too. "Oh, I don't suppose I'm ready to drive yet."

"No," he said. Why don't you call your insurance company while I wait, and we'll see what follows that. I would hate to see you stranded here for a while. It's still a little chilly out here at night. Why don't you get in my car, and we can wait until someone comes for yours, and then I can take you home, if you like.

Cheryl looked at him and hesitated a moment, as though she were about to refuse. He smiled. Then she smiled and said, "My kids are waiting, and I must get to them. I am supposed to pick them up on the way home. They get off the school bus at my aunt's house after school and stay until I get home."

"That's not a problem," Kevin said. "Why don't you go into Walmart after you call the insurance company, get what you were after before you started steaming, and I'll wait here for the service truck. I'm sure they'll be taking it to the shop tonight. I'll call you when he gets here and hold him until you get back out here. Then I'll take you home, and you can pick your kids up on the way."

He was afraid she was going to refuse but she said to let her make the call, and she would hurry to do her brief shopping. She gave him her card with her telephone numbers including her mobile number. It said "Cheryl Inmon, Assistant to the President." The card was headed "New Bank of Pulaski." She made her call to the insurance company and headed into Walmart. Fifteen minutes later, the service truck was pulling up to her Expedition. She had given them the row and space number. Kevin was not surprised at her efficiency. Cheryl was hurrying back as the driver was pulling her vehicle up on the tilt bed of the truck. She signed the authorization paper and the driver took off for the Ford dealership.

Kevin helped her put her things into his Blazer and asked, "Where to?"

"If you don't mind, my kids are on Pebble Beach Drive," she said. "If you take me there, my aunt can take me home."

Just let me take all of you on home," Kevin said, "and you won't have to move your groceries." There was no answer.

They arrived at her aunt's house, and Cheryl said, "I'll just be a moment," and dashed out. In a moment, she came back and opened the passenger door. "Mr. Henry, my aunt wants the kids and me to have dinner with her and my uncle. She will take us home. I thank you so much for your kindness. We'll just transfer the groceries to her car. I have the keys."

Kevin got out and helped her move the groceries into the trunk of her aunt's car. She extended her hand again to him. "Thank you, Mr. Henry."

"You're welcome" he said and backed out of the driveway. "Mr. Henry! Mr. Henry!" Kevin said aloud to himself as he drove back onto Hinson Road and headed toward Napa Valley. He still had an appraisal to finish and was glad he had his office at home now. "What would it take to be just Kevin? I can't be that much older than she is. Well, so much for luck." He drove home and into his garage on St. Charles.

CHAPTER 6

Kevin picked up two more clients, a mortgage company and a bank. Those plus the others were keeping him busy. He was shocked to see an order on his fax machine for an assignment from New Home Mortgage to appraise a property in Chenal Valley. There was a sale in a new subdivision and a rush was requested.

Carol Fleichman, the new manager of New Home Mortgage Company, signed the order. *Strange*, Kevin thought as he read the order. *I thought I would never get another order from them.* Carol Fleichman had been an assistant to Kennon Foster and was promoted by New Bank of Pulaski to fill the vacancy after the death of Kennon Foster.

The next morning, he arrived to pick up the plans for the new construction, and Carol Fleichman walked out of her office to greet him. "Mr. Henry, we are pleased to have your services," she said warmly. "You must be good friends over at New Bank. They requested that none, but you do this appraisal. They called us in advance and said this application was coming. Are you a regular appraiser there?"

"Just Kevin, if you will," Kevin said. "I am about to choke on the misters. Well, I am acquainted at New Bank of Pulaski. But you may know that when I did the last appraisal for your office, I was castigated heavily. I am surprised to receive this assignment.

"Kevin, please call me Carol. I think we can cool the formalities." She smiled as she said that. "Yes, I do remember that appraisal report. It was quite interesting when that came in. I came in from an errand after you had left. But I think Mr. Harley wanted you to know he has confidence in your quality of work. I am told your work is good. This builder needs the loan to start the job soon, and we hoped you could get right on this. The job contract, as you see, is for $375,000."

The rules called for the appraiser to receive a copy of the contract. The copy was to show the appraiser the conditions in the contract, if any, which would affect the value shown in the appraisal report. Kevin looked over the contract when he got back to his office and proceeded to work on the appraisal.

Kevin was curious though why he was given this assignment in view of the fury he created when he did another appraisal earlier this year. Kevin's mind was racing. *New Home Mortgage Company…Kennon Foster, previous manager, dead. New Home Mortgage Company…owner, New Bank of Pulaski…Frank Harley, president…Cheryl Inmon, assistant…the warehouse appraisal he refused…* he wondered. *Now, this simple assignment with no strings?* Things were not making sense, he felt. *I'm glad for the assignment, but why me?* he thought.

"Okay," he shook his head to clear it. I'll finish the appraisal and see what follows.

Two days later, he walked into Carol Fleichman's office with three copies of the appraisal report. There was no problem with the value; the value was found to be $5,000 greater than the contract. "Good morning, Carol," Kevin said. "Thanks for the assignment."

"Good morning, Kevin. That was quick," Carol responded. "I'll have more work for you, if you wish, and they usually won't be rush jobs. You are in demand, it seems."

Kevin thanked Carol and paused a moment. "I'm sure you're aware of the furor created by the low appraisal I did just before Kennon died. How have I survived that?"

Carol laughed. "Well, that's a good question, and if Kennon were still here, we probably would be afraid to have you do other work after what happened. I don't know what brought about this appraisal assignment for you, but its okay with me. If we can get enough jobs through to keep going, we'll be okay. I think you know how to be reasonable. So let's be reasonable and make some money." And she laughed.

Kevin left to work on some more jobs. He was glad he was in demand but still thought this was strange in view of the uproar that occurred on his first assignment there.

———

Blunt Force to the Back of the Head! the headline of the article said. The forensic pathology report stated that Kennon Foster had died from a blow on the back of the head. It seems his chair had overturned, and he hit the back of his head on the credenza behind him, and he bled to death. He might have been in his office alone, early that Saturday morning, but that could not be determined for sure, and it was said that he sometimes left the door unlocked while he worked. There had been no appointments scheduled, and he was known to go to the office and work to catch up. The newspaper said authorities considered the case still ongoing and would have further statements if anything developed.

Mr. Frank Harley, president of New Bank of Pulaski, thanked the authorities for their diligence and hard work.

———

Kevin returned to Little Rock and saw three assignments on his fax machine. One was from the First Trust Bank of Arkansas. It was for a purchase of a residential property in southwest Little Rock. There were two more requests direct from Frank Harley to do an appraisal in the Pleasantree Subdivision and one in Pleasant Valley Subdivision. "What is going on?"

Two days later, Kevin walked into the New Bank of Pulaski to pick up some paperwork for the assignments. The receptionist greeted him and asked him to have a seat, and she would get the papers for him. Cheryl Inmon came from her office and extended her hand for the formal handshake. "Mr. Henry, it's a pleasure to see you again.

She smiled warmly, then said, "Mr. Harley wants to see you, if you can wait a few minutes. May we bring you some coffee or other drink?"

"Yes, if we can drop the formalities of Mr. Henry and make it just Kevin, I would like some coffee—black," Kevin said and smiled.

Cheryl paused and then said, "Mr. Henry, our management's policy states that proper exchanges should be maintained at all times when conducting business in our office."

She brought the coffee. "Mr. Harley will be with you soon," she said and walked back to her office.

Well, la de da, he thought. *How cold can proper business be?* He looked at the cup and saucer in his hand. He took a sip and noticed a tiny piece of paper under the cup. He took it quickly and jammed it into his shirt pocket.

Frank Harley called and said for Kevin to come on in. He was sitting at a round table with four chairs—a nice setting for close conference. "Have a seat, Kevin," Harley said in a warm and informal tone. "Would you like some more coffee?" Harley said warmly when Kevin had seated. Kevin said no, and Harley took his cup and set it aside.

"Kevin, I am glad to see you're getting several appraisal assignments from our bank and the mortgage company. I would be happy to see you continue to have a close relationship with our network. Sometimes, our situations can be arduous and demanding, but there is where the big bucks are. James Carpenter said you were sharp and knew how to handle yourself in difficult situations." He was speaking quietly and watching Kevin's face closely for his reactions. Kevin was aware of that and maintained a poker face. He wondered what this would lead to.

His memory was too good. When he was at Central Arkansas Workers' S&L, there were several arduous situations. They infringed heavily on his Scout's Oath. He had always taken that oath seriously, but things had gradually chipped away at his conscience until he allowed himself to be talked into unwanted actions. It had gotten to bother him severely, and he had gently slipped away from that business. *Now, could this be following him after two years away?* he wondered.

James Carpenter had become known as one who would help a struggling businessman to keep his head above water and give him a chance to survive long enough to recover or a homeowner who was fighting to pay bills. Several had been helped. But finally, there were too many who were sinking. Everyone was hoping the economy would recover quickly enough to cover the shortages.

The loans carried by the S&L were at fixed rates, and the discount rates had gone much higher, savings accounts were requiring much higher interest rates and the difference was having a high impact on the association's profit margin and the bottom line. Collateral could not be raised sufficiently to back the loans, and the loan insurance was hit again until the Federal Savings and Loan Insurance Corporation said no more and investigations had begun, but that was after Kevin had left.

James was in trouble. The Savings and Loan was closed, and the members were screaming for blood. Kevin felt sorry for James. He had been sincere about trying to do something good for the members who were also investors. He had gotten premium fees plus a high rate of interest when he made those weak loans. The fees and interest contributed to the growth in the association's income. The members liked that until the good interest rates they were receiving could not be paid. James Carpenter had received some bonuses in his annual pay but nothing extraordinary.

When Kevin was the in-house appraiser, he had gone to bat for James when he needed a high appraisal and signed off on some weak loans with James just to kick the can down the road. The appraisals were those that were borderline, and any discrepancy could be charged to lack of good judgment rather than fraud. Finally those loans became obvious to examiners and the alarm was sounded. There went James. Kevin had been gone a year, but his signature was still there on lots of deals. He had received no extra salary or bonuses, but he had been accused of that. They couldn't prove it, because there was none.

Now…Frank Harley was coming on with some innuendos as he carefully tried to prepare Kevin for his requests. "I visited with James about some of the activities at your old S&L," Harley said. "I think you and I can do some business. The fees can be lucrative. Real Estate business can be profitable if managed right. We are entitled to make money when we make other people money," he reasoned.

Kevin was beginning to have feelings. They were not good feelings. He couldn't let Frank Harley know his feelings yet. He wanted to hear more and determine what he was up to. He knew he and James Carpenter had gone out on a long limb at times to help a borrower. He didn't know all that James had done as the manager of the S&L to make some deals work, but he knew James was being investigated and was still in trouble. Kevin wondered what he had told Frank Harley.

"Mr. Harley, what are the arduous situations you think might happen?" he asked. I know the Feds are combing the books over and over at Central Arkansas Workers S&L. I hope James Carpenter is cleared. I know some say he's in trouble. What do you think?"

Harley leaned forward and said in a low voice, "First Trust Bank of Arkansas has sources that claim all kinds of havoc will break loose if certain things come to light. We try to make sure these things don't happen here." Then Harley leaned back. Kevin kept a straight face but was wondering what First Trust Bank of Arkansas had to do with the S&L and what was Frank Harley's connection with First Trust Bank of Arkansas. These were not things that were discussed between different banks so readily... or were they?

"Mr. Harley, we might continue this discussion later. I must move along for now. I am snowed with work," Kevin said and stood.

"Yes, Kevin, I know you are busy. Remember the source of several of your recent assignments. Would you like for them to continue?" Harley watched for his reaction. He nodded toward the packages Kevin was holding in his hand.

"We can talk again later this week if you wish," Kevin said. "Now if you will excuse me, I will move on. It's almost 4:30, and I must be somewhere soon." He didn't want to say it or imply it, but somewhere was any place but here. He didn't feel he was too free to cut Harley short and fire these assignments back to him. He wanted to know more. Why this pursuit was a burning question now.

He quickly left the bank and got into his Blazer and happened to remember the note he had stuffed into his shirt pocket. It was from Cheryl and said, "Please call me tonight."

CHAPTER 7

At 7:30 in the morning, Kevin was in the midst of shaving when his phone rang. It was Cheryl Inmon. "This is not Ms. Inmon, Kevin, this is Cheryl. You didn't call me last night," she said. "I want to tell you I am sorry for the formalities, but they are necessary. I am worried and would like to talk to you more. We need to meet, but I think it should be discreet. We could be seen in a public restaurant, so would you mind having dinner tonight at my house? Even that should be discreet. My aunt and uncle are keeping my children tonight for a sleepover at their house. The kids were looking forward to it, and we can have a quiet dinner and talk about some serious things. My garage is in the rear of my house, and I'll let you park in the garage while we eat and discuss these things…then you would go," she said hurriedly and laughed.

"Cheryl, is there some danger for you involving this?" Kevin said seriously.

"Yes, but…"

"Well, suppose you meet me in the Walmart parking lot on Bowman, and I'll get in the car and ride with you to your house? I can stay hunkered down. That way no one will see a strange car pulling in. Deal?"

"Deal," she said. "I'll get dinner ready and pick you up at dark, about seven."

She hung up, and Kevin was wondering again. What could this lady have on her mind that called for such a clandestine meeting? These recent events were in the back of his mind all day as he worked. He didn't run into any irregularities on these jobs. *I wouldn't have been surprised if I did*, he was thinking.

His old job at the S&L, his old boss James Carpenter, the New Home Mortgage, New Bank of Pulaski, now First Trust Bank of Arkansas were all running through his mind. What about Kennon Foster, the former manager of New Home Mortgage Company?

Kevin knew this was not supposed to be a date, but he went home and showered anyway. For good measure, he shaved again. It wouldn't hurt to look decent in front of this good-looking lady. After all, she is now calling him Kevin. He changed into some slacks and a blazer. He needed to wear them some. They didn't get worn, as much now that he was doing all appraisal work. Crawling around shrubbery, while measuring houses, was not conducive to wearing dress-type clothes—that was jeans and cotton khakis.

He tried to drive normally as he pulled into the Walmart parking lot. He parked his Chevy Blazer and waited. It was dark, but the parking lot lights were making it lighter than he wished. He saw the Ford Expedition coming, and he got out to meet it. She stopped, and he got in quickly. *She looked amazingly beautiful, dressed in dark slacks and a pink blouse. Her trim figure graced the clothes*, he thought. "I'm glad it doesn't have to be Mr. Henry still. I want to talk a little more down to earth," Kevin blurted out.

Cheryl laughed. "I do appreciate your coming tonight, Kevin. I have been worried for some time now, and when you rejected that warehouse assignment, I felt you had integrity. I am hoping I can trust you," she said very seriously.

"Trust me? Does she think I may not have the right intentions, or is she concerned about the things we are to talk about?" Kevin wondered quickly. "Cheryl, you mustn't think I am not aware that

I am in the presence of a beautiful and attractive woman, because I am very much aware. But I do know how to behave myself," he said.

She laughed again. It was a more relaxed and melodious laugh. "Thank you, Kevin, I needed to hear some compliments as any woman does, but I am talking about trusting you with the things we will be discussing." She turned off Hinson Road and onto Beckenham Drive and drove in silence for a little while until she pulled into her driveway and around to the rear of her house. She opened the garage door and pulled inside. Her windows were tinted, and he hadn't needed to hunker down after all. She closed the garage door, and they got out of the vehicle. The garage was clean and neat, he noticed.

"Come inside, I'll set the dinner on the table, and we can eat, then talk. She took the rolls out of the oven and dumped them into the basket. A pot roast with potatoes and carrots was set on the table. She poured some iced tea and invited him to sit at a chair. It was a round glass table, and they sat across from each other. Kevin remembered his manners and waited for her to be seated, but he didn't hold her chair. Maybe that would be inappropriate in these circumstances.

Cheryl sat quietly for a moment with her head bowed, then raised up and told Kevin to skip any formalities and help himself to the pot roast. He held the dish to her, and she took a helping and passed it back. "Kevin, I am always thankful for what I have today. You are the first man to have dinner with me since Johnny died. We always said grace at the meal. Johnny was a good man."

Kevin had noticed the couple's picture on a grand piano in the living room. "When did your husband die?" Kevin asked. He had not known John Inmon.

"Johnny died in a car wreck shortly after Jonetta was born. He said she was so beautiful and would come home each day from the bank and pick her up to dote on her. He always played awhile with each of the girls. They were daddy's girls. Johnny was always so careful about our cars, but the brakes apparently failed, and he lost control going down Herndon Hill at the sharp curve.

They ate in silence for a little while; then, Cheryl excused herself while she made some coffee and served him a piece of apple pie. "I made this last night," she said.

"Boy, now we go from this to talking business?" Kevin quipped.

Cheryl laughed and poured the coffee. "Now for business," she said. "Kevin, I am going to talk to you about something that could cost me more than my job, if you betray me," Cheryl said seriously. "I must talk to someone though."

"On my Scout's honor, I promise I can keep confidence. What's on your mind?" Kevin said.

"I have been working at New Bank of Pulaski for about seven months. I have the feeling that not all is as it should be. There are files that I would normally have access to, but they are locked in a vault, and only Mr. Harley can bring them out. He studies them sometimes when he makes certain calls. He puts those calls through himself, but he has the receptionist put his other calls through. He has meetings with other bankers and makes notes that he keeps in those secret files," Cheryl stated frankly.

"There is a small vault room behind his office where he has the file cabinets. One day, he left suddenly, and in a hurry, when his daughter was in a car wreck on her way to Hot Springs. She was pulling a ski boat and couldn't make a curve. She was speeding as usual, they said.

After he left, I noticed the door was open to the vault room and went in to close it. I then noticed the file drawer was pulled out and saw the files labeled New Bank of Pulaski; that didn't strike me as unusual, but then there were files labeled First Trust Bank of Arkansas, New Home Mortgage Company, Central Arkansas Workers Savings and Loan Association, and…Franklin Savings and Loan of Texarkana. That last one was really a surprise to me. Why would he have a file for Franklin Savings and Loan? Why would he have those other files?

When Mr. Harley returned, he was seemingly distraught, and I asked him if everything was all right. He said, "Oh that wild daughter of mine wrecked her Ford Bronco and the ski boat, but she's fine. She was moving it to the marina, and I had told her it was too early.' Then he quickly dropped that subject and very sternly asked me if anyone had entered the office vault room while he was gone. That was one time I felt afraid to admit I had been in the vault room, so I told him the room was secure, and I had locked his office. He didn't press me more."

"Now, Kevin," Cheryl said, and her voice dropped a little. "On Friday, the day before Kennon Foster died, Kennon and Mr. Harley were in a very heated argument. I overheard something about the Wemberly Warehouse property and Mr. Harold Wemberly. Kennon kept saying, 'No! No!' I couldn't hear what Mr. Harley was saying.

"I am fearful that Mr. Harley will wonder what I may have heard, what I may have seen in the vault and what I may know. Kennon Foster was not a clumsy person. His chair was said to have overturned. All these things make my mind become muddled," Cheryl said.

Kevin could see the worried look on her face. He wondered how much more she might be carrying in her mind.

They got quiet. A car had stopped on the street out front. Her house sat off the street about fifty feet. The doorbell rang. She jerked. "Don't answer that," Kevin said.

Then her phone rang. "It's Mr. Harley," Cheryl said. "I have this feeling."

"Don't answer it," Kevin said.

The answering machine responded, and Harley started to speak, "Cheryl, I saw your lights in your house and wanted to be sure you're okay. Call me when you can. Uh…I was wondering if you were in town and wanted to invite you to a cookout at our house tomorrow."

"He's lying," Cheryl stated quickly. "He has never invited me to their house. I think Mrs. Harley is above any employee of the bank. And why would he be coming to my house? Why this time of night? Why didn't he call, anyway? That was a sham." She was firing off the questions in rapid fire.

Kevin agreed. Did Frank Harley suspect something from when he and Cheryl were talking in the office? He would have been watching for something. "Cheryl, do you own a gun?"

"Johnny had one, and it is still here. It's a 357 magnum that he used when he spent some time as a policeman before we married. We used to go to the firing range together after we married. I learned to handle it and shoot it fairly well, but I have kept it locked away and unloaded because of the children."

"Cheryl get it and keep it handy—but unloaded. You might find it handy as a bluff at least," Kevin told her. "Now, we have the problem of getting me back to Walmart to get my Blazer."

"You can't stay here," she said with concern. Then she laughed. "I didn't mean that as an accusation of your intent," she said apologetically.

"No, no," Kevin said. "I suppose that would be a natural assumption because of the logical solution. But I don't want that to be a solution either," he said to reassure her. "I think we both have problems with our personal safety now. We don't want Harley to know we are communicating. In your office, we should be as formal as your policy calls for. Yet I want us to communicate and find what's going on. I wonder about Kennon Foster."

Cheryl poured each another cup of coffee and sat down at the table. "What are we going to do? Since I didn't answer the phone or the door, if he sees the Expedition pulling out from the house, he may follow us. I don't want an encounter tonight."

"Let me sneak out the back and scout out the area, discreetly. I'll see if he is parked nearby. Now I wish I had worn a dark outfit. This jacket and shirt will reflect light and make it easier to spot," Kevin remarked.

"Okay," Cheryl said. "If you don't mind wearing them, I still have some dark clothes that I have kept since Johnny died. I think they will fit you. Let me get them, and you can try them on. You can wear them home and return them later," she said as she was going to retrieve the clothes. She came back with a black polo shirt and dark trousers.

Kevin changed clothes quickly and went out to scout the area. He eased around the house and stayed close to the brick wall. There was a car coming. He quickly hid behind the tall shrubbery at the front of the house. It slowed down as it neared the house, but...across the street, a garage door opened and the car pulled into that garage. *Whew, there for a moment,* Kevin thought. After carefully observing that there were no cars parked on the street, Kevin went back to the back door and knocked gently. She let him in.

"Now, let's get into your Expedition, and you can take me back to get my car. Take your pistol with you tonight so you can have it when you return," Kevin suggested. "First, do you have a roll of duct tape?" He opened the door of her SUV and taped the light button of the passenger door. "When we get to my Blazer, I want you to slow down, and I will get out quickly while you are moving. This will prevent the light from coming on when I exit your vehicle."

They drove into the Walmart parking lot, and she slowly drove down the aisle of the parking lot where Kevin was parked. "Kevin, take my car phone number so we can communicate. I have your number stored in my mind. I am not storing it in the phone memory, in the event someone might see it."

"I'll do the same," he said. He committed the number to memory when she spelled it out. "I'll watch for a couple minutes to see if you are followed. Circle the parking lot once to see if you pick up a follower," Kevin said as he quickly exited the vehicle. He walked down to the basket storage, looking around as he eased along. He got into his Blazer and sat for a little while and waited for Cheryl to circle the parking lot. She came by once and then headed home.

There was no one following, so Kevin drove home, and when he was sure she had time to get home, he called her and confirmed her safety. He was very concerned about her safety now.

CHAPTER

8

Kevin sat at his breakfast table and read the morning paper. He had also seen the news on television at ten o'clock the night before. The blood! The question, posed by the reporters, was whether it was a hemorrhage or was there another cause of death. There had been no health issues known by his friends and acquaintances. Everyone was speculating about what happened, the paper stated. Kennon Foster was well known in the finance industry. He had been a branch manager of a large branch of the Franklin Savings and Loan Association of Texarkana, Texas, that failed in 1989, after hanging on through three years of investigation.

Franklin S&L was a huge organization with depositors from a wide-reaching area of Texas and into south Arkansas. Shelton McKinley, the chairman of the board of directors had almost been indicted but escaped when his congressman came to his defense. The prosecutors were not satisfied and still had their sights on him. McKinley was wealthy and owned several thousand acres of prime farmland in east Texas and several warehouses in Texarkana that he had acquired during the 1970s and early 1980s. He was thought to have interest in several banks in Texas and some in Arkansas, but no one actually knew which ones.

Kevin had heard his boss at Central Arkansas Workers S&L speak of McKinley. When McKinley spoke, they considered it would happen. Things happened the way he wanted them to happen. Kennon Foster had left Franklin, and everyone assumed he had crossed McKinley, but he was able to take charge of the office of New Home Mortgage Company. Supposedly, Frank Harley knew his capabilities and gave him a chance at a much-reduced salary.

Tuesday's paper had news update about the Kennon Foster death: "The coroner's report is not yet complete. Authorities are still investigating the death. Kennon Foster, a newcomer who had gained prominence quickly, the paper said, was a rising star in the Little Rock mortgage industry and was slated for a promotion. He was expected to move into the New Bank of Pulaski soon. 'His experience in major financing was needed,' Frank Harley had stated. 'We will definitely miss his knowledge and experience in the finance industry.'"

Kevin left his office and headed to Cabot where he had to do the preliminaries of two residential appraisals. There were two pre construction appraisals to do. He had picked up the plans from one of the other banks and had to work the comparable sales and head back to his office. *These are a piece of cake*, he thought.

CHAPTER 9

The annual meeting and seminar for appraisers and loan originators to meet with the Federal Housing Administration (FHA) was this week in Hot Springs, and Kevin was there. He was standing in line to sign the registration when an appraiser he had known from his days at the Central Arkansas Workers S&L. got in line with him. Charley Larkin was a big talker and usually had a story when they saw each other. Charley was partially instrumental for Kevin's starting his own appraisal business when the S&L was having trouble.

They shook hands and slapped each other on the back for a moment. "How have you been?" Charley asked. "Are you getting all the appraisal work you want? I have been swamped." Kevin knew appraisers say that often, even if they were hungry and couldn't pay their bills, but he knew Charley stayed busy.

"I stay pretty busy, Charley. I had to turn down an assignment last month to appraise a warehouse." Kevin said without saying more.

"Oh! Speaking of warehouses, did you hear about Jim Hammons and his woes? It might be in the newspapers in a few days. The state banking department is investigating," Charley said in a quiet voice. When Kevin shook his head no, Charley continued, "It seems old Jim appraised the Wemberly Warehouse and sixty acres of land on Riverside Drive last year for $11,200,000. The problem is, he appraised the same property two years prior for $10,000,000, and there haven't been any improvements since. In addition to that, there is a greater surplus of warehouse space in this area. I hear the owner is in trouble and can't make his payments. I think the stuff is about to hit the fan, if you know what I mean."

"Well, do you suppose Jim's good luck is coming to an end?" Kevin said. He didn't mention to Charley that the assignment, they tried to give him, was on the same property.

What was Frank Harley up to, trying to get me to appraise that property? Kevin was wondering silently. *This is going to be interesting. What about Cheryl? Is she wrapped up in this also?* Kevin hoped not. He hadn't heard from her since the dinner. *Maybe he should give her a call.*

—⁂—

"Appraisers and loan originators, cover your backsides. Don't get caught in some of the flip schemes," warned one of the speakers from the attorney general's office. There will be people who go to prison over some of these schemes. "Don't get sucked in!"

Kevin looked across the room where some of the New Bank of Pulaski people were sitting, but he didn't see Cheryl. He hoped she would get the warning.

Burnie Burnside, who was staff appraiser for FHA, was doing his usual talk on flaws in appraisal reports and some downright fraudulent and misleading reports. He was showing slide pictures of actual conditions of a house where he had done a routine follow-up. The report showed the roof condition as good. The pictures showed a worn out roof with curling shingles and several missing ones. Burnie Burnside was a popular speaker who told several jokes while making his presentation. His job back in the office was to provide a source of information for appraisers when they had questions about FHA requirements.

Carol Fleichman was in a group with the New Home Mortgage and New Bank of Pulaski people. She seemed to mingle well with the other people and was promoting her office with the Realtors. Always promoting, that was the function of successful people in the real estate industry. You scratch my back and I'll scratch yours, as the saying goes. It works!

CHAPTER

10

Monday morning was a busy day for appraisal work. Kevin had set appointments for two inspections to start two appraisals. They were both in Jacksonville. He usually liked to do the preliminary work with the measurements of the property, photographs, and the necessary details describing the property including the condition of the property. He was more efficient that way when he had two in the same area. He could then go to his office, which was now located in his home in Little Rock, and put things on the computer. He took his film to the photoshop for development and dropped it off. He could work on these that night and partially finish the reports, or he could complete them the next day. There was rumor of improvements that would allow reports to be sent over the Internet. But that was thought to be a few years off yet. The Internet speeds would need to be better. They were also talking about digital cameras that could download pictures to the computer, and printers would print pictures to ordinary paper.

Kevin had not talked to Cheryl since Saturday evening. Tonight, he would call. He had a call recorded on his new answering machine. It was blinking. It said the call was recorded at 4:37 p.m. *Good, Cheryl has probably left me a message to call,* Kevin thought. But it was Frank Harley.

"Kevin, call me today if you get this message in time," Harley said. Kevin didn't want to talk and decided to wait until tomorrow. Besides, he wanted to see how Cheryl's day went first.

It was five o'clock when the phone rang. Kevin jumped to pick it up, thinking it would be Cheryl. "Mr. Henry, this is Winston Kenwood, president of First Trust Bank of Arkansas. How are you and the appraisal business today?" Kevin had met Winston Kenwood in the past when he was associated with the S&L. Winston was a big mogul in banking in Little Rock and Arkansas. He swung a big stick, most people said. He financed much of the large businesses in the city and around part of the state. He was a leader in many of the organizations including the banking organizations. Kevin didn't know that Winston Kenwood knew he was an appraiser now.

"Hello, Mr. Kenwood. It's good to hear from you. To what do I owe this pleasure," Kevin said courteously.

"I'll get right to the point, Mr. Henry. My banking committee is looking into the quality of the appraisals that the finance community is relying on. You have an additional background in the finance business, and we are thinking of adding someone, like you, to our committee. Could you meet with me in my office tomorrow morning to discuss this idea?"

"Mr. Kenwood, I am honored to be considered for something like that. However, I am self-employed, those committees usually take a lot of time, and I don't have much of that at this time," Kevin replied. He didn't want to be on a committee. "Now this is strange. Why is he calling me? I'm not a wheel in anyone's machine," he was thinking.

"Kevin, just come in and talk. I'll be sure you get some appraisal work that will compensate you for the trip. We have a large house in Chenal that's to be built, and there should be a good fee for a good appraiser. You could be that appraiser. This committee will be considering some of the defunct S&Ls," Kenwood dropped that in, seemingly in passing.

That struck a note with Kevin. *What is this guy up to?* he thought. *That's old business. I've been out of that long enough now to not have to be answering questions about that.* Kevin was getting concerned. *Maybe I should find out what he's up to but I'll try to not let him know it matters to me, though.* He silently considered.

"No, I don't think you need to talk with me. James Carpenter may be able to help you. But if you want me to consider the appraisal on the big house, I'll try to come by about nine o'clock tomorrow morning," Kevin told him.

"Good," Kenwood said. "I'm handling this one, and I would like to go over the plans with you. Come to my office, and I'll see you right away." Kenwood hung up at that point.

Kevin knew Kenwood was pulling one out of a hat to bring him in. He probably knew about the job and was sidetracking it to me to bring me in, he surmised. *Well, at least I'll get a nice appraisal assignment, and if all this is on the up and up, maybe I'll gain a client.*

―⚘―

He thought about Cheryl again. *Something's up*, Kevin thought. *But I want to talk to Cheryl.* He called her car phone number, but she didn't answer. He called her house, but no answer. "Cheryl, answer your phone!" Now, as if he hadn't already been concerned, he began to worry. *But maybe she's shopping, picking up the kids—that's it, the kids. Maybe she's having dinner again with her aunt and uncle. I'll wait*, he thought.

Kevin sat down at his computer and began to work up the reports on some appraisals. That kept his mind away from the tension he had been feeling. This one appraisal was a doozy. It was on a property in Lonoke with an old house built in 1885. It had seven of the lots in the original platting of the subdivision, and the house was one of the larger houses in this small agriculture town of four thousand people.

There were no comparable sales. Lonoke was about twenty miles from North Little Rock and Little Rock, probably twenty-five or more miles from anything similar to this house. Kevin decided to wait until tomorrow to hunt for comparable sales. The rules of appraisal required that a comparable sale be found in close proximity and a similar neighborhood. Boy! Well, he'd have to think about that for a while, so he set out to compute the cost of construction. That required some judgment for this old hundred-year-old house and its condition after having been remodeled three times.

He had just finished the computation of the cost approach, and the phone rang. It was Cheryl. "Kevin, I'm sorry I haven't called you earlier, but I've had a very hectic day at the office, and Patty was sick when I got to my aunt's house. I had to take her to the emergency room. She's much better now, but we just got home.

"I'm concerned, Kevin…" she said and paused. "Mr. Harley had me in his office three times today asking me about when he left the door open in his office vault room. I don't know if he is paranoid or if he left that open on purpose and has set some sort of entrapment to test me. My fingerprints could be on something in the vault. I suppose he might find some…if he went that far to have it inspected. He kept quizzing me about whether anyone had gone in there. I was beginning to wonder."

"Was something missing? Did he say?" Kevin asked.

"He didn't say anything about anything missing, but I remember that each time he called was right after Mr. Winston Kenwood of First Trust Bank of Arkansas had just talked to him. I had taken the call and transferred it to Mr. Harley. As soon as they hung up, Mr. Harley called me into his office."

"Cheryl, speaking of Winston Kenwood, he called me today. What time was his last call to Frank Harley?" Kevin asked. "He called here about five o'clock."

"Mr. Kenwood called Mr. Harley about 4:15," Cheryl said.

"He must have hung up from a conversation with Mr. Harley, then turned around and called here. I wonder what the connection is between those two. Cheryl, I want you to play it safe at the bank. Don't work any past the normal close of the day. Leave work when the others are leaving. I don't mean to scare you, but I think it wise to play it safe," Kevin advised her. "I am wondering if there is a connection to all of this and my meeting with Winston Kenwood tomorrow. Something's going on, and I guess we'll see."

Cheryl was beginning to feel a more constant tension now. She needed this job and didn't feel she could just walk out. She wished she did not work in such close relationship with Mr. Harley. Before coming to New Bank of Pulaski, she had worked in the First Trust Bank of Arkansas, as a secretary to one of the loan officers there. The pressure was not the same, but it didn't pay as much either. The work here was interesting and kept her busy, which she liked. But this pressure from Mr. Harley and his strange actions lately were beginning to make this job more stressful and maybe dangerous.

Get hold of yourself, she mentally admonished herself. *What if the actions by Mr. Harley were, in fact, sincere and harmless?* These thoughts were going through her mind as she drove to work. She was glad she worked. She had kept herself occupied after Johnny's death five years ago, but a regular workday felt good in many ways. *Now I—we have involved another person in what might be a danger. But it seems too that there is some comfort to me, knowing there is one to whom I can go,* Cheryl was thinking as she drove along. *I don't know why Mr. Harley is bent on bringing in Kevin Henry to be involved in an appraisal of the warehouse property, even after he resisted.*

CHAPTER

11

Kevin was leaving for his appointment with Winston Kenwood when his car phone rang. It was Carol Fleichman, the new branch manager at New Home Mortgage Company in North Little Rock. "Kevin, would you please come by our office when it's convenient for you," she said. "I may need your help."

"Okay, let me call you later when I'm free," Kevin replied. "It's about time I heard from your office again. You haven't sent me an assignment lately," he chided her. "I'll call you later." He couldn't help but let his mind review this manager of the mortgage company. *She was a good pick, at least for the image*, he thought. *She's a good looker and very sharp. She's very professional but warm at the same time.*

His mind continued to review Carol. He remembered a Carol, a little, from college, he thought. She was a freshman when he was a senior, so they never ran across each other very often. He had not seen her since college but could see she was doing okay, job-wise.

She had a natural look with her noncolored blonde hair in a ponytail. Her trim figure was attractive with her tall five-foot-ten height. She looked as though she had been a basketball player—good personality too, he thought. *I'll give her a nine, maybe a ten. Hah!*

Kevin drove into the parking garage at the Arlington Building where the First Trust Bank of Arkansas was located. He noted his parking space number and locked the doors of his Blazer. The air was a little nippy, but otherwise, it was a pleasant day. He felt good. He rode the deluxe elevator to the seventeenth floor. "Winston Kenwood, President, First Trust Bank of Arkansas" the sign said over his door.

The receptionist greeted him and offered the usual coffee. She was very nice and professional. "Mr. Kenwood will see you now," she said and moved toward his door. Kevin followed and viewed the large suite. It had a large walnut desk with glass top and a large overhang at the front for the guest. Over in the corner was a round table with four chairs. In another corner, there was a room with toilet to the left and a break bar in a room at the right.

Winston Kenwood rose and walked around the end of his desk to greet and shake hands. He was a large man with rimless glasses. He had a deep voice and seemed to be one that would be in charge at any gathering. "Good morning, Kevin!" His voice boomed out. "Thanks for coming in. Did Ms. Elton offer you coffee or soda?" he asked. Kevin shook his head yes, and Kenwood motioned toward the round table. "Let's talk over there," he directed. He let Kevin be seated, and then he set his large frame down in one of the deluxe chairs on wheels.

"Thank you, sir," Kevin stated. "You must be a busy man Mr. Kenwood. How can I help you?"

"Just call me Winston," he said warmly. "We don't need formalities, if you don't mind. Kenwood paused and retrieved a cigar from a humidor on his credenza. Kevin smelled the nice aroma from the humidor. Kenwood handed it toward Kevin who declined, and Kenwood put the cover on and set it back on the credenza. He had been a heavy cigar smoker until the smoking ban in public buildings was being pushed. He had quit smoking, but he still kept an unlit cigar in his mouth, most of the time.

"I'll get right to the point, Kevin. You'll be getting this appraisal assignment for a new construction in Chenal Valley. It is being built by one of our prime builders and a large customer of the bank. The house is being built for one of the heart surgeons who has plenty money. I want someone reliable to do this one and feel you would be the man. You know how important appraisals are to builders, having been in the finance business as well as the real estate business." He went to his desk and picked up a set of rolled up plans and a manila envelope with a copy of the contract and the assignment papers with it.

Kevin opened the plans and looked at what would be a twelve-thousand-square-foot house with elaborate fenestration, several bathrooms, four fireplaces, and a four-car garage. The roof would be tiled. It was to have a thirteen-hundred-square-foot guest-house and, in a separate entry, showers and dressing room for the pool users. The contract showed a finished price of 2,400,023 dollars. The specification sheet was included and provided for top quality features. A nice house! This would be the largest and most elaborate house Kevin had appraised.

"Winston, this is a large project, and it will be a time-consuming effort," Kevin stated after he rolled the plans back and placed the rubber band around it. "Has the bank set a fee for the appraisal job?"

"Yes, I know it will be time consuming. If the appraised value is sufficient to cover the contract, the fee will be twenty-two hundred dollars." He sat back and looked at Kevin as if to see his reaction to the answer.

Twenty-two hundred dollars. Kevin realized the fee without exhibiting any response. *With that fee, he could finish paying off his Blazer. That would be nice, and he could do many things with the fee,* Kevin was thinking. "If the appraised value is sufficient to cover the contract—" Winston had said.

"Winston, the fee is adequate, but I can't accept it on the terms you just stated. I can't accept the assignment if it is conditioned on the value reaching a certain number." He handed the rolled up plans and contract over to Winston Kenwood and laid it down on the table. "The appraiser's code of ethics and the conditions statement provides that there must be no pre conditions to the assignment. I can't accept one on that basis. I just want to remind you of that virtual law."

Kenwood sat back in his chair and just looked silently at Kevin for a moment, then said, "Kevin, this doctor is very wealthy, and we can put the fee higher, if that will help you." And he pushed the plans back across the table.

"Mr. Kenwood," Kevin said firmly, "I don't think we should discuss this anymore." He rose and started toward the door. *What is this guy trying to do? I wonder if he's trying to set a trap*, he was thinking.

"Wait, Kevin," Kenwood said as he rose from his chair. "You have passed the test. I want you to know my committee on quality and dependability is checking with appraisers in this part of the state to see if their credibility is worthwhile. I'm sure you're aware of the banking and S&L problems that exist and what it is costing the public to save the banks. I want you to take that assignment and appraise it to your best ability."

"Now…let's sit down and talk some more, okay?" He looked at Kevin.

Kevin was not sure about this. He knew Kenwood was on some banking committees, but this still didn't sit well. He knew what was expected on the appraisal report for this project. "Mr. Kenwood, I accept your explanation of the test, but I know what is expected, and I can't help but feel that expectation. Please do me a favor and make a clean assignment to another appraiser," Kevin stated to Kenwood. "Just send another one my way some time if you wish."

"You are turning down $2,200, then. You don't have to do that to prove your integrity," Kenwood said.

"I know, but if the value should be short in my calculation, I would feel I would be letting someone down. I just feel someone else should complete this appraisal. Thank you for the opportunity though," Kevin said and rose to go.

"Wait, wait," Kenwood said and motioned for Kevin to sit down. "I still want to speak with you about other matters."

"All right, what did you want to talk about?" Kevin said and sat down again.

Kenwood leaned forward and looked straight at Kevin. "Some things have been happening in the Little Rock area that concern me a lot. You are aware of the Kennon Foster death. The police have not solved that case yet. Some files might be missing that he had charge of when he died. Have you heard anything about those files?" He watched Kevin closely as though to see his reaction.

Kevin kept a poker face, and then he feigned surprise. "Why would I know about files? I don't work at that mortgage company. I would ask Mr. Frank Harley," Kevin said innocently. *Why is he grilling me about this?* He was wondering. "Has anyone checked with the manager at New Home Mortgage?" Kevin asked. *This is why he wanted to meet with me, but still, why me? Why does he think I might know?* Kevin was thinking.

"Now, Mr. Kenwood, uh, Winston"—Kevin changed to informal—"why do you think I might know about files that I have never seen or have any way of seeing. Do you know if there are files missing or just wonder if they might be missing?" Kevin queried Kenwood. "Is this a banking committee investigation?"

"Well, you might say that," Kenwood answered vaguely. "We know Ms. Cheryl Inmon has approached you about doing appraisal work. Has she ever said anything about any missing files?"

Aha, there are some critical files in that vault room behind Frank Harley's office. Harley has screwed up and left the vault door open and is extremely worried that someone has seen something that he doesn't want seen. Why is he bringing in Winston Kenwood of this bank? Kevin was wondering.

"Winston, I don't know if Ms. Inmon knows about anything. She was sent to try to entice me to do a certain appraisal but did not talk about any missing files or any files. Someone is on the wrong trail," he said firmly. "If you'll excuse me, I will get back to work on my appraisals," Kevin said.

"Yes, yes," Kenwood said. "Do that, and keep in touch. Let me know if you hear anything and…keep this conversation quiet, please," he asked.

Kevin nodded affirmatively. "Now if you'll excuse me, I must go on. Thank you for the confidence on that assignment," he said and left.

Kenwood was looking a little perplexed and shook his head negatively.

Kevin walked out and retrieved his vehicle. *The test…$2,200…I turned that down.* He was pondering that. He felt the assignment was tainted, although Kenwood had wanted him to take the assignment after the test. *No way!* he thought. *It's a no win. If it came in short, my name is mud. If it appraised okay, they could think I still bowed to the condition. Too bad*, he thought and dismissed it from his mind.

CHAPTER 12

One more stop before getting back to appraisal work. Maybe Carol Fleichman has an assignment for me, Kevin wondered. He called her and said he was on his way.

Carol met him at the door, and they shook hands. She was there by herself. "Come on back to my office. Everyone is out hustling," she said. "I'm glad because I want to talk confidentially about something that's bothering me, and I hope you can keep this to yourself," she said quietly. She turned and led the way to her office. Kevin noticed the slender figure and the shape of the calves of her legs as she seemed to walk with effortless motion. Her movements flowed like an athlete, maybe a former basketball player, ready to spring for a jump shot. She walked behind her desk and motioned for him to sit in the chair in front. "Kevin, you have been in the real estate financing business and probably remember the general systems and office procedures of this type business.

"We have been looking for some files, and one file is not here. We have crosschecked to be sure it hasn't been misfiled—it's not here. We have the ledger showing the loan record that has always been kept in this office, but there is no file folder to match. I called Mr. Harley about this, and he said to not worry. I said we must be in balance on everything, or we could be in trouble if we are audited. He said don't worry. That's not like him. He wants everything perfect. I expected him to start yelling like he usually does when something is missing, but he said don't worry about it and forget it.

"Kevin…those folders were here not long before Kennon died, and I know because he had been discussing the case with Mr. Harley. When the police checked everything after Kennon's death, they said nothing was missing. Mr. Harley had told them that. They wouldn't know about every file folder. Here is the printout of the ledger. It's the Wemberly Warehouse property, and it shows the loan made last year and each time before. The year before, it was $1,100,000 less, and a new appraisal had been ordered for last year. The year before that, it was $2,200,000 less, and a new appraisal had been ordered each year. Each year the appraisal met the amount needed for the new balance. There were file folders with the appraisals for each year. Now the file folders are missing. They had the loan applications and the appraisal reports in them."

"Today, Mr. Harley called me and asked if I could find those file folders. He asked as though they had never been missing. I reminded him we couldn't find those folders earlier, and he had said to don't worry about it and forget it. Then he denied he said that. He said the bank examiners were coming, and he wanted me to find them. He said they should be here, and I should be able to come up with them."

"Kevin, I don't like what I 'm seeing here. I am a little frightened, and I had to talk to someone about this besides Mr. Harley," Carol said.

They heard someone coming, and it was one of the loan originators returning. "Here, this is an appraisal assignment. Be looking at it. I don't want any of the others to know I am talking to you about this other. You can do that appraisal and turn it in at your leisure," Carol said.

They both stood and shook hands as Kevin was leaving. *A pretty strong handshake for a woman*, Kevin thought. "I think you're right in not talking to any of the others here about this. Let's think about this for a while and see what else turns up about it, Kevin told her. He didn't say anything about the effort to entice him to appraise that property for a number they wanted at New Bank of Pulaski. *That is still something I'm wondering about. Why did they pick me, one of the newer appraisers? True, I have financing in my history. What happened to that file folder? Why has Carol called me to discuss the disappearance of the folder?* he pondered.

Kevin placed the assignment papers in his attaché case and headed for west Little Rock. He had an appraisal to do off Cantrel Road. There was a tract of land with thirty-five acres that was planned for a new subdivision. An eight-foot brick fence was planned, and a creek ran through the middle. The owner was planning a series of dams to bring some water into the picture. He planned to cause the dams to hold enough water and provide a pond at the backs of the houses. "He's a sharp developer, and the idea might work well," Kevin felt.

His mind kept drifting back to his meeting with Carol Fleichman. *Not a bad looker*, he was thinking. He hadn't noticed her when he had picked up the controversial appraisal assignment before Kennon Foster's death. *How could I have missed her? She couldn't have been there either time he was there. She's too eye catching to miss! Well, in fact, she is downright beautiful*, he thought. *There, now I've said it. I must admit, these mortgage companies tend to hire beautiful women for their offices. Carol looks familiar*, he thought, and he asked himself where he could have seen her before, maybe several years ago. *That blonde hair with the ponytail. She's just cute too. I'll have to think. Should I know her?*

Back at his home, Kevin went directly to his office and sat down to finish the two Jacksonville appraisals. They were fairly simple, and he finished them quickly. He printed out the eighteen pages of each appraisal report and pasted the photos onto the photo pages. *The glue—that smell, and they say the stuff is made from horses hooves?* His mind was wandering back and forth from the task at hand and the strange happenings at New Bank of Pulaski and New Home Mortgage Company. *That was strange too, at First Trust Bank.* He felt.

He packaged the three copies of each appraisal report in their respective manila envelopes and put a copy of each in his file cabinet. *The file cabinet.* His mind wandered back to the missing files at New Home Mortgage Company, and then it stopped on Kennon Foster. Kennon Foster is dead. *Was that an accident that the chair overturned backward and hit the credenza?* He thought he would like to look at the chair and the surroundings. Obviously, that couldn't be done with other people watching and curious about what he was doing.

CHAPTER 13

After delivering the reports, Kevin pulled into Sam's Wholesale Club on Landers Road. He was about out of legal size copy paper, and he thought he'd pick up a case of that while he was in the area. The place was mildly busy when he walked in, and he showed the greeter his membership card. "Watch that guy. He may be an imposter," the voice called out. He turned and saw the old friend, James Carpenter, his former boss at Central Arkansas Workers Savings and Loan Association. They shook hands and slapped each other on the back. Kevin had always liked Carpenter and missed him since those difficult days of the S&L's demise.

"Let's finish here and go grab some dinner together, if you have time?" Kevin asked James. "We need to catch up with each other," he said. James said that was a good idea, and they could meet at Red Lobster for a steak. "That is if you're buying!" he said with a grin.

James had aged a lot since he had seen him, Kevin thought. They hadn't been around each other much since Kevin had left a couple years ago. He knew James had been through the wringer with the difficulties at the S&L and the pressure from the Feds. The association had closed and government workers had descended upon it with efforts to find wrongdoing. It was all he could do to fend off strong charges. It seemed everyone felt he had a duty to find something whether or not it was there. Kevin knew there were things that were on the verge of being improper at times, if not improper. He had helped James at times to cover up some shortfalls, but they couldn't keep it afloat. Federal Savings and Loan Insurance Corporation (FSLIC) came in and tore everything apart to try to find irregularities.

The FSLIC was fighting for survival. It had served a purpose. The employees were still trying to justify their jobs.

James and Kevin had struggled through these times, and James had lived through investigation after investigation. So far, he was surviving. Of late, he had been in Oklahoma working for a large bank.

They met at Red Lobster, and after the server had taken their orders, Kevin sat back and looked at James. "You're a sight for sore eyes," he quoted a favorite local expression. "I have wished many times I had your counsel on some happenings. In fact, some things are happening now that are beginning to get sticky." He confided a few of the recent happenings. "They have been asking me to appraise the Wemberly Warehouse. I remember we looked at that loan down there once. Now the New Bank of Pulaski is involved and wants an appraisal for $2,250,000 more than it appraised for two years ago, which was more than it appraised for the previous year. The overall warehouse space in the Little Rock area has excess vacancy, and values have diminished."

"Kevin, watch yourself now. I have been through a lot in the past few years that make me leery when someone starts pursuing me aggressively. But you have a head on your shoulders and should be able to handle yourself. Just be careful," James admonished. "You need to know that Kennon Foster inherited that Wemberly Warehouse situation when he came here from Texas. I don't know if he knew what he was getting into though."

Kevin looked at Carpenter's once dark-brown hair that was now almost white at age forty-five. The wrinkles around his eyes told of stress, and he had a little stoop now. James had always been a strong and vibrant man and had built a thriving S&L in the central Arkansas area. He was a caring and good man who tried to help too many people without really thinking enough of his own risks. Maybe that was some saving grace when the sharks ascended on his S&L. They didn't see greed.

"Now Kevin"—James Carpenter leaned forward—"the finance world is one that sometimes works in a very high-dollar range that is beyond the average person's vision, and in that range, motives get distorted, and methods get even more distorted. Sometimes it calls for the insistence on certain people playing ball. If they don't play ball, fingers get mashed, and sometimes heads roll. The actions can be subtle. They can be insidious, or they can be rash and sudden. It behooves you, who are young yet in the business, even at age thirty-five, to be wary and really stay heads-up. But I know you'll be okay. Carefully select those you trust, watch for the slick ones, and don't let them suck you in. I wish I were here to help because I think you are beginning to face some serious challenges."

James Carpenter needed to leave for another commitment, and Kevin told him to go ahead. Kevin wanted to stay for a couple minutes because he had noticed another party out of the corner of his eye and wondered why he seemed to be looking in their direction occasionally. He ordered another cup of coffee and sat there for a while pretending to make some notes on a notepad he took from his pocket. The other party started to leave when James left but sat down again when Kevin stayed. *Strange*, he thought. He didn't know the man but noticed he had been furtively looking in the direction of his table. Kevin could see the ruddy complexion and deep acne scars on each side of the face, and he wore a bushy mustache with a crew haircut.

The server brought the coffee, and Kevin asked for the check. When the check came and he paid, the party rose and went out. *Now what*, Kevin thought, *am I getting paranoid and why? That may not have anything to do with me.*

"Watch yourself," James had admonished. "I don't think he meant physically?"

The crowd was getting thicker, and Kevin moved out to the outside and the parking lot. He kept his eyes moving all around to see if he could detect anything unusual. He saw the same man sitting in a red Ford pickup truck. "What am I doing?" he asked himself. "I am getting skittish. If that guy is tailing me, I think I can handle him, but…I think I'll ease around to Walmart and see what they have in a pistol. I don't want to carry a gun, but maybe this is a time for caution."

He drove into the parking lot at Walmart and didn't see the man but decided to pursue his original thought. The clerk at the gun counter showed him a small assortment of pistols. One was a Ruger 9 mm. He filled out the paperwork and purchased the pistol and some cartridges. He had fired that type pistol in the past and felt comfortable with it. "Now that I have this thing, it will be illegal as ever to be carrying it. I can't get caught with it, but can I afford to be caught without it?" he reasoned. "How can I explain to police that I need protection?" He admitted to himself he may be overreacting, but he couldn't help but let his imagination run. "These recent events have stirred my imagination," he reasoned.

Kevin drove across town and onto Saint Charles Boulevard. He pulled into his garage and closed the door. He felt a little relief but still not secure. He left the lights off and watched the street. An occasional car went by. Finally, he went to his office and sat down at the desk to check his calls. "Am I paranoid, or what? I feel like a hunted deer." There was a message from Cheryl. "Please call me when you come home. I didn't want to call your car phone in the event you were with someone."

What does that mean? Kevin wondered.

"I didn't want to call your car phone in the event you were with someone," she stated.

He pondered that for a moment, *I was with someone, it so happens. Is she psychic? Oh well.*

He dialed the residence number of Cheryl's house, and there was no answer. It was now nearly nine o'clock, and he thought she would've been home with the young school age children. He turned on the television and tuned to the ball game. March madness was here, and Nolan Richardson's Razorbacks were beginning to get more national attention. They were in the middle of a red-hot game against the University of Tennessee. The game was tied with six minutes left in the third quarter. Todd Day and Lee Mayberry were hot-hot. They were pumping in one basket after another. For some reason, his mind went to Carol Fleichman. He wondered if she were watching the game. He had a hunch she was.

The game was over, and the Razorbacks held true to form. They won again. Arkansas fans were gloating about their state's flagship team. *We love a winner*, Kevin was thinking. "Does this team have the makings of a championship team? Oh boy! That would be nice."

The pistol was in a box with the Ruger emblem showing profusely. He looked at the box and told himself it will not be very useful like it is. He picked up the box, broke the seal, and lifted the pistol out. It fit his hand well enough, and he lifted it up and down a few times to test the weight and the feel. He worked the mechanism a few times and then got the clip out. It holds nine cartridges, the paperwork said. The nine bullets fit perfectly, and he inserted the clip into the pistol. That made it heavier and the balance better. He left the chamber empty for safety, then laid it into his attaché case that he carried with him when he was out. It would be left in the car with the case when he was away from the car.

"Tomorrow, I'll take a trip to an abandoned gravel pit to practice some shooting." He decided.

He tried Cheryl again at her house but no answer. It was now ten-thirty. Then his phone rang. "It's Cheryl," the voice whispered. "I'm calling you from my car. I have not been home since I called you earlier. There is a strange pickup truck that has been driving by slowly. I pretty much know the vehicles that usually are seen on our street. I guess I'm paranoid, but this is not a regular. I have taken the kids to my aunt's house, and I may go back to her house tonight. I don't feel safe. I hate to bother you, but are you free?" she asked.

"Yes, what did you have in mind, Cheryl?" Kevin couldn't believe this was happening.

"I would like for you to come and see the pickup and see if you have seen it around any of the offices. Kevin, I'm sorry, but I don't know who else to call on in this case. I want my uncle to stay at their house with my aunt and the kids. Mr. Harley continues to quiz me about who might have gone into the vault room the day he left it open. He is really concerned about something. I don't know what to think about him," she added.

"Okay, I'm on my way," Kevin said. He lived only a three- or four-minute drive from her house. "Where are you now?"

"I'm in my car. I just drove by my house a moment ago, and he was coming up behind me, so I continued on. I am afraid to go into the house until I know what this guy is doing. I am near my uncle and aunt's house, and I'll wait here and let you see what's going on. I am hesitant to call the police yet. I don't know if that would solve the problem that has caused these weird goings on."

"Good, you stay where you are and keep an eye out. I want to see this pickup too. I am almost to your house now." He had thought to bring his new pistol with him and had it lying in the seat by the console. He pulled over to the curb and worked a cartridge into the chamber and put the gun on safety. He pulled onto Cheryl's street and saw a Ford pickup parked near her house. He was glad he had the spotlights installed last month. He had felt they might come in handy sometime for various reasons.

He slowed, and as he got closer, he turned the spotlight on and shined it directly on the pickup. It was a red Ford truck, like the one he had seen at Red Lobster in North Little Rock. The man had a cap on now. Kevin couldn't see the face, but he suspected it had pits from acne. The truck pulled away from the curb, in a hurry, and took off as Kevin memorized the tag number. "What is that guy doing? First he's tailing me, and now he's watching Cheryl's place, and who is he?"

Kevin moved on away, to avoid attention of the neighbors, if he could help it. *Now…will this guy return? What does he want? Where is he from? Maybe he won't return tonight since he knows someone is onto him*, he pondered. He picked up his phone and dialed Cheryl.

"Kevin?" she answered the phone quickly. "Is everything okay? Was he there when you arrived?" she asked in rapid fire.

"He is gone, at least for now. I have no idea who he is or why he is stalking you and me. I'm sure there is a reason, but we'll have to find out or figure it out. I'd like for you to ask Mr. Harley tomorrow if he has any idea why this guy was tailing you. Don't say anything about his tailing me. Watch his face closely to see if there is any surprise or other reaction. I wonder if this is his doings or if there is a tie someway. You might try going home now and then watch the front. I'll try to cover the street for a while to see if he returns."

"Okay, Kevin, and thank you! I didn't know anyone else to call in this circumstance."

Kevin watched her street from a side street and decided the guy was not going to return. He called her and told her he hoped everything was clear but to keep her pistol handy. He headed home and kept an eye in his rearview mirror. He hoped the guy had quit…for tonight, at least.

What does all this have to do with appraisal business or the finance business? Kevin wondered. *There is some reason for it, but what?*

What have I done that has put someone on my tail and why is he tailing Cheryl?

Cheryl watched through the partially opened plantation blinds in her front bedroom with the lights off. She had her Smith & Wesson pistol in her hand with it loaded. *I need to practice shooting this thing*, she thought. She was thinking about where to practice when Kevin called and said he was leaving and going home. *We need to be able to talk to each other without being afraid of being seen. This is ridiculous*, she was thinking. She closed the blinds and called her aunt who insisted that she leave the girls there tonight and pick them up for school tomorrow. "I am alone…oh stop it," she told herself. The urge to invite Kevin to come by the house was strong. *"Would he think of me as too forward?"* she thought. "Oh well," she muttered.

As Cheryl reported for work the next morning, she greeted everyone and went straight to her office. She felt hesitant to mention last night's events to anyone. For some reason, she didn't want to go into details about what happened; she didn't want to be answering questions. Now though, Kevin had wanted her to approach Mr. Harley about the guy tailing her. *I wonder if he had something to do with that. He has been terribly pushy about that vault room event and…and…* She saw Harley as he walked into his office, and she could tell he was in a grumpy mood today. *What's new since he quit smoking?* Cheryl thought.

"Cheryl, please come to my office," the voice on the intercom said. Harley's voice betrayed his countenance when he arrived.

"Yes, sir," she responded and went to her boss's office.

"I know I have been pushing you lately, and I want you to know I appreciate your loyalty to me and our bank. That is always important, and I'm sure you realize how crucial it is that you be discreet in all of our business here. There are many things you will become aware of that is not for public consumption," Harley went on. "If there is anything you have questions about, be sure to come to me so we can talk in confidence." He sat back in his chair and looked at her expectantly.

Now what is he referring to? First the vault room has been a concern. Does he know about last night and wants to see how I react to that? Cheryl was wondering. "Yes, Mr. Harley, I am aware of the loyalty needed in my position. I have always tried to be responsible...always. Has there been a time when you have doubted that?"

"No, oh no, no," he responded. "I just want you to know that if you have questions about any of the bank's business, you must let me know. If there was anything you saw in the vault room recently that you want to know about, please feel free to ask me," Harley said warmly and sat up straight in his chair.

The vault room! Is it going to continue? Why? she thought. "Mr. Harley, I have told you the way things were when you left, and they were that way when you returned. I have no more to add to what I have already said!" Cheryl said firmly. "We have discussed this for three days now. It's making me nervous. Are you missing something from the vault room?"

"No, nothing is missing," Harley said and rose from his chair and walked to the front of his desk. "Cheryl, Mrs. Harley and I want to host a cookout at our home, a week from this coming Saturday, for you and the other personnel and a few other guests. I want you to prepare an appropriate invitation and mail it to their homes. I hope you will accept," he said softly.

"Yes, Mr. Harley, I will accept and be happy to attend," Cheryl replied. She held her hand up to stop Harley as he was about to dismiss her. "I want to tell you about something that happened to me last night," she said.

Harley walked back around to his chair and sat down. "Go ahead, what happened to you? Have a seat. He looked up at her, and she sat down.

Cheryl looked straight at Harley and told him about the man sitting in a parked pickup on her street, near her house. She didn't tell him about Kevin coming and running him off. Harley showed no emotion but said, "I'm sorry. Have you had that happen before?" He moved some papers around on his desk.

"The man was parked on the street near my house when I arrived. He moved on, and I assumed he had left. I went into the house with my girls. A few minutes later, I looked out and saw him parked there again. That worried me, so I took my girls to my aunt's house and left them. When I came back to my house, he was parked there again. This was going on quite late last night," she explained. Cheryl had been watching Harley closely.

"Cheryl, have you called the police? Maybe they should know about this." He picked up a folder from his desk, opened it, and started reading it. Cheryl felt dismissed.

"Yes, sir!" she replied. I'll get right on those invitations." She excused herself and returned to her office.

CHAPTER 14

Early Saturday morning, Kevin was in his office at home, reviewing the plans for a big house the head of a stock brokerage was to build in Chenal Valley. Winston Kenwood had sent an appraisal request with plans and specs and a letter requesting the appraisal. There was a copy of the contract. The letter asked Kevin to please render this service for us and was signed by Winston Kenwood, president.

The contract showed 2,300,000 dollars to build. A well-known builder, Roger Blansing, was to build the house. The specs showed that it would be top quality. Kevin got on the Internet and searched the Multiple Listing Service for some comparable sales. He found one sale of a similar house built by Blansing and two others by other builders that were similar enough to use for comparison.

Kevin spent a part of the day estimating the cost approach, then folded up the plans and got his camera and attaché case. He had his pistol and extra cartridges in the case and loaded things into his Blazer. The attaché was locked with a code as usual. He pulled into a gas station, filled the tank, and headed for the Chenal Valley area. These houses were large, and he had the powerful lenses on his camera so he could take adequate pictures from the street.

His first comparable was on the right side of the street, so he drove down a block and turned around so he could drive back and take pictures from the driver's side window. He had learned that when he got out of the Blazer to take a picture, sometimes the owner of the property saw him and would come running out to see what was going on. They then had questions that he couldn't answer because of confidentiality. So it was better to quickly take the photo and go on. He would usually drive up a little way and make his notes. This usually avoided the curiosity and questions. They sometimes were offended when he couldn't answer their questions.

The first set of pictures was taken without event and he went on to the second house. He pulled up to the second house, and there were three people standing out on the front lawn visiting. It was not good to take photos with people wondering what he was doing, and he didn't want to have to return, so he drove up in the driveway and courteously ask if he could take pictures of the property to use in a comparison in the appraisal of another property. "Do we know the house that's being appraised?" the lady asked.

"It is a new construction," Kevin replied.

"Well, who is building the house?" the man asked.

"I can't give the name of the party because at this time it is confidential," Kevin told him.

At that the man's expression changed and he responded, "Well, then you can't take any photos of this one. Sorry about that," he said. "You should just leave. We'll just keep this one confidential."

I handled that wrong, Kevin thought. He hated that because he had only three good sales for comparison, and he needed this one. "Thanks anyway," he said and backed down the driveway and drove away. He knew he could return when there was no one outside the house and take the photos. He could not be prohibited from taking photos of a property from the street because it was the public's right to view properties from the public streets.

He drove on to the next property and took photos from the street. These were three good sale comparisons, and he made his adjustments to the grids and felt good about the appraisal so far. He found the subject vacant land, a beautiful piece with three acres and a small stream running through it that had small dams to hold water. It gave a pleasant atmosphere that would provide a nice setting for the house. "It's looking good," Kevin thought, and he decided to go on and headed out to find an abandoned gravel pit where there would be a remote place to practice firing the new Ruger pistol.

The car phone rang. He wondered who might be calling on Saturday, and he thought about not answering it; but curiosity got the better of him. He picked it up, and it was Carol Fleichman. "Kevin, I hate to bother you on a Saturday. You probably don't want to think about work today," she said in a fresh, upbeat voice. She seemed to always speak in a cheerful and happy tone. Kevin wondered how she could maintain that tone when she should be loaded with issues of her job.

"Good morning, Carol, you must be ready for a ball game," he joked.

"Yep!" she responded. "I just finished an early one on one with my neighbor. I beat him too!"

"I should have known better than to ask. What are you up to today? Are you looking for that appraisal report for the assignment you gave me? I've been taking my time on that, but I'll get it back to you soon if you need it," Kevin asked.

"No, I am thinking about the last call from Mr. Harley. He called me yesterday and kept implying that I should be able to find those files on the Wemberly Warehouse. I think he knows we don't have them here, and he keeps bugging me about it to see how I respond. It's weird," Carol said. She still had the upbeat voice even though she was worried about the situation. "Kevin, I have an idea that I would like to talk with you about but not on the phone. If you have time, can we meet somewhere, sometime, without risking being seen together?"

"Sure, I am heading out to a gravel pit on Downing Road, off of Highway 10. I want to practice firing a new pistol. That place is remote, and we would probably not be seen."

"Hah, Kevin, you're talking like a teenager." She laughed. "You must promise to not act like one, and I'll bring my little pistol to practice also. I bet I can outshoot you," Carol declared, still with the bouncing and happy voice. *Maybe I wish he would act like a teenager—just a little bit,* she thought. "Hah," she said as some mischievous thoughts popped across her mind—it had been a long time.

"Good, I'll be at the gravel pit. Call me when you get to Downing Road, and I'll direct you from there to the pit," Kevin told her.

What does Carol want to talk about? Kevin wondered. His mind was going back to the conversation they had about a week ago. That was about Frank Harley and his demand that she find those files regarding Wemberly Warehouse.

He drove down the narrow road to the old abandoned gravel pit and got his Ruger pistol from his attaché case. He loaded the clip full and inserted it into the pistol. Then he got some of the metal cans from the back of his Blazer and set them against the wall of the old gravel pit. He backed off about ninety feet and drew down on the cans and fired once. He hit the can the first shot and sent it flying. "Wow," he said aloud. He aimed again and fired two shots rapidly. He hit with the first shot but missed with the second shot. "Aha," he said. "It kicked the nose up with the first shot, and I didn't allow for that before I pulled the trigger for the second shot."

His car phone started ringing, and he walked over to answer it. It was Carol. "Kevin, there is some dude in a red Ford pickup truck who I think is following me. I am going to drive past Downing Road in the event he is following me. I'll drive down a mile or so and pull over to the side of the road and stop. If he stops, I'll take off again," she said.

"Sounds like a good idea. Carol, I'll tell you about that pickup truck later, but I want you to be very careful. Don't get caught in a trap where you can't get by him. Shake him if you can and then come back to Downing Road, turn off, and drive until you come around the first curve and stop to see if you are followed. I think the dirt road is still wet enough to keep the dust from fogging behind your vehicle."

What's going on with this pickup truck guy? Kevin wondered. *Should I go out and confront him? Is Carol in physical danger at this moment? I feel though that it could be detrimental if we were seen together, especially if this guy is tailing people for some information gathering, which I suspect he is.*

Kevin waited with some trepidation. He liked that girl and was still wondering if he had known her from somewhere. She seemed to be smart and confident, so he could tell in her voice, and she seemed in control of herself. Maybe she can handle this pickup truck tail and get rid of him safely, but he still felt the need to go help.

The car phone rang, and he was glad he had stayed nearby. "It's Carol," the voice said. "I was just pulled over by a policeman. He said I was going ninety miles per hour in a sixty-mile zone. I told him about the pickup truck following me and that I was trying to get away from him. I think he had doubts, but he said he had noticed the red pickup close to me before I increased my speed. He said he was giving me the benefit of the doubt and just gave me a warning ticket, but next time, he would just take me in. Kevin, I don't see the guy now. I'll head back that way and see if he follows."

Kevin laughed! He could envision the scene with Carol trying to convince the officer of her concern for the pickup tailing her. He could see her constant expression of confidence and no fear.

Then, he imagined her concern for the pistol in her vehicle, if the officer decided to do a check of the car.

In a moment, his phone rang again. "It's Carol again, whew, I think I have gotten rid of that guy, and I am headed toward Downing Road. Tell me where to look for your location."

"Good…turn on Downing Road and drive to the first curve, pull over behind that old abandoned shed, and wait to see if you are followed. If not, continue on down the old dirt road two miles and look for a virtually obscure trail by two vertical crossties that form a gateway. That leads to the abandoned gravel pit. I'll be looking for you."

Carol didn't see the pickup truck anymore and turned on Downing Road. She wondered why they called it a road. It was seldom traveled now and had bushes growing close to the lane in places. She felt it should be called Downing Trail or something like that. She saw the curve, pulled around behind the old shed, and waited to see if she were followed. She was feeling some anxiety and her heart was pounding more and she wanted this thing to settle a little bit.

After a moment, Carol headed down the trail slowly for about two miles. The scene was hilly with some wooded area of semi-sparse trees. Several pine trees dotted the landscape with some oak trees mingled in. A few shrubs and plants were beginning to green up. She saw an old watershed pond along the way on the down side of the trail. It was full of water and appeared large enough that it could provide a little fishing. She liked to fish.

Up ahead, she saw Kevin's Blazer. He was watching for her. She saw the two vertical crossties for the gateway and turned into another little trail. Kevin followed her, and she drove down the trail until she approached the abandoned gravel pit. It appeared that the gravel had been mined thoroughly and the hole left. Those pits always left an ugly scar in the landscape and sometimes marred nature's beauty, she felt. She drove down to where she saw the end of his previous tracks and parked. Looking around, she saw a few clumps of grass here and there that looked like sage grass.

Kevin pulled in behind Carol and felt a flood of relief come over him. He realized how worried he had been. *Hey, this isn't supposed to be happening*, he was thinking. *I am just a real estate appraiser, trying to make a living. She is a customer. Here we are making a clandestine rendezvous.* He got out of his vehicle and felt like running to her and gathering her in his arms for a good hug of relief. He approached her slowly, though, and noticed her facial expression. It had that familiar look of confidence and her smile, though not as radiant as he remembered her normally, was still beautiful. *Darn it!* She wore jeans and a light-green jacket and a light-green cap with her blonde ponytail sticking out the back. He thought he'd give her a strong ten.

"Carol these are strange happenings for Little Rock, Arkansas!" Kevin said as he walked up to her. "What's going on? Do you have any idea what this truck is all about?" He told her about the same truck parked near Cheryl Inmon's house, and he thought the same man who seemed to have been shadowing him."

"I don't have any idea why that man was following me, but I will find out and handle it. That is ridiculous!" Carol said with emphasis. "I may have to get a larger pistol." She laughed. She got her little .32 caliber pistol out and some cartridges. "Here's what I have. I don't know if this would even scare anyone, but it might would if they cared about having a little hole put in them."

"All right, Carol, let's try a few shots and see if we can pop a few cans. I have a sack full in the back of my Blazer." They walked over to a spot to where they had a good view of the cans. "Now try your best, and I'll see if I can beat you," Kevin told her and backed off so he could watch.

She brought the pistol up to about shoulder level and held it in front of herself with both hands like a policeman would. *Gosh*, he thought. *She is no novice at this. That's a professional posture.*

Carol aimed for a moment and shot four times in a row without missing a shot. She had the cans bouncing.

"Good gracious, where did you learn to shoot like that?" he asked.

She chuckled and smiled. "Kevin, my ex-husband was a policeman. Back in our good days, we went to the police firing range a lot. He taught me how to shoot, and I suppose some of it has stuck with me."

"That figures," Kevin said. But he thought to himself, *Why is she single, and why would even an idiot let her get away?* He walked to the standing spot and raised the Ruger automatic with the 9 mm cartridges loaded into the nine-shot clip. He remembered the upward kick and tried to concentrate on that as well as his aim. He still had five cans lined up and aimed at them. He too held the pistol with both hands to control the aim. He looked at Carol and back at the cans. *Pow, pow, pow.* Three times he fired and the cans went flying. The fourth time he missed, but he got the fifth one.

"Well, I got four too!" he declared and looked at Carol, who was smiling. "Unh hunh," she chuckled and stepped forward again. She had reloaded the six-round pistol and was ready. "Look where those cans have landed. I am going to shoot them where they lie." She drew down on them and fired six times rapidly. Four cans were knocked to new locations.

"That's good, especially in rapid fire and at the scattered cans," Kevin said. He knew that was good. Now watch, and I'll shoot three cans twice each." He fired at the first can, hit it, but missed the second time. The second can he hit twice, and the third can was not shot at. A rabbit that had been hiding nearby apparently had all he could take and struck out across the field. Kevin shot once and missed but got him with the second shot.

The rabbit leaped into the air, and Carol said, "Hold it!" She ran and picked up the rabbit. She held him up by his back legs and said, "That's a head shot. Is that where you were aiming?" She smiled at him as she said that.

"Of course." Kevin smiled. "You know I wouldn't shoot him anywhere else because that that would ruin the meat." They both laughed.

Then Carol looked more serious and walked back to Kevin. "I do want to talk to you about something that is beginning to bother me, and I'm not sure how I should handle it."

"Go for it," Kevin responded.

"I have worked for New Bank of Pulaski and New Home Mortgage Company since I graduated college. I was there when Mr. Harley took charge of the bank and all of its holdings. He bought a large portion of the holding company's stock and was made the chief executive officer. He has been a hard driver and very persistent in what he wants," Carol explained. "He knows me, and I have told him we don't have those files on Wemberly Warehouse. He continues to ask for them. Something is wrong. I have felt he might have the files, but if he does, why would he still be asking? When authorities were investigating the death of Kennon Foster, he told them nothing was taken. Of course, I don't know how he would have known, for sure, and I don't know why he would have made that statement. I really don't know how he would have known."

"How strongly do you think *he* has the files?" Kevin asked. He was thinking of Cheryl Inmon's predicament. Harley was persistently asking her if anyone might have seen things in the file vault room behind his office. *If we knew someone who could get into the office and look inside the vault—but I suspect that is impossible,* he was thinking.

"I still worked at the bank a while after Mr. Harley came there, and I know the combination to the vault room if they haven't changed it. I think I could skim those files fairly quickly if I could get in," Carol said. "I don't have a key to the bank anymore."

Kevin's mind was clicking, but he was hesitant to speak these thoughts aloud. He thought maybe Cheryl had access to the bank but knew she might not too. She was Harley's personal secretary, but that didn't mean she would necessarily have a key to the bank. First, there were the exterior building doors to enter, and then the interior doors had different codes or keys. Then…Carol knew the code to Harley's office vault room. If Carol could give the code to Cheryl—but he thought, *Not yet. I don't know what relationship these two have with each other. I'll have to find out. Give me time.*

"Do you have someone at the bank you would trust or to whom you could give the vault room code?" Kevin posed the question and watched her face closely. She showed no emotional response but gave no answer.

"Let shoot a few more shots," she replied.

They exchanged pistols with each other and fired at the cans a few more times, and then Kevin let Carol leave first. He watched as she drove away. "Where have I been these past years? She has been there for several years, and I have been in the area most of the time since the university." He looked at the blonde ponytail and remembered it from college. She was a good basketball player, even as a freshman.

CHAPTER 15

One more photo to take of that comparable sale. *I'll get it if there are no people in the front of the house*, he thought. He pulled into town and drove down the street. There was no one in sight. He paused a moment with his window down on the driver's side and fired a photo shot toward the house. He pulled up a little bit and took another shot. He had the wide-angle lenses on and got two good pictures. "Good!" he gloated and chuckled. He drove on down the street, and suddenly a car was behind him and the horn was honking persistently.

"Oh no, it's Mr. Sourpuss," Kevin grumbled. He pulled over to the curb and watched in his rearview mirror as Mr. Sourpuss parked and walked up hurriedly.

"I told you no pictures of my house," he shouted angrily. "You cannot take pictures of my property without my permission, and I'll have your appraiser's license. Give me that camera. I'm going to show you a lesson." He reached his hand toward Kevin as though he expected Kevin to hand him the camera.

"Sir, just calm down!" Kevin said calmly and quietly. "You may not be aware that the view of property from a public street is free to the public and photographing things of public view is legally permissible. I don't think that will damage anything, and I'm sorry if you feel offended."

"Then why did you ask my permission earlier?" he yelled back, still very angry; Kevin felt the guy had had a bad day. The man wasn't backing down. "I'll have you arrested. I know my rights," he yelled absurdly. Kevin wondered how a man with this attitude and character had accumulated the wealth to build or buy a house of this magnitude—2,400,000 dollars.

"Sir, I asked your permission because you and some others were standing in front of the house, and it was a courtesy I wanted to extend. Now please excuse me, I must go."

The man was still shouting obscenities as Kevin drove away. When he returned to his office, he called the Realtor listed on the MLS sheet and asked him who that guy was who had bought that house. "It's no guy who bought that property. It's a wealthy widow lady." The Realtor chuckled. "He doesn't own the house or anything else. He is her uncle who lives there freely and wants to appear bigger than he is. You just met Mr. Big Dog—hah!"

"One more experience." Kevin sighed and laughed a little. "Everyone needs one more experience, I suppose."

CHAPTER 16

Tuesday morning, Kevin was buried in reviewing specifications and calculations of the big house to be built in Chenal. He was trying to finish up that project when his mail arrived, and he stopped to bring it in. He opened an envelope from New Bank of Pulaski. It was an invitation to a Saturday cookout at the Frank Harleys. *Now this is a bit unusual*, Kevin thought. *I am just an appraiser.* He had been accustomed to courting the banks and mortgage companies for their business, not their courting him. *Is it very often that appraisers are invited to office parties of banks? Well, I wonder about Frank Harley. Maybe I should get to know him better. Springtime is here, and it may be nice for a cookout*, Kevin thought.

He called Cheryl and asked her why he was included in the list of guests. "I think…well, I am not sure why, but your name was on the list," she responded. "You may be surprised at some others who are on the list. Please come, Kevin. I think you are more than welcome."

"Please let me give it some thought," Kevin told her. "I have several things I need to get done next weekend, some that will be difficult to put off," he lamely offered. "I'll let you know by tomorrow if possible." As he was speaking, he was looking out his office window and saw a red Ford pickup truck passing by slowly, but he couldn't see the driver. *Is that the guy with the acne pits?* he wondered. He watched to see if the pickup made another pass and to see if he could check the license plate number. He took his pistol from his attaché case, inserted the clip, and laid the pistol beside him on his desk.

After a few minutes, he decided the pickup was not coming back. *Now, what am I coming to?* he thought. *Am I getting paranoid? That probably was just another similar truck. There are lots of red Ford pickup trucks.* But that got him thinking about the incidents with the three of them, and also he remembered that they started when he was having dinner with James Carpenter. *Is there any correlation?* he wondered.

Kevin turned to the work on the Chenal appraisal for Winston Kenwood at First Trust Bank of Arkansas. He had purchased a little fancier cover for the report since it was a larger project and for the newer customer. He knew this bank handled several large loans, and the fees would be higher.

The cost approach was more complicated and more time consuming on this one. It had elaborate fixtures and finish. The fenestration was extra nice. It appeared it would cost a lot extra to build this house per square foot than most houses. It had three full stories and a large basement. The elevator was to be a high grade and fancy. The kidney-shape pool would have a 1,300 square feet pool house that could serve as a separate guesthouse. The landscaping was estimated to cost $120,000. The three acres of land would be designed for an elaborate garden.

Kevin completed the sketch with the Apex Sketch program and finished calculating the cost approach. It was good. The comparable sales were working out nicely, and it appeared the value was there for this assignment. He packaged the pages of the report and prepared extra copies. He could deliver them tomorrow. He backed up his files on the floppy disk and put it in the fireproof file box he kept in his kitchen cabinet. He turned his computer off and changed his password. He usually did this periodically. That lesson was learned when the hard drive crashed at the S&L, and they had a terrible time restoring the data. The password was a habit from being in an office with several people, and he felt it a good practice.

The work file for the Chenal assignment was put away in the file cabinet, and the plans were rolled up and placed in the plans rack where he usually kept them. As he walked out to get into his Blazer, he grabbed his attaché case. He had made this a habit and was especially conscious of keeping it with him lately since these strange things were happening. He had placed the appraisal report in the case as well as the Ruger. *Oh well*, he thought. *There goes my paranoia.*

His car phone rang as he got behind the wheel, and it was James Carpenter. "Hey, buddy," he said. "Join me for dinner tonight. Let's do a steak at Red Lobster. I'll buy." Kevin was surprised that he was in town again after being here just a few days ago. But he liked James and considered him an old friend. "Red Lobster it is," Kevin replied. "I was just leaving my house. I'll head that way."

He pulled in to Red Lobster and saw James Carpenter parked toward the back, and so he joined him in the next space. "Thanks for joining me," James said. "I hate to eat by myself, especially when I'm out of town."

"What brings you to town this soon?" Kevin asked. "You were just here last week." James was walking and let the question pass for the moment. He glanced around the parking lot a couple times and headed into the restaurant. Kevin couldn't help but look around the parking lot also. He saw nothing of interest. The traffic on McCain Boulevard was moderate. Shopping at the McCain Mall nearby was usually moderate on Tuesday evenings.

They fell in behind a waiter who was standing ready. "A booth please," James requested. "I'm tired." He plopped down into the booth and leaned back to relax. "I just drove in a few minutes ago. I have been in Fort Smith and thought I would come to Little Rock. How have you been? Anything happening?" James asked.

"Some," Kevin answered briefly. How about you? Are they still hounding you, James? I hope they have quit by now."

"Kevin, do you remember the Wemberly Warehouse loan application we had one year not long before we shut down? You know we turned that down because of the amount they asked to borrow on it. Well, I was contacted about that and asked if I could locate the file on it. I don't know where that file might have gone. Do you have any idea where it might be now? It seems the information they want might have to do more with the financial statement and the associated documents. They are pushing me now for the file and inferring that I have destroyed it purposely."

The waiter took their drinks order, and Kevin happened to look out the window and saw a red Ford pickup going by. He said nothing. It could be anyone. He couldn't see the driver.

"I'll have the New York Strip, medium rare," he said when the waiter returned. *He was a young man, possibly a college student,* he mused. The college student took James's order, and Kevin turned back to James and asked him what was in the file that made it so desired. James looked at Kevin with a tired look.

"That file contained the information of who the actual owners are and who controlled the inflow and outflow of items stored there from time to time. Much of it was not for public consumption. That file was not found when I left the office and the Feds took control. They wanted the files. I couldn't provide it. Do you remember it and maybe what has happened to it? I have battled this thing for the past three years." James gave a soul-piercing look straight into Kevin's eyes.

"Sorry, friend," Kevin stated. "I remember the case that you handled, and I did some of the research for you and had your files but returned them to you. I never did a case review on that one. I'm sorry, but I can't help you on this one. Is this a mafia deal or can you tell me?"

"Then it's better that you know nothing about it," James replied. "I'm serious. It has some very personal information about some of the principals. That is one that I wish had never graced our doors. We were supposed to be a simple operation. We didn't make the loan, but we did establish a file. Everyone wants the copy of the file. It could be that it was destroyed in the routine of destroying old files. That one could have been inadvertently destroyed too early.

Their steaks were served, and they ate in silence for a while. James ate his steak slowly and said very little during the meal. "Let's have some dessert," James said. Kevin agreed, and they waived the waiter over. When the dessert was finished, James wanted a last cup of coffee and seemed more relaxed. "Kevin…" James said, "I've been invited to a party Saturday at Frank Harley's place. I don't think I'll attend. I would have to drive back from Oklahoma, and I just don't care for that party now. I am not in that crowd anymore, and I don't know why I was invited."

"Aah, that's interesting," Kevin said. "They must be inviting half the finance world. They even invited me, and I don't know why I was invited. I have been doing some appraisal work for them, but that invitation seems strange to me. I haven't decided whether to go."

He told James about the red Ford pickup truck. James seemed too tired to get very excited about it, but said "Kevin, be careful and keep your eyes open. I'm glad I am in Oklahoma now."

The conversation drifted to memories of some good times and happy events at the old S&L, and they talked for another half hour, and they both seemed to feel a little better. James headed for his motel, and Kevin headed home.

It was late when he pulled into his driveway and pushed the button to open the garage door. He was glad to get home and get to bed, and he started pulling his jacket off as he walked into the house. "Man! What in the world?" He looked around at the disarray of things in the kitchen. The cabinet doors were all swinging open. Kevin set his attaché case down quickly and pulled his Ruger out and shoved the loaded clip into the handle.

He held the Ruger in front of him with both hands on the grip. He checked each room and stuck a hand around the doorway and flipped the light on and jumped in quickly and took a quick look while any possible intruder might be getting his eyes adjusted to the light. The search revealed no one. Then he discovered the back door had been unlocked by the glass being broken and the burglar simply reaching in and unlocking the dead bolt and the button on the doorknob. *How simple*, he thought. That wasn't a very secure way of locking my house.

Computer Stolen

He immediately looked for the fireproof box where he kept his more important documents and his backup floppy disks. He found it lying in the living room floor with the lid ajar. It had been slammed to the floor and broken. All the folders were gone, and the other things had been rummaged through.

The floppy disks were all still in the box, but they were scrambled. Each disk was coded, and only he could identify any of them. It appeared someone had tried to gather them up but had dropped them and left. Kevin wondered if he had surprised the burglars. The data disks contained copies of his appraisal reports and his data on various researches. *What were they after?* he wondered.

Kevin advanced his observations to the office. "Oh, man!" he exclaimed. The file cabinet drawers were open. "And hey! The computer is gone." His mind raced in near panic. "Wait," he said aloud, to himself. "That red Ford pickup", he remembered. "Maybe that was that guy at Red Lobster parking lot whom I saw passing through. Was that circumstance? Why? Would James Carpenter set me up? He's my friend!" Kevin sat down in his office chair and pondered. Was he kept away from his office to give a burglar time to rummage his house and get his computer?

"What to do—police?"

No, he answered himself mentally. *I don't think I'm ready to get them involved at this time.* For some reason, his mind went to Carol Fleichman.

Kevin dialed Carol quickly, and she answered. "Carol, have you seen that red Ford pickup today or tonight?" he fired at her rapidly.

"What's up, Kevin, I thought that guy had left town. Have you seen him?"

Kevin was so frustrated, he thought that was irrelevant. "Maybe I saw him tonight, but I can't say it was that guy. It could have been someone else. I wonder if someone thinks I have those missing files. Have you found them yet?

No. I think they are in Harley's possession at the bank. He keeps pressing me, but I think that is some kind of ruse for some reason, which I don't know. What's up with you? You sound urgent!" Carol pressed him.

"I have been burglarized tonight, between 5:00 and 8:00 p.m. I went out to eat and was hit while I was gone. They stole my computer," Kevin explained. "I am not sure which way to turn. If I bring the police in, there goes what privacy I have. The newspapers and television news will jump on it. I don't want all the questions."

"What about checking with the pawnshops tomorrow morning, after someone has had time to pawn it? If it is a druggy, he'll sell it quickly. Do you have the serial number of the computer?" Carol asked.

"Yes, I have that and the operator's manual in the file cabinet, and I'm looking at it as we speak. I'll take that and check the pawnshops tomorrow. I need that computer. Actually, I can't think of anything on it that anyone should want it for. But I will have to get a new one and reacquire all the programs I work with including the appraiser software. That will be a major job for me.

"Now, Carol, I'm wondering about something. I have been invited to the cookout party at Frank Harley's house Saturday. Have you been invited?" Kevin asked her.

"Hah! Yes, I think everyone under the sun has been invited to that party," she said. "I really don't want to go to it though. I have something else in mind. Are you going?"

"I haven't decided, but I really don't want to go. I don't see anything to be gained but to hobnob with the bigwigs—maybe that would be advantageous," Kevin mused. "Maybe I should go. I wonder if other appraisers will be there. Now that might be a reason to go. I have a strange feeling all the while that my business relationship with this bank is more than just my service to them."

"I'll tell you later what I had in mind, but I think my absence would be conspicuous, since I am an employee," Carol guessed. "But I can think of better things to do. I suppose I will show up even if it is a Saturday and my free time as an employee," Carol moaned. "C'mon, let's go, maybe we can enjoy the atmosphere—keep our eyes and ears open. There is something rotten in Denmark, don't you think?"

"Okay, I'll be there," Kevin said. Actually, he was thinking about the two employees in this banking system that made his association more appealing. There were two especially attractive women. Life in the business world was getting more interesting.

—⁂—

The next morning, he was on the streets hitting the pawnshops in search of his computer. He checked with the first two, and they had not received any this morning. The third one had a new one, but it was not his, for sure; it was the wrong brand. The fourth shop had one that looked like his and had just been pawned that morning. He showed the shop owner his papers and the serial number. It had been pawned by a pimple-faced man who said he had to make a trip immediately and would be picking it up this Saturday. They checked the serial numbers on the case, and the owner just handed it over to him. He didn't ask if he had a police report. *That's luck*, Kevin thought.

By now, it was afternoon, and he thought he would just go back to his office and get his work lined out again. Cheryl called. "Are you going Saturday?" she inquired. She sounded hopeful. "I hope you *will* come," she said. "I'm not looking forward to the party. Maybe we can talk a little without raising much suspicion of anything except normal business relationship." She spoke in a low voice. Kevin could envision Cheryl in her blouse and long skirt and high heels. She was the epitome of an executive secretary.

Harley knows how to pick 'em, he thought.

"Cheryl, I have some extra work to do in my office, but I'll plan on it. Well, I'll just say yes. I'll be there," he said more firmly this time. He hoped to gain more information from her and from Carol Fleichman about the workings of this bank.

—❦—

Kevin set the computer into the slot where he always positioned it and began to plug in the cables and lines. "What a mess," he grumbled. *At least maybe I can get everything working and get things back in order*, he thought. He got up from the floor and brushed his hands and knees off a little. "I've got to dust this floor today." He missed Marylyn in many ways. She kept things immaculate. Kevin kept things, but he could use more of the woman's touch. The place under the desk where all the wires were had a way of collecting dust and lint.

Everything was hooked as they should be, and he turned the computer on. The Microsoft flag appeared, and he looked forward to getting on line. He looked for the Total software icon, the appraisal program software. It was not there. Several other familiar icons were not showing up. He pressed the buttons to pull up his document files. They were different. There were only a few and not his. He checked the properties of the hard disk. It was a different hard drive. His hard disk had been removed and another installed. He checked the serial number on the case. It was the same number.

"Now it figures," he said aloud. "They didn't want a computer. They just wanted my hard drive." He had been using this computer for three years and had owned it as his own since before he left the S&L. "What do they want with my hard drive? Now, I must start from square one and rebuild my computer with the new programs and reload the data from the backup floppy disks." He didn't trust this hard drive that was now in the computer. What if it is bugged?

His phone rang; it was Carol. "Hey, Appraiser Man," she said. "I have an appraisal assignment for you to pick up if you want to come by about five o'clock. Do you have your computer going?"

"Guess what! I did find the computer in a pawnshop, but the hard drive was changed out. There is a different one in there. I think they just wanted my hard drive and then put another one in and got rid of it at the pawnshop," Kevin explained.

"Why would they want your hard drive only? Do you have some files in that hard drive that would be useful enough to someone to cause them to steal it or have it stolen? Do you have your files backed up?" Carol asked.

"Yes, I always back up my files on floppy disks each day. I have three years of floppies with backup data. They had been ransacked, but they couldn't figure out the right one and apparently didn't take any of them. They might have been scared off when I arrived. I think I'll buy a new computer and upgrade it while I'm starting over. I can restore my data on it. I'll do some checking on old data while I'm doing that."

Old data! That suddenly struck a chord with Kevin. The old data reaches back to his last year at the S&L. Those backup floppies had been stashed in storage boxes in his ministorage building. He had not bothered that storage building in a long time.

He and Marylyn had bought that ministorage facility a year before she died. When he left the S&L, he stored some boxes of old memorabilia from ten years at the S&L. No one knew about the things there, and he had not thought about them in two years. There was no wonder the intruder had not taken the backup floppies. He could tell they weren't old enough. *That's why he wanted the hard drive*, Kevin thought. The hard drive…that had been replaced shortly after he left the S&L when his hard drive crashed.

Kevin drove up to the New Home Mortgage Company at precisely 5:00 p.m., and Carol met him at the door. "I'm glad you could come now. The rest of our crew has gone to the Harley's to help prepare for the party Saturday. I knew you wanted a chance to look at the office where Kennon Foster died. See what you think of the circumstances here," she said as they walked back to the office.

Kevin looked at the desk and asked Carol if any of the furniture had been moved to different positions since the death. She said it was all still in the same location, and the chair was still there; although she had moved it to the corner and had a different one for herself. Kevin moved the other chair behind the desk and looked at the chair and the credenza. He sat in the chair and pushed backward. It rolled smoothly and freely across the hardwood floor and came to a stop against the credenza. "There goes the theory about his rolling back and it tipping over so that he hit his head on the credenza," Kevin surmised.

"If he was on the floor when he was found dead, I would think he had been put there after he was hurt, so it would look like an accident. If he had a blow to the back of the head, that would not likely be a suicide. Isn't that something *rotten in Denmark*? It doesn't smell right," Kevin ventured aloud.

"Take this appraisal assignment and get gone. I think it is not safe for you to be here with the two of us alone. They'll pull you into this quagmire more than you are," Carol said.

"Right, thanks for giving me the opportunity to look at the situation. I don't know why there has been no advancement in this case."

He was detecting the faint fragrance of perfume. It was very pleasant and caught his attention. *After all, Carol is an attractive woman,* Kevin almost said aloud. He looked at Carol, and she was not frowning. "But she did say I should get gone," he admitted.

Kevin pulled away from the New Home Mortgage Company office, and behind him was a red Ford pickup truck. He slowed down to let the truck pass but the truck's driver slowed down also. He drove slowly along hoping the driver would pass so he could check the license number. Unfortunately, in Arkansas, there are no license plates on the front of the vehicle. Finally, the pickup turned off, and Kevin couldn't see the license number. Was it the pock-faced man? That was always the question when he saw a red Ford pickup. Was that guy tailing him always? Why?

CHAPTER 17

The Party

The party was more than a cookout. There were cars parked up and down the street, and the long driveway was full of big cars and little cars. There were Arkansas license plates and some Texas license plates. Kevin looked and wondered facetiously if there would be a red Ford pickup. He parked down the street and walked up to the gateway of the large mansion type residence. The grounds were immaculate and extravagant. *It must be nice to be a banker*, Kevin thought. Frank Harley had been successful, undoubtedly. He had several bank branches and six mortgage offices now.

He was greeted at a table in the front yard and asked to sign in. "We welcome you to our home, The Harleys" the large sign stated. He was given a name tag with his occupation and title stated, and he was directed to the backyard. A waiter and waitress stood at a drink box where he was offered his choice of drink. Beer and sodas were being snatched up, and he took a soda.

Kevin wondered if the scar-faced pickup truck driver would be there, but he doubted it. He walked through the beautiful garden of sculptured shrubbery. There was no question but that a gardener or two spent full time working on this landscape—it was beautiful.

The hostess, Penny Harley, walked up and greeted him. "Welcome to our party, Kevin. Frank wants you to join him at the pavilion and meet some friends."

Of course, Kevin thought. *I am one of the bunch, and I will just fit right in with these bigwigs. I am an all-powerful appraiser. Hah! This is strange.*

"Come on over, Kevin." Harley boomed out as he stood with a group of men. I want you to meet some of my friends. "I think you know Winston Kenwood." Kevin stepped over to Kenwood and shook hands with him. "Now, I want you to meet a special guest today, Shelton McKinley. Shelton has driven up from Texarkana to join us. Gentlemen, this is Kevin Henry, one of our independent appraisers. Kevin formerly worked at the Central Arkansas Workers Savings and Loan Association. He worked with James Carpenter."

"Yes, Kevin, it's good to see you again," Winston said.

Shelton McKinley stepped forward slowly as he studied Kevin. "Of course, Kevin, I'm glad to meet you. I'm sure I've heard James Carpenter speak of you through the years," he said.

Kevin wondered about this statement and felt strange. *There's more to this than readily meets the eye—three bankers, one larger bank, one huge Arkansas bank, and the head of a giant savings and loan and conglomerate of other things. Yes! Now what do they want with me?*

Kevin had expected Shelton McKinley to be a large man with a strong voice, but instead, he saw a slight man who walked with a cane and had one shriveled leg and arm, probably from polio. His voice was gravelly and not strong. He had heard, though, that McKinley was a very shrewd man who had manipulated a small beginning into an empire. He had piercing eyes that seemed to engulf a person and look deep inside him at the same time. Kevin wondered if McKinley could read his thoughts.

"Kevin, may I introduce my wife, Elizabeth," McKinley said. She was a dazzling blonde about forty years old, Kevin guessed. He guessed McKinley to be about sixty-five, at least. Elizabeth smiled warmly and extended her hand. "We must get to know you, Kevin," she said. He caught a glimpse of Cheryl Inmon out of the corner of his eye. She was watching his reaction.

"Kevin, how long ago did you leave the savings and loan association?" McKinley asked.

"Mr. McKinley, I left there a couple years ago, maybe longer," Kevin replied. "I worked several years there with James Carpenter. He is a good man. Did you know James well?"

"I knew James only slightly," he replied a little hesitatingly. "We saw each other only at some of the regional meetings of S&L leaders and bankers." Elizabeth looked at McKinley quickly. Kevin noted that.

"Mr. McKinley." Frank Harley's voice boomed out. "We are fortunate to have Kevin Henry to serve on our appraiser panel. He is very talented and knowledgeable of the market in the Little Rock area. He understands the finance end of this business also. Kevin, I thank you for coming, and I hope you will stay and enjoy the party." With that, he motioned to Cheryl Inmon. "Cheryl, would you show Kevin around and introduce him to some of the other guests?" With that, Kevin felt dismissed.

Cheryl walked over and invited Kevin to walk with her. "I'm glad you could come," she said as they walked along a flower and shrubbery lined pathway. "Do you feel like you were getting the once-over?" she said. "Mr. McKinley always seems to be analyzing you. He gives me the creeps sometimes."

Kevin laughed. "I think I know what you mean. But I'm glad we can talk here by invitation, and maybe it won't set off suspicion. How have you been? Has the scar-faced man followed you anymore? That is a concern to me. All of this banker business is strange, and I think there is something interwoven, and it may be tied to the Wemberly Warehouse files. Was Harley the one who was pushing my invitation or were you giving me a chance to mingle and hobnob with the bigwigs?"

Cheryl smiled. "Mr. Harley had told me to make sure you accepted the invitation. Kevin, I'm glad you accepted and came," she said warmly. Kevin didn't find it unpleasant to walk with her as they visited with other guests. She was a beautiful woman, and any man would be glad to be in her company. She was wearing more relaxed clothing and flat shoes. After all, it was a relaxed party. "Is Harley still pressuring you about what you might have seen in the vault room?" Kevin asked her.

"Not as much," Cheryl replied. "It does make you wonder what is in there, doesn't it? There must be something of utmost importance that is not for other's consumption. It does raise one's curiosity. I'm almost afraid to even think about what's in there." Cheryl smiled and then had a little frown on her face.

"What's wrong?" Kevin asked her.

"I think about the things that have happened and wonder if there may be a killer in this crowd. I think Kennon Foster was murdered, and the killer could be among us," she replied. Are you being careful all the while, or do you feel a sense of danger? I sometimes get too nervous and wonder if it shows."

"Cheryl, we must get to the bottom of this somehow," Kevin said. "I wish you knew what is in that vault room of Harley's, but don't take any chances. We must figure out something to see what that place holds."

They walked around meeting many people in the banking crowd. Kevin tried to be observant about the people he met and realized he had to be careful not to appear as searching everyone when he was introduced by Cheryl—but he was.

Kevin looked across to the return pathway in the garden and saw Carol Fleichman talking to Jim Hammons. *Interesting*, he thought. Jim has been one of the more lenient appraisers in the area, but it was rumored he had become more conservative since the financial meltdown of some banks and the senate investigations of the failed S&Ls and banks. He had been called in to answer a lot of questions. Appraisers were being routinely blamed for giving false values. Some were being charged with crimes of different sorts. Less was being said about the finance people who pressed for artificially high appraisals to back their loans.

Carol looked his way and flashed her white toothed smile. She moved along, and Jim Hammons was staying right with her and talking hard. Kevin wondered what the conversation might be.

Cheryl had noticed the couple and said, "It appears Carol has her hands full. She was told to contact Jim Hammons to see if he is still as conservative as he had become. We need some fearless appraisers," Cheryl said and watched for Kevin's reaction.

Kevin kept a relaxed face and hid his feelings about that remark. *Just what are you saying, Cheryl?* Kevin thought. "Well, I heard Jim used to hit the numbers pretty well, but then he had a close call with the FDIC boys, and it nearly scared the britches off him," Kevin said with a grin and watched Cheryl. She didn't respond.

"You never know what might happen in this business," Cheryl said a little sadly. "Carol has been told to talk to Jim about some appraisals we need to have done." They moved on down the path and approached another group, which consisted of several Realtors. Kevin stopped and Cheryl kept going.

One of the Realtors was Jenny Lafferty who stepped forward and introduced herself. "I'm Jenny Lafferty," she told Kevin loudly and proudly as she stuck out her hand. She was holding a drink cup from the bar and seemed to be imbibing heavily. Kevin knew her, and she had known Kevin for many years. They had met when he worked at the Central Arkansas Workers S&L and before he became an independent appraiser and came up with the low appraisal on her sale. She turned around and looked at the other Realtors. "Kevin is an accomplished real estate appraiser," she said. "He is *very* accomplished, aren't you, Kevin?" Jenny said in deriding tone.

"I supposed that's in the eyes of the beholder," Kevin responded with a slight smile and started moving down the path, away from the group.

"Kevin, don't you want to explain to this group of all you have accomplished? I'm sure they would like to know," she said in a loud and syrupy tone, and the others laughed. Kevin didn't know if the laugh was in sympathy for him or joining Jenny's sarcasm. "Maybe Cheryl can pull your irons out," Jenny continued and laughed loudly.

He ignored the remarks, and they headed back toward the group of bankers. They arrived at the group just as Carol and Jim Hammons were walking up. Kevin and Jim Hammons shook hands and walked off to the side as the ladies started talking and picking up a soda at the table.

"Kevin, I'm glad to see you in this crowd. I'm not sure if I'm glad to be here. Are you doing a lot of business with this bunch now?" Jim asked him. "They had virtually quit me for a while, but I was called back this week for a commercial job," he stated. Kevin hoped he would stop there. He didn't want to know what Jim might be about to tell him.

"Jim, these banks and mortgage companies do a lot of business and order a lot of appraisals. I think the pressure could be there if they get a little crack in your armor. Be careful!" Kevin stated in a friendly way.

Carol Fleichman walked up and asked Kevin if he would like a hamburger or hotdog, and he was glad for the opportunity to chat with her for a while. She looked like the girl next door and a breath of fresh air. She had on a denim skirt and matching denim shirt. Her feet were clad with a pair of red canvas shoes. Her hair was done in a simple ponytail. "How's that for a mortgage company manager?" he asked himself.

They prepared a hamburger and moved over to a table where they were alone. *Carol looked at Kevin with her constant smile that seemed a little more vivid*, he thought. "How's this for luck," she said in a low voice. "I wanted to talk with you, and now I can officially do so because of my assignment."

Carol glanced subtly toward the banker's tent and back to Kevin. Still with the constant smile on her face, she said quickly, "Kevin, I have been told to get Jim Hammons to appraise the Wemberly Warehouse property. We still need an appraisal on it, and you haven't wanted to…so I'm told." Old Jim has been appraising for a long time and knows his business. He has always been a liberal and cooperating appraiser until he tightened up a year ago. He hasn't accepted the assignment yet. I'm worried about this." In an even lower voice, she said, "I'm hoping he doesn't yield to the temptation. Mr. Harley is to talk to him also about taking the assignment." Kevin looked in her eyes and could see the concern in her eyes even as she had the constant smile in her face.

CHAPTER 18

Rachel, one of the girls from the New Home Mortgage Company office walked up to Kevin and told him his car phone had been ringing almost constantly for the past half hour. "Uh-oh," Kevin said. "I need to check that out. It sounds important. He excused himself and left.

When he walked up to his Blazer, which was now sandwiched between two cars, he was suddenly hit from behind with a club and went to the ground. He could feel hands going into his pockets, and then he passed out. When he awoke, his keys were gone, but his Blazer was still there. His wallet was still in his hip pocket and nothing had been removed. People were crowding around, and Carol and Cheryl were running up. There was a huge knot already on the back of his head, and he could barely sit up. He could hardly focus his eyes and see clearly.

"What happened?" several were asking.

"Did you faint?" someone asked. He keeled over again, and someone caught him as he went down.

"Call 911," someone said. That was the new emergency system being advertised on the police cars and around town.

Carol yelled at Rachel to come to her. "You said his car phone had been ringing for the past half hour. Is that true?"

"There was a gentleman who told me that it had been ringing and would I let him know," she said. "I didn't know the man but just came to tell Kevin," Rachel said.

"Has anyone called 911?" Carol shouted. No one answered. "Never mind then, I'll take him to emergency. I'll get my car, and someone help me get him in." Her car was near, and she turned it around quickly pulled up to where Kevin was now sitting up again. "Help me get him in the front seat," Carol instructed. By this time, others in the party were arriving. She saw Frank Harley and Winston Kenwood running up, but she didn't wait. She drove off with Kevin sitting up in the front seat.

"Take me home, Carol." He told her his address. "I think that's where I need to go immediately," Kevin said. He was beginning to think clearly now. "My keys are gone, and I think I know why."

Carol looked over at him and said, "Look at me, Kevin." When he looked toward her; she could see his vision seemed normal, and he was sitting up straight. "Okay, we are headed toward your house." And she speeded up. "Why do you think we should go there now instead of the emergency room? You have had a whale of a lick on your head. You really should be going to the emergency room," she said but kept driving.

"I'll be okay," Kevin said. "I have a headache, but that'll go away," he claimed and leaned back against the seat. "I think the person or persons who got my keys would be headed to my house, and I want to stop them before they ransack the place. There has to be a connection between this and the other break-in."

"I gotcha," Carol responded and speeded up a little more. They were approaching Kevin's house. She glanced over toward him, and he had passed out. She immediately turned her car and headed toward the hospital. As she looked in her rearview mirror toward Kevin's house she saw a red Ford F150 pickup truck cruising down the street. She couldn't tell if it stopped. She speeded up and hoped she hadn't done the wrong thing by obeying Kevin's request to go to his house. A brain concussion was what she feared now. She headed to the Baptist Hospital emergency entrance. Thankfully, she had put emergency numbers in her car phone and she dialed the number. They acknowledged her call and were waiting when she drove up.

Attendants parked her car, and other emergency people put him on a gurney, and she ran with them into the hospital and explained what was going on. Doctor and nurses took him immediately for examination. Frank Harley and Winston Kenwood appeared and seemed to be very concerned about Kevin. "What do you think is going on, Carol?" Harley asked.

"That's a good question, Mr. Harley," Carol replied. "Why would they target him, an appraiser guest?"

"Well, you stay with him and see that he's taken care of. If there is any expense to him, the bank will take care of it," Harley said. "He was our guest." He and Kenwood then left.

The nurse came to Carol and told her Kevin was conscious again and was calling for her. When she went into the room, he tried to raise himself up, but they pushed him down and told him he must lie as still as possible and on his back for the next twenty-four hours. He had a concussion, and it was a dangerous one. "But, Carol, I'm okay, and I need to go to the house as quickly as possible," Kevin was insisting.

"Is there something I can get for you?" Carol asked him. You might really hurt yourself if you don't stay down. What can I do?" She looked at the nurse who said she would excuse herself for a few minutes if need be. Carol nodded yes, and the nurse left.

"Carol, I think whoever knocked me in the head was after entry to the house, but on that key ring were some other important keys. One is a key to a padlock I have on a ministorage rental unit. For several years, I have made a duplicate key ring for all my keys I carry with me. I keep it hanging inside the kitchen cabinet located to the right of the sink. I want you to do me a favor and go buy a medium size padlock for the ministorage at Hanson's

Storage on Camp Robinson Road in North Little Rock. You will need to go get my Blazer.

"You don't have your car keys, Kevin," Carol chimed in quickly. "How can I get that?"

"Okay, I always keep a spare key in a little magnetic box located under the fender well of the right front fender of the Blazer. That little box, if it hasn't fallen from the fender well, also has a key to the house. If the key is there, I want you to go into the house and get the spare key ring. After you have gotten a new padlock, go to Hanson's ministorage and change the lock on unit 37. They may not have any idea that I have a ministorage unit, but just in case, I want to change the lock so they won't have a key. I think that is the most important thing now. Don't bring the police into this yet. I think it's best."

"Okay, Kevin. I'm gone, and you should stay down and get quiet. Do what they tell you. You must give your head time to go back to normal," Carol admonished him. She could tell he was getting nauseous, and she went to get the nurse. She went on to get the Blazer.

Carol found the little magnetic box and took off in the Blazer to check on Kevin's house. She had never been to his house but knew where he lived. Probably an hour had passed since they had found him after the attack, and she wondered what she might find. The street was abandoned at the moment. She pulled into the driveway and saw no vehicle, so he or they hadn't arrived yet or had been there and gone already.

Oh migosh! My pistol…I wish I had it, but it's in my car, and that's no good now, she was thinking. Suddenly, cold chills ran up her back. *What if they're in there.* Carol stopped at the door and listened. *There is a noise inside, but there is no car or truck out here in the driveway or on the street*, she was thinking. She listened again carefully. There was no sound. "Maybe it was my imagination," she told herself. "Wait, Kevin's pistol should be in his Blazer," she remembered. She ran back to the Blazer and searched until she found the pistol in the console where it was handy for him.

Carol crammed the loaded clip into the butt of the pistol and worked a bullet into the barrel. "Now," she said to herself, "maybe my chances will be better." She walked to the door and tried the key. The key fit the lock perfectly, and she opened the door quietly. Carol remembered the police training her husband had showed her, and she searched the house thoroughly until she got to the back door. It was wide open and the burglar or burglars had gone. She locked the back door and went back through the house. Kevin's office had been ransacked. The computer was gone. It had been stolen again. *Okay, it's too late to stop that, but I've got to get to the storage unit now. Maybe they know about that and maybe not.*

Carol jumped into the Blazer again and took off for the Hanson Ministorage on Camp Robinson Road in North Little Rock. She must pick up a medium size padlock on the way. She remembered Levy Hardware on Camp Robinson Road. If she could reach it before they closed, that would be the quickest. Otherwise, Walmart would still be open, but that would take longer. She drove into the parking lot of the hardware store just as they were starting to lock the door, but they waited for her. "A medium size heavy duty padlock is what I need, and I'll leave quickly so you can close," Carol told the clerk. He showed her the padlocks, and she picked one that looked strong, paid the man, and ran out the door.

"Now to get there before the burglar does," Carol told herself. She pushed down on the pedal and looked to see if a patrol car was in sight. "In luck so far, Carol. I feel this is probably the more important part of the mission, anyway," she said aloud. She slowed the vehicle to a normal speed and pulled into the lot, pushed the code numbers Kevin had told her, and waved to the caretaker. He waved back, and she proceeded on to unit 37. There was no one there. "Maybe they don't know about it," she said hopefully.

She took time to open the unit and look inside. Everything was stacked neatly and in some kind of order. There were boxes of things but not marked so that one could tell whether it had floppy disks or some other supplies. *That's good, Kevin*, she said mentally. Carol closed the door and put the new padlock on the unit and got back into the Blazer, which was parked outside the door.

There was a car moving slowly down the driveway between the columns of storage units. A sense of fear came over her. Could that be the burglar coming to check the unit? Carol moved the Blazer on and made the turn around the end, turning back into the next driveway between the next two columns of units. She parked the Blazer, got out, and walked over to furtively look around the corner toward Kevin's storage unit. The car had gone on down to the end, and a woman was going into another unit. "Whew, I must be running scared," she said aloud to no one.

Back in the Blazer, she headed toward Little Rock for Baptist Hospital and Kevin Henry. She pulled the Ruger pistol from her skirt waistband and tucked her blouse back in. The pistol had provided some feeling of security. She placed it in her purse and went inside.

In room 2215, there were several people waiting in the hallway. Frank Harley and Winston Kenwood were inside the room visiting Kevin. Cheryl Inmon was outside with some others. "Where have you been?" Cheryl asked. "Everyone has been asking about you."

"I had to make a quick trip to the office and check on some things to be sure they were done and sent off this week," Carol lied quickly. It seemed that what she had done was not what everyone should know. *Who is communicating with this burglar about Kevin's actions and plans?* she thought.

Carol waited until the group had visited Kevin two by two, and when Cheryl came out, she told Carol that Kevin was asking for her. "He said you did a good job, and he wants to thank you for what you did. The rest of us are going home. He needs rest, of course. Concussions can be bad." Cheryl said and walked down the hall and out.

Kevin was lying flat when she walked in, and he started to rise when he saw her, but the nurse pushed him back down. "You must stay flat," she told him sternly. "Promise me you will, and I'll give you some privacy."

"Okay, if I must. Thanks for the reminder. I'll do what I must do," Kevin replied.

The nurse left the room, and Carol moved closer and started talking in a low voice. "Kevin, have you recovered any old files from the floppies to your new computer?"

"No, I intended to, but I took all the floppies to the storage and haven't had a chance to get all of them and put them back on the computer. I want to buy a new computer and then go through all of them to see if I can see why they want them. Don't tell me they have ransacked the storage unit," Kevin inquired quickly.

"No, but they had beat me to your house and had ransacked it and stolen your new computer.

"Hah!" Kevin replied. "They got the old computer again. I haven't had a chance to go buy a new one, and I have hidden the backup floppies in my Blazer. They probably did not do any searching of it. I think I'll let them keep it or take it to the pawnshop again. But, Carol, I need your help more if you can. Find a locksmith to change the locks on my house and include a deadbolt at each door. Also look in the pocket on the back of the rear seat in the Blazer, and you'll find the floppies. Since they have the key to my Blazer, I don't want to take a chance of losing the data on them. Although, there is nothing on them but what work I have done since the last theft."

Carol looked at Kevin and couldn't help but smooth his hair back and look deep into his eyes. "Kevin, you have been pulled into something that is a mystery to me, and I guess you too. But know this—I am glad to be with you. I remember seeing you in college and wishing I could be in your group of friends, but you…" She pulled away as he looked up at her. Her face reddened a little.

"I'll take care of those locks for you tonight. I'm on my way."

—⚜—

The locksmith said he would meet her at the house and install new locks. By now it was dark and nearing ten o'clock, and Carol hoped the day would be over shortly. She had had enough excitement for the day. She pulled into the driveway and saw dim lights inside the house, like flashlights, but they went off. "What the… there's someone in the house," she said. She grabbed Kevin's pistol and ran around to the rear of the house. She figured they saw her car lights and would leave that way again. Carol was rounding the corner of the house when she saw the two figures running across the backyard. "Hey," she hollered. "Stop right there."

One of the figures fired a shot in her direction and kept running. The bullet hit the brick on the corner of the house, and particles of brick stung her face and some went into her eye. It was a small particle, but she held her fire. *I hope we don't bring the neighborhood here. Neither Kevin nor I want that. It's best we don't have that publicity at this point*, she was thinking. *I can get this grit out of my eye by myself.*

"Apparently the figures jumped over the low metal fence and crossed the backdoor neighbor's yard to the next street where they must have been parked. That's why she hadn't seen a vehicle each time she had driven up today. Now they have a key," Carol reasoned. "Well, that ease of entry is about to stop. The locksmith will be here soon."

The locksmith drove up just then and got out of his truck. "I hope you haven't been waiting long," he said with a friendly greeting. Why the sudden need to change locks tonight? Surely there wouldn't be any unwanted entries in this neighborhood. Are you locking your hubby out? Hah," he kept yakking. She let him keep talking and just ignored him. He went on talking as he installed the new locks.

He was finishing up when she noticed a red Ford F150 drive by. She could not see the numbers on the license plate but wondered if that were the burglars. "My gosh!" she exclaimed quietly. "Are they not going to quit?" Carol paid the locksmith, and he drove off with a parting comment, "Now you and your man should patch things up. Life is too short, you know. Hah!"

The thoughts raced through Carol's mind in response to that. *If he were my man, I would not be locking him out.*

She ignored that remark, though and pondered what to do. *Will those guys return and try for something else. There must be something that someone wants very badly*, she thought. She still had the Blazer, and they had a key to it. *I know…I'll pull the Blazer into the garage. They don't have an opener to the garage. It's rather late to get someone to pick me up. I'll just bunk here. Uh, I wonder what Kevin would think about this*, she thought and chuckled. Carol pulled the Blazer into the garage and took Kevin's Ruger with her. If they come inside the house, I'll shoot first and ask questions later. They'll have to break in to get in now," she muttered to herself. Her face had the ever-present smile again. It had disappeared when the shot was fired at her, but a look of determination was there now along with the smile.

Then, as a light coming on, she thought, *I can't do this.* "I don't want to be seen leaving his house tomorrow morning and having the neighbors starting rumors. The bank would probably not like that either. Oh well…" Carol went back into the garage and got the floppy disks from the pocket behind the rear seat that Kevin had told her about. She went into the guest bathroom and looked around. "There." She found a place and hid them. *Let them try to find these now. If they get into the Blazer and steal it or search it, I suppose they can have at it*, she thought. She drove back to the hospital and asked the nurses if she could stay and watch after Kevin. They gladly granted her permission.

CHAPTER 19

The night was short, but Carol napped a little in the chair and was present when Kevin got a good report on his condition and was released with instructions to move slowly and carefully. She told him what had happened during the night, and they went down to the parking lot to pick up Kevin's Blazer. It was gone! "The floppies...?" Kevin looked at Carol. "Did you get them?"

"Yes, Kevin." She laughed and pointed to her purse discretely. "I have your Ruger pistol also, but they may be watching. Let's go back into the hospital and call the police. Those guys are determined. I think now is the time to turn in a police report for a stolen vehicle. Hopefully, you won't have to tell the whole story. You may never see that vehicle again, and you will want your insurance to cover you," Carol said.

"I think you're right. I'll also call for a rental car until I can resolve this thing about my Blazer. I'll have to take you back to your car. I suppose it's still at Frank Harley's place."

"It should be," Carol replied. They probably are wondering why I haven't picked it up.

Kevin called Enterprise Car Rentals and got a car headed their way. As soon as the police came and took their report and the rental car arrived, they returned the driver and headed back to Frank Harley's place. Carol had parked near the house Saturday, and when they drove up, Frank Harley came out of the house. "Hey, Kevin, I'm glad to see you are better. You gave us a scare. Do you have any idea who did that to you?" he asked.

"No, but I'd like to find out and give them a sample of their own music. It didn't feel good," Kevin quipped. He didn't elaborate on the other things that had taken place.

"Kevin, I'm sorry this happened to you. What's going on? Do you have some enemies who might be out to get you?" he enquired. "Do people get that upset over low appraisals?" he said and laughed. "Just kidding," Harley said.

Kevin wondered if he were thinking about the low appraisal he had given on Jenny Lafferty's sale. He looked at Harley and grinned as he thought he might have been expected to do. "Some people do get upset," Kevin replied.

"I'm going to have someone look into this. This has happened for some reason. Carol, thank you for taking care of Kevin. Are you okay?" Harley asked her.

"Yes, Mr. Harley, I am just picking up my car that I had to leave yesterday." She was not going to elaborate either. "If you both will excuse me, I am going to leave now." She didn't mention that she was going home to take a shower and get some sleep. She wanted to hand Kevin the new keys and his Ruger pistol but not in front of Frank Harley.

They watched Carol drive away, and Frank Harley motioned for Kevin to join him at one of the benches in one of the pavilions. "Kevin, would you please join me for a chat this morning, or I would like for you to come by the bank one day so we could visit. You have experiences that are beyond appraisal work that may be an advantage to you."

Not now, Kevin thought. "Mr. Harley, I haven't had breakfast yet and am still not feeling up to par. I'll be glad to talk later, if you will please excuse me," he said courteously.

"Of course, yes, of course," Harley said in his booming voice. "How thoughtless of me—call me one day later and we can talk. Go now, and get some rest too"

Kevin excused himself, left and drove straight home.

The phone was ringing when he walked in. It was Cheryl.

"I called the hospital, and they said you were dismissed. I hope you are all right," she said. "That must have been a very nasty lick you got. What is going on, Kevin? I am terribly sorry this happened. I feel I have brought you into a dangerous situation." Cheryl said in rapid-fire almost before she could take a breath.

"Good morning, Cheryl. Yes, that was a nasty lick. I don't know if they meant for me to recover. I'm glad you weren't along. This is getting to be dangerous. Have you had anything happen in the last twenty-four hours?" He thought he should mention Frank Harley's invitation to talk and did. "Do you have any idea what Harley wants to talk about?"

"No, but I saw Mr. McKinley and him talking, and I heard Mr. Harley tell him he would visit with you about it. I don't know what the *it* was. Mr. McKinley was in our office Friday, and he and Mr. Harley visited for a long while. Winston Kenwood came in later, and the three of them talked for an hour. I heard they have had some common interests in the past but don't know if they still exist."

It's interesting that Frank Harley, Winston Kenwood, and Shelton McKinley were at the same party and that they all seem to have an interest in me, Kevin wondered quietly.

Cheryl went on. "Kevin, they seem to all have a worry about the vault room behind Mr. Harley's office. When they got together in Mr. Farley's office Friday, I heard Mr. McKinley asking Mr. Harley if he were sure that the vault room was secure at all times. I couldn't hear Mr. Harley's answer, but they got quieter and talked awhile longer. After the others left, Mr. Harley called me in and asked me if I had run across the Wemberly Warehouse files."

Kevin was pondering all these recent events and actions of these people and tried to think what might be the connecting link to him. He is a real estate appraiser? True. He has worked in a savings and loan organization? True. He was a loan officer there? True. He also did real estate appraisals there? True. He is now an important figure in the real estate industry? False. "So why are they all so interested in Kevin Henry?" he questioned himself.

So with the consideration of a few facts, Kevin began to try again to reason what is happening. Someone wants something he might have on his computer. They had rummaged through his backup files and then didn't take any of them. They have stolen his computer twice. Albeit, the same one. "Hah! I wonder what they thought when and if they realized it was the same one. What could it be that they wanted from my computer files?"

"Kevin? Kevin?" He heard Cheryl saying on the phone. "Are you still there?"

"Oh, excuse me, Cheryl," Kevin said. "I guess my mind was wandering off and back to some of the recent events. I didn't mean to ignore you. You were saying Harley wanted to know if you had run across the Wemberly Warehouse files. I think Carol said he is asking her the same thing. Do you think they are in the vault room behind Harley's office?"

The Wemberly Warehouse files! The Wemberly Warehouse files! Why does that keep popping up now? They must be somewhere, and these two women don't know where they are? Or do they? Why do they keep telling me about them? Kevin was thinking.

"Cheryl, do you think Harley has the files in the vault room but wants to see if you will tell him they are there?" Kevin asked. "You know he apparently doesn't know whether you saw any files in that room when he inadvertently left the door open. Didn't you kinda evade answering his question that day and told him you secured the door. He didn't question you further then, but maybe he now wishes he had."

"You may be right," Cheryl said. I wish I could get into that room and search for those files. "I don't think I can since the security is so tight in this building. Do you know any magic?" she asked and chuckled.

"I don't, but I wish I did. I wish I had a good crystal ball to see what's coming next," Kevin remarked. "I think we need to hone in on what is so important about my files they want."

CHAPTER
20

Monday morning was another day. Assignments had come in from two other mortgage companies, and he needed to get on those, but he had no computer. An appraiser with no computer was in bad shape. Kevin decided that might be first priority and he should go shop for one. "Uh-oh, I suppose my insurance might cover that, but I'll need a police report for that, but do I want the police involved? He knew they may ask some questions he didn't want to answer but decided to chance it. He called Little Rock police and was surprised at only a few questions. "We don't have many break-ins in your area," the officer said. He followed with another question but none as to why and recorded the loss.

Kevin shopped a couple places and found a good computer with upgraded speed and storage capacity. He hooked up the computer at his office, called alamode, the software company, to help him set up his appraisal software; then next was the restoration of his files. Now for the floppies that had the files, and what did Carol do with them?

"Yes," Carol answered the phone. "Have you recovered from the weekend? I think I caught up on the lost sleep."

"I think I am ready to get some work done with a new computer," Kevin responded. "I have looked everywhere and cannot find the elusive floppy disks. You must have done a good job hiding them if they are in this house. I compliment you," he said. "I give up. Where are they?"

Carol laughed. "Good, I hoped they would be hard for the intruders to find if they came back. Look in the toilet tank in the guest bathroom. I turned the water off at the cutoff valve, drained the tank and dried it, then wrapped the floppies and your pistol in plastic wrapping paper, and hid them in the tank."

"Kudos to you," Kevin said. "You're a woman after my own heart."

"Really, Kevin?" Carol teased as she picked up on that.

"Well," Kevin responded. He thought about that and let it pass, but his mind was racing.

—⚎—

When the large bundle of floppy disks were unwrapped, he began the process of restoring the files to the computer. As he did so, he briefly scanned the contents. When he had finished, he had noticed nothing in them that seemed worthy of someone stealing them. "What is it they want?" he asked himself. He hid the floppies again and went to work on his appraisal assignments. During that day and into the night, he kept wondering why the persistent effort of someone to get data records from him.

By Wednesday, he decided to go to the storage building and search for the files he and Marylyn had taken there before she died. That was after he had left the Central Arkansas Workers S&L. They were backup floppies of when he worked at the S&L—maybe a clue there?

Kevin retrieved the Ruger pistol from the desk, where he had put it, and loaded the clip into the pistol. Come on, guys! If it's action you want, let us have it. He retrieved the floppies he had hidden and took them to his rented car. *The computer...* he thought, *what can I do about that?* He went back in and unhooked the computer tower and carried it to the trunk of the car. "I may not keep them from breaking into the house while I'm gone, but they'll have a fight on their hands before they get the floppies or the computer tower where the data is now."

It was almost dark now. Since he would have no car phone in the rental car, Kevin called Carol from his office to tell her what he was doing. "Wait and let me go with you and ride shotgun or maybe stay at your house while you are gone. I just bought a new Glock .45 caliber, and I am not afraid to pull the trigger on it," she said. Kevin pondered that for a moment and regretted he had called her. "No thanks, Carol, never mind. I may not go out there." He didn't want to expose her to that kind of danger. "I may wait until another time," he lied and hung up the phone.

Kevin got into the rental car and headed for Hanson Ministorage on Camp Robinson Road. It was secured and had access control with coded entry. He watched the rearview mirror and saw no pickup following. He arrived at the storage unit but toured the premises and found no one around. It was now dark. He used the intruders' method and parked the rental car one driveway over and walked up to his personal unit and opened the new padlock. It appeared to have been tampered with but had held in place. Carol had gotten a strong padlock. He raised the door and used the flashlight he had brought. Turning on the unit light was a little risky tonight, he thought. He had left the car one aisle over, and he knew he was exposed. Carol's suggestion to ride shotgun now seemed a good idea, and he wished he had taken her up on that.

He stood in the doorway, looking down the drive between the rows of storage units. They were all made of steel structure with corrugated sheet metal walls. The driveways between the units were covered with asphalt. *Well, I guess I will have to risk going into the unit and find the floppies that Marylyn and I stored here more than two years ago*, he thought. The Ruger automatic was fully loaded and handy on his hip. He moved a few boxes without success and tried to remember where the floppies were placed. "Maybe Marylyn had put them in here?"

High in a stack of boxes on top of an old file cabinet was a box marked "Floppies." Kevin retrieved the box and opened it with his pocketknife. "What the…" It contained nothing but some empty jars they used when they canned some preserves together. They had enjoyed those projects as they worked side by side. That memory touched him deeply for a moment. *But why were they marked floppies? Of course.* He remembered the codes Marylyn used when they wanted a measure of security in something important. He removed some of the jars and found the key to the file cabinet. Kevin opened the top drawer, and there they were, in trays.

Just as he removed the trays of floppies and shut the drawer, he heard the sound of a vehicle pull up to the closed entry gate. He turned off his flashlight and went to the doorway of the unit. He could not see the gate from where he was but could hear it open and the vehicle drive through. The headlights were bright as he saw them coming around the corner, and it turned down his aisle. All he could see was headlights, and he couldn't see the vehicle. He couldn't tell if it were a truck or car. The headlights eased along, and he shrunk back into the unit but the door was open. Kevin pulled the Ruger out of the holster and flipped the safety off. It was ready to fire.

"Man!" Kevin muttered to himself. There he was with no protection; his only light was the flashlight and no protection even from the headlights. "If it's the intruders, I've had it if they move up and shine those lights in here," he surmised. They moved. He thought about firing into the vehicle when it parked and left the lights shining into the unit. *I'm a sitting duck*, he thought as he squirmed around and flattened himself against one of the walls. He fired the Ruger pistol out the doorway and moved quickly to another position. A shot rang out, and he heard the bullet ping as it went through the metal wall of the unit.

"Kevin! Oh for Pete's sake!" It was Carol. "I thought it was the intruders helping themselves," she yelled.

"Carol, what in the world are you doing here? I could have shot you. I couldn't see and was about to start shooting into your vehicle. She entered into the headlights, and he could see her. He felt like chastising her, and at the same time, he wanted to hug her—-so he hesitated momentarily then gathered her in his arms. She quickly reached up and put her arms around him. He held her tightly and when she tilted her head back to look up at him, he couldn't help but meet those compelling lips. *Carol… Carol*, he whispered.

"I knew you were probably coming out here anyway and felt you needed some backup. I was afraid you were about to get killed," Carol said. "You shouldn't have come out here by yourself, Kevin. These people mean business. They have already taken a potshot at me."

"Let's close this unit up and get out of here," Kevin said. "There could be some police arriving, and I don't want to go through explanations and have this thing hitting the news yet. You can take me around to my car, and we'll get out of here fast." He locked the door of the unit and jumped into Carol's car. They pulled around to Kevin's rental car, and he jumped in. They left the premises of the ministorage facility. They were driving slowly along on the highway and met a couple of police cars headed their way. They kept moving along and watched as the police continued on toward the storage facility.

A close call, Kevin thought. *That was lucky.* He could feel the clammy sweat from his T-shirt and realized he had been sweating it back there. *Carol was cool—some gal*, he thought. *I need to get to know her even better.*

―⁂―

Kevin went straight home and called Carol at her house. She was okay. "Thanks for coming to cover for me," he said. I know it could have been pretty bad if the intruders had been there instead of you. "I owe you," he said. "Somehow there must be a way for us to get together without Frank Harley becoming too concerned about a relationship with her loyalty to someone other than him and the bank," he was thinking.

"Kevin, you are very welcome. I know we have gotten you involved in something, of which I don't know the extent. Somehow all of this stuff is tied together. I just have that feeling, and the incidents are not just happenstance. That's my thinking. I don't want to leave you hanging out there by yourself."

"Okay, thanks, Carol! I think I am going to put these floppies on my computer and research them to see if I can see any correlation in these happenings."

"I'll see that you get enough assignments to keep you going while you work on that," Carol mentioned and hung up.

—⚏—

Kevin started the long process of restoring the floppy disks over to his new computer. He started with the oldest ones, which were three years ago, back when he was still at the Central Arkansas Workers Savings and Loan Association. As he went along with the project, he skimmed through the files and organized them as he copied to his new computer. That was quick reading and required little study of them, but when he was scan-reading in the *W*s, his attention was given to Wemberly. It was the Wemberly Warehouse records of when the corporation had applied for a large loan. It was $6,000,000. He had done some precursory work on the loan, and James Carpenter had called it off. *He said it was a loan that was more than our S&L could handle at that time.*

A further reading of the record showed a search that had been made to determine the identity of the owners of the corporation that was applying for the financing. Kevin had been involved in the search at the Secretary of State's office and had found it quite entangled with a web of filings of the corporate organizing. He was reminded of the famous quote of Walter Scott in the writing of Marmion and the battle of Flodden Field. "Oh what a tangled web we weave when first we practice to deceive." It seemed these incorporating procedures were woven to cover up who actually controlled the property. The filings seemed to attempt to deceive anyone who wanted to know who the principal might be. It was a huge project and encompassed many government storages and other large shipments stored temporarily in the warehouses.

Also, buried in these files was the story of the Wemberly disappearance. The files told about when a group of men had gone hunting in the wilds of Gruntington's Island on the Arkansas River in the late 1980s. Harold Wemberly, one of the developers of the huge project and whose name the project bore, was a member of the group in the hunting trip but never returned. It was said they thought he had gotten lost, and the long search for him was without success. All kinds of theories came forth. The project was almost complete, and when finished, it bore the Wemberly name, although none knew the true owners. The five-thousand-acre island was searched for seven days before the sheriff finally called off the effort.

Harold Wemberly was thought, by some, to be still living on the island. Sightings were rumored of evidence of someone living on the island. That could be possible many claimed. The island was five miles long and over two miles deep at its deepest place where the Arkansas River curved. Much of it often flooded in the springtime. Tug boats pushing fleets of barges sometimes stopped and tied to trees near the bank during high waters that became turbulent. Some thought he caught a southbound barge and rode to New Orleans. Others thought he was dead and buried. He could have been taken deep into the forest. He could have gotten lost and wild animals had eaten him. His ghost was seen at times by hunters who would never hunt there again. Rumors were circulating rapidly and wildly.

Wemberly Warehouse back at home still bears the name, but to the superstitious, the warehouse was cursed. During the first three years, an accident caused a death each year. It was rumored that Wemberly's ghost was walking the premises looking for revenge. There were other notes in the file that were recorded in the computer files. Kevin skimmed over much of the notes and moved on, just catching the highlights. Wemberly Warehouse files—Kennon Foster had been working on a loan for the Wemberly Warehouse. Those files may or may not be somewhere at the New Home Mortgage or at the New Bank of Pulaski. Frank Harley kept inquiring with Carol Fleichman who said she didn't have them. Kevin guessed that the missing files would be those that Kennon Foster started. He wondered if Kennon had added anything to the file.

The night was late, and Kevin was beginning to wear; his eyes were beginning to blur also. He decided to stop for the night, and he called Cheryl Inmon. She answered with a sleepy sound, and he apologized. "I'm sorry, Cheryl, I forgot the hour. I just wanted to ask you if there were some way to get into that vault room some time and see if you could locate the Wemberly Warehouse property file. I think it may be in that vault room. Don't say anything, but just see if it is there."

"I'm glad you called, Kevin. I wondered if you were all right. We're all concerned about you. What have you been doing since you got home?" Cheryl inquired. "Are you getting some rest?"

"Of course, Cheryl, I've been in the house all evening," Kevin evaded the question. He was, in fact, feeling very tired at the moment.

"I'll try to get an opportunity to look in there for that file and let you know. I would like for us to find a way," Cheryl continued and said she would be helping the kids off to school in the morning.

"Okay, Cheryl, thank you. I'll talk to you tomorrow or tomorrow night."

Kevin wondered what he might be asking of Cheryl. How limited is she in gaining access to that vault room? Is it as risky as she thinks? He left it at that and called it a day.

CHAPTER 21

The Wemberly Warehouse property was a property of vast size and was only partially filled with revenue producing occupancy. The land lay along the riverside and had value, but how much value was a big question. Properties along the riverside sold occasionally but not often enough to establish a good measure of value. Frankly, it was thought to be a better indication of value to put more weight on the cost approach and the income approach. There were rumors of an effort to establish a new factory of a major company on the sixty acres, but no one knew whom to see about that. The property manager kept such a secret; no one knew whom to contact.

Kevin remembered that when he and James Carpenter considered the property, the cost was sizable, but the income was low at that time. *Now…the increased appraisal value the bank is asking for, for the second time, is rather bizarre*, Kevin thought. "Why are they doing that? For what do they want this additional money? Don't they know it will be difficult to get an appraiser to take the chance of repercussions if he gives the value they are asking for and something happens to the loan?"

It was late in the afternoon, and Kevin decided to grab a meal at his favorite Chinese café in downtown Little Rock. Kevin let his mind wander back to the story about the disappearance of

Harold Wemberly. He was never found. What happened to him? This thought held his attention as he walked into the cafe. There was old Jim Hammons. "Hey, Kevin, come on over and join me," Jim said. "I've wanted to visit with you a little about your perspective on these new appraisal laws and rules."

Kevin ordered his food and thought about Jim's statement. *What about my perspective?* Kevin thought. *I wonder what his perspective is now.* He knew Jim knew the business.

"Jim, I suppose we must take them seriously and just work and report so that we don't have to be looking over our shoulder or lying awake at night fearing if we might be challenged with something we can't defend," Kevin answered. "What's your perspective?"

"Well, Kevin, you know I've been on the carpet a lot in the last couple years. They threatened me with jail time and fines at times because of some of my values I had used. But I'll tell you," he said and raised his hand in gesture. "Those birds who are coming down and are saying we had unsupported values just don't know the pressures that bankers and Realtors put on us. They made us hit those damned numbers," he said angrily. "Kevin, there were times that they told me that if I didn't hit the number they wanted, they'd just find another appraiser and forget about me, and they would put out the word that I was too conservative. Other banks would stay away from me then. I had two kids in college and a sick wife. I couldn't stand to lose my business.

Now that they have lost money on these loans, they want to blame me for overvaluing the collateral. It just ain't right," he said solemnly. "I know I'm not the only one who had pressures like that. What do you tell a bank or mortgage company who asks for a ridiculous appraisal value? Now, this job"—and he gestured in the direction of Wemberly Warehouse but didn't name the case—"they are offering a very handsome fee for this job…I just don't know…" Jim paused and looked up at Kevin. When Kevin said nothing, he asked, "Kevin, what do you think I should do? I need the money. The feds fined me $5,000, and I still have part of that to pay."

"Jim, if you didn't need the money, what would you do? I think you might want to back off and look at the pros and cons of what they are asking you to do. You know, another round with the feds could mean a prison sentence. That would be much more loss than that fee. That would probably mean your career also. From what you say, you may be lucky to have a license now. Think about that, Jim." Kevin felt that old Jim had been beaten down so much and had lost his judgment on things that would previously have been simple to handle.

"I just don't know," Jim said again. The food was served, and they ate quietly. Jim would look up at Kevin occasionally but say nothing. Kevin felt sorry for him. Here was a man who had been an appraiser for many years but had succumbed to the pressures that all appraisers had to face in the daily business life of working in the industry. He had been caught up with in the mortgage meltdown. The Feds had chewed him up, and now he had lost his balance.

Kevin knew the pressures that some Realtors and finance people applied strongly on a regular basis. The Realtors needed their commission and would put pressure on the mortgage lenders to get the loans through to finance a property they had sold, so the lender would put the pressure on the appraiser to come up with the number needed. He had lost a few of the clients over just two years of his independent appraising career. They don't like an appraiser with a strong enough resistance that he will turn in a short value when it comes out that way. Some lenders would cut an appraiser off after the first short appraisal value, but some would give a warning.

Jim had a hard time walking the tight rope that every appraiser must walk to keep his business. The loan originators who worked on a commission were under pressure from the Realtors to make the loan application work. It was a vicious cycle. The realtors and loan originators didn't make a buck unless the sale closed. *Ugh, what a system*, Kevin thought. "There are too many opportunities, in the system, for greed to overcome honesty and integrity. The buyers and sellers are at the mercy of all of that—but that's the way it is."

Jim finished his food and took the last sip of the Chinese tea. He looked up at Kevin. "Would you go partners with me on this job?" We could make a good check on this," old Jim said.

"Probably not…I have several things going," Kevin said. "Anyway, you haven't told me where it is and who ordered it."

"Okay, it is the Wemberly Warehouse property. I have appraised that property at least five times in the past years—maybe more," Jim said. "New Bank of Pulaski ordered the appraisal." Jim looked up at Kevin hopefully. "You wanna do it?" he asked. "I haven't started it yet, but I have all the measurements from past times."

Kevin decided to level with old Jim. "Jim, I wouldn't touch that assignment with a ten-foot pole. I think that deal is too hot to handle. Don't you think the figure they want is way out of reach?"

"Well, they're the bankers, and it's their money to lose." Jim said.

"Jim, how far back do your files go? You said you have appraised it several times." Kevin knew that his own files from Central Arkansas Workers S&L had some details from his research when they decided to not make the loan. He had actually conferred with Jim at that time. Maybe old Jim had something interesting.

"Okay, sure, I tell you what! Just come on over to my house tonight and I'll show you some stuff that might be interesting to you. I live alone now, you know, since the missus passed away a couple years ago," old Jim explained. "How about eight o'clock tonight. I have some things to do kinda early this evening."

"All right, Jim, I'll see you around eight," Kevin said. "I'm buying lunch. See you tonight!"

CHAPTER 22

Kevin left the café, went home, and sat down in his office to work on the two appraisals he had started today. They should be easy. He had dropped off the film for the pictures. They would be ready to pick up tomorrow, as usual. He put new film in the camera and set it out to take with him to Jim Hammons' place. There might be some interesting things about the Wemberly Warehouse that he could photograph if old Jim permitted.

The sun was down as he left home to go to Jim's house. Jim lived in North Little Rock, and it was about a half hour drive, depending on the traffic. Kevin drove across the Arkansas River on I 430 and saw a tugboat maneuvering a group of barges. They were headed for the dam to be lowered to the next level. It was interesting how the dam worked for the water transportation on the river. The river was quite large at that point.

Kevin turned into the Shady Valley Subdivision. Jim lived in a nice house toward the rear of the subdivision where it was quiet and very peaceful. Jim's house was a quite large brick, one and a half story, with a three-car garage. It had a cedar shake shingle roof as required for all the houses in that subdivision. Jim and his wife had waited for years until they could manage and had built this house as their dream house. It was on a larger lot than most and about a block distance from the nearest neighbor. The front porch light was on, and he pulled into the driveway. Jim came to the door and yelled for him to come on in.

Kevin had not been well acquainted with Jim Hammons but had known him for many years. He was likeable, helpful, and always tried to please everyone. "Kevin, come on into my office, and we'll look at some of the information I have accumulated through the years on that warehouse. I have files going back to about the time it was built. You knew Harold Wemberly disappeared about the time the building was being finished. I hunted with him some on that island. That was a prime hunting place. That was around 1986 when he disappeared. We never knew what happened. I helped hunt for him. Some said he had gotten onto a boat going down the river and headed for other parts of the world. He and his wife were seriously at odds and had already divorced. He hated her and she hated him…they say," Jim said.

"Who were the principals in the project, Jim?" Kevin asked. "I know there were some corporations, but I don't know who the shareholders in the corporations were."

"Yeah, that was the darnedest thing. There was a corporation called the Wemberly Company Inc., and it's still named that. That corporation had shareholders that were a number of other corporations whose shareholders were a mystery. I'm not sure that can be done that way anymore. I know some banks and finance organizations from out of state were involved. I think one was in Atlanta, one in Dallas, etc. I don' know…" he trailed off.

"Here's where I measured the entire building structure the first time. That was not very long after it was completed. It filled up quickly back then. It was nice," Jim said and smiled. "I enjoyed appraising it each time I did it. I talked to Harold Wemberly when they were building the warehouse. He told me then how the ownership was set up. I can't remember the details, but they are in this file right here," he said.

"Jim, that is one document I would be interested in having a copy," Kevin told him.

Jim smiled widely and stuck it out toward Kevin. "Here, take this whole file and make a copy. This contains all my files on the Wemberly Warehouse work. It's quite large, but you can bring it back when you have made your copy," Jim said. He went on to explain his conversation with Harold Wemberly. "Harold talked about the trouble he and his ex-wife were having and the strained relationship. He was a little fearful of her, actually," Jim surmised. Then he shifted in his seat and looked seriously at Kevin. "Do you think I should give them the appraisal they want. I could use that money. You can go in partners with me on the appraisal."

"Jim, that appraisal assignment is one that is going to get someone in trouble. They want to make another huge loan and want that appraisal to back up what they are doing. They may place a government guaranteed loan on it…and, Jim…there you go…the Feds again. The Feds have been after you in the past, and they might be watching you closer. Why not back off and look over this situation before you do that. As for me, I want no part of it," Kevin told him.

"Okay, Kevin! Thanks for coming. I'm going to do what you say and think about this for a while."

Kevin took the file and said good night to Jim. He got into his rental car and eased along through the subdivision. As he pulled onto Osage Drive of this residential area, he saw a red Ford F150 pickup truck. It was backed up into the carport, and he couldn't see the license plate. "Oh well, why am I so paranoid? There are lots of red Ford pickups," he told himself. He drove out of Shady Valley Subdivision and through the long Osage Drive.

He turned onto John F. Kennedy Boulevard. *JFK*, they called it for short. It was named for the assassinated president. That reminded him of Kennon Foster, whose cause of death was still not determined, at least publicly. His mind dwelled on that until he drove into his garage. He couldn't help but be cautious when he entered his house. He had his gun in his hand when he opened the door, and then he looked through his house to be sure there had been no intrusions. His computer was still there, and there were no signs of disturbance.

—⚋—

The next two days were filled with hard appraisal work, and one appraisal report was for New Bank of Pulaski. He dropped off that report to the receptionist. Cheryl Inmon came into the reception area and motioned for him to come into the office. "Come in and sit down," Cheryl said. She closed the door and sat down at her desk. "Have you heard about Jim Hammons?" she asked him.

"Well…no!" Kevin said. He hesitated to mention his visit with Jim a couple nights ago.

"Kevin, old Jim was found dead in his home early this morning. One of our employees heard on the police scanner about a fire in Shady Valley Subdivision in North Little Rock. The fire department responded and put the fire out, but they found old Jim dead in his garage. He was lying on the floor in his blood as though he had fallen from the pull-down ladder to the attic, they said. He might have fallen backward and hit his head on the concrete floor, they were thinking. They thought he might have been going up in the attic to check out a smoke smell and maybe had a heart attack. They have not announced the cause of the fire though. It appeared to have started in the attic because the shingle roof was burned pretty badly."

"Cheryl, we saw old Jim at the party last weekend. I talked to him briefly. He was a good man," Kevin remarked.

"I wonder if his office had been disturbed," Kevin said. "I wish we could see it." He noticed that Cheryl said nothing about the appraisal assignment they had asked Jim to take.

"Maybe we'll know when the story hits the news media," Cheryl said. "That's a good question, but why would someone be after something in his office?"

"Kevin!" It was Frank Harley's booming voice. They shook hands. "It's good to see you out. Are you working and feeling good?

"I'm feeling fine Mr. Harley," Kevin said. I am working, thanks to your bank, and I just turned in two assignments."

"That's good. That's good," Harley repeated. "If you feel like it and have time, I'd like to take you to lunch. Can you go?"

"How can I turn down a free lunch? I think I can make some time for a good client," Kevin said and smiled.

"All right, that's good. Cheryl, call the Top of the Arlington and make reservations for us. We want to see the town," he said and laughed.

CHAPTER 23

Kevin had insisted on driving his own car and meeting Harley at the Arlington Building. They met in the lobby and rode the elevator to the top where they were met by a greeter in the restaurant. She guided them to a cubbyhole table and seated them in the little room. That was a little more elaborate than anything he had experienced there before, and he was curious about why that room instead of a regular table. *Oh well, the bank has the money*, Kevin thought.

Harley cleared his throat. "Kevin, I'll get right down to business. You have a background that gives you a wide range of experience, training, and education. We need a man at the bank who has those qualifications. I think you could be a tremendous asset to us," Harley said. "You have experience in the S&L field as a loan officer, an appraiser and next to James Carpenter in the management side, and you have been a good baseball player"—he laughed at that—"but seriously, I need someone here who is flexible, whom I can assign to take on a variety of responsibilities," Harley continued.

The server brought the drinks and took their orders. He closed the door again as he left.

"Mr. Harley, I'm very flattered that you have that confidence in me. Of course I'll give due consideration to what you are thinking. What are some of the specific responsibilities you have in mind?" Kevin responded. "At this time, I am independent, and I have enjoyed this independence tremendously. I don't mind working, and I know that if I am not productive, I don't make any money, so I work hard. I kinda like that, although all the grunt work is mine to do, and it is limiting."

"Right, I need a man who can take the ball and run with it. I need someone who can cover my backside, and I want someone on whom I can depend and who will be loyal to me. I will pay. I will set up a remuneration plan you probably wouldn't expect. The bank can afford to pay. I don't think that will be an issue with you," Harley said quietly in his rumbling voice.

They both sat in silence and sipped on their drinks. The server brought in their lunch and asked if they would like to see the desserts. Harley motioned at Kevin, who said no. "Let's dig in, Kevin, and enjoy," Harley said and started eating.

"Do you have troubles you are dealing with that I might be advised to know about?" Kevin asked. He thought he would try to get a little bit of an idea of what was prompting Harley to take this step. He knew Harley had seemingly been very concerned about the security of his vault room behind his office. He had been asking questions of Cheryl about what she might have seen. He also had been quizzing Carol about the Wemberly Warehouse file, strangely.

Kevin knew that Harley had met last week with Winston Kenwood, who is not only a fellow banker, but also the chairman of a state banking committee, and the meeting included Shelton McKinley from Texas. Kevin had no idea how McKinley fit into the meeting or how anybody fit into that meeting. They apparently had a serious meeting, and then they were all at the large cookout.

"I suppose that's a fair question, Kevin. You know we lost Kennon Foster not long ago, and there have been things that disappear that cause me concern. Cheryl has had some concerns, and I can't be sure what is going on in several ways. I want someone who is astute enough to ferret out these answers and help me avoid a tragedy," Harley answered.

Kevin noted that Harley had not mentioned Jim Hammons's death. Maybe he hadn't heard about it yet. *And all that's interesting*, Kevin thought. *I've been wondering where Harley fit into many of these questions. Now I wonder about everyone.*

"Give me some time to consider all this, and I'll give you an answer later, if that's satisfactory to you," Kevin said.

"Sure, Kevin, I wouldn't expect a quick decision. You should think it out. Let me know when you reach a decision."

They left the little room and waited for the elevator as Kevin stood a little while, looking out the window as the café slowly revolved. He watched the city and could see across the river into North Little Rock, about where Shady Valley Subdivision held the house of old Jim Hammons.

He left Frank Harley and drove to the new car dealer to see what was available. His Blazer would have to be replaced if the police didn't find it. *What kind of vehicle would he need? Would he be driving one type if he reached an employment agreement with Frank Harley or would he want a different type if he continued working as he now worked? Well, I may as well take a little time and automobile-shop while I think about everything. Right now my brain is spinning at too fast a pace*, he was thinking.

Kyle Chevrolet let him try a new Impala to drive overnight. He left his rent car there with them. He had to discreetly remove his gun from the rental car and carry it into the Impala. That was tricky because the salesman kept trying to tell him about all the new features. "Now let me know what you think about how this one handles," he told Kevin.

Kevin drove away and thought he would drive across the river to North Little Rock. He missed his car phone. He drove into the Shady Valley Subdivision and on around to old Jim Hammons house. The yellow tape was up around the house. That meant they were considering it a crime scene. "I would like to go in and see the place now," Kevin wished. Old Jim had let him take some photos of him and his new home office where he had been working since he built his new house. The file cabinet space was large and undoubtedly held thirty or more years of files. The office was neat. Kevin wondered if it were neat now.

He drove by the New Home Mortgage. He dropped in to see if there were any assignments to pick up while he was that close. Carol saw him and asked him if he knew about old Jim Hammons. "Yes," he said, "I took some reports by the bank today, and Cheryl told me. I haven't seen any new report yet, but I drove over and saw the house and where the roof had burned. It looks as though they got there quickly, and the fire was contained in the attic and roof. It makes me wonder if the fire was started on purpose or was from wiring. That was a fairly new house, or so it looked." He didn't want to appear to be too knowledgeable yet.

"Well, I had been thinking about how life threatening it was to be a mortgage banker, but now it looks like even real estate appraisers can go too," Carol said, and she had that continuous smile on her face as she glanced toward him.

They had no appraisal assignments for him, and he went on home. When he went inside, he checked the house for intruders and saw none. "Boy! Am I getting paranoid?" Kevin thought. By then, it was time for the evening news, and he turned on the TV. "Long-time real estate appraiser died last night and was discovered when the house was burning. Jim Hammons, age seventy-eight, was found dead in his garage. He was found at the foot of his pull-down ladder where he might have had a heart attack while trying to climb the ladder to check on the fire. He had already called 911 who dispatched the fire trucks."

"What to do with that large Wemberly Warehouse file Jim had loaned me to make copies?" Kevin asked himself. He hadn't made the copies yet and thought he might not make copies of them now. It would be hard to explain when he had gotten the file. He might immediately go under suspicion of murder, if it's murder. "Right now, I'll need to keep the files a secret." He picked up one folder and began to sort through the papers. It had the plans indicated to be somewhere to pick up. He lifted another folder out of the box and saw that it contained notes of the research at the Secretary of State's office. Old Jim was trying to determine the ownership control. He had talked with one of the owners personally and made notes.

Aah, this is rich, Kevin thought. "I remember some similar research I had done when we considered this loan a few years ago. Does someone want to get that information from me?" They've gotten my computer once. They've searched the files of others. Old Jim is dead." That made Kevin wonder. He strongly suspected murder. "The circumstantial evidence is strong. If I could tell the criminal investigators, they might have a better resolve to pursue that theory. He couldn't afford to let them know he had Jim's files, so he placed the folders back in the box and wondered where there was a good place to hide them. The intruders seem to have a way of coming on in if they want," he was thinking.

The phone was ringing, and he answered. It was Cheryl, and she was whispering. "Kevin, a customer was just in and talking about a radio report about Jim Hammons," she said. "He talked about how he was found dead, and they are not sure whether it was foul play. The customer said they were wondering if Jim had a heart attack and fell backward, but he said Jim had told him he had just had a physical, and it showed him to be in good shape. Kevin, this situation is looking more and more dangerous all the time. I feel I must tell you, we had asked old Jim to do an appraisal for us—the first assignment we had asked him to do in a long time. It was to appraise the Wemberly Warehouse properties. That's the one you turned down. I don't know if Jim was going to accept the assignment. It makes me feel that it might be the kiss of death to be asked to do that appraisal. Kennon Foster was to get someone to appraise that property and was working on that file at the time he died," Cheryl said.

"Cheryl, are you in the office?" Kevin asked her. "And does Harley know you are telling about the assignment?"

"He is not in the office, or I wouldn't have been telling you that now. I just didn't want to wait until tonight. I think you should be doubly cautious with all this strange stuff happening. I am beginning to be more and more scared," Cheryl said. She had lost a little of her professional edge talking there in the office. Maybe it was because of the greater familiarity. "Kevin, Mr. Harley seemed a little hesitant but had asked Carol and me to see if old Jim would do the appraisal for us. I am not sure why he was hesitant. Jim seemed to be reluctant at first until I told him what the fee would be. He hesitated a moment and then said he would think about it. Mr. Harley had told me to ask him if he still had all of his old files on that property—I must go, Kevin, Mr. Harley is returning. 'Bye!" She hung up.

CHAPTER
24

What a wrinkle, Kevin thought. He felt he had a greater need to safeguard this box of Wemberly Warehouse files and also the floppy disks. He decided to take the Impala back to Kyle Chevrolet and get the rental car so he picked up the box of files and the older floppy disks and loaded them in the car to take to the ministorage. That would have to suffice for now. He backed out of the garage and turned toward North Little Rock. He drove to the I 430 freeway and merged with the traffic. Behind him was a red Ford pickup truck. He was gaining on him, and Kevin pulled into the right lane. The truck passed, and Kevin breathed a little sigh of relief. He wasn't ready for any confrontation at this time.

The traffic was light, and Kevin made it to the Levy exit shortly and pulled off and onto Camp Robinson Road. He soon would be at the ministorage unit. He passed the Dairy Queen and noticed a red Ford F150 pickup there. "Uh-oh," he said to the Impala. "I think I'm hung up on red Ford pickups. I can't help but notice all of them, and there are many." Kevin laughed at himself but kept an eye out, nonetheless.

He pulled up to the ministorage gate and entered the code for entry. He noticed the red Ford truck passed by. Now the hairs on the back of his neck were beginning to rise. Be cautious. It may be no one, but play it safe. The gate closed behind him. He knew a vehicle couldn't come in behind him unless they knew the code, but between the fence post and the building was a gap through which a person could squeeze. That worried him. He pulled down the aisle to his unit but eased on around the row and kept going back toward the gate. Sure enough, the red truck had pulled up to the parking area in front of the now empty office. The driver had left the truck, so that meant he had entered through that little gap. "Curses on that gap! I've got to have that changed," he muttered.

Kevin pulled his Ruger out and moved the safety off. He laid the pistol down in the seat and eased along in the Impala. He could see no one. The person had gone somewhere, and Kevin couldn't help but feel that that was someone up to no good. He eased on around to the last aisle, and there was a person standing at a unit putting a key into a lock at one of the bin doors. Kevin drove on by the person who looked up and waived to him innocently. "Yuck!" he said. "I guess the guy forgot his code. He has a key for his unit," he exclaimed as he pulled around the corner of the row of bins.

He drove the Impala on around to unit 37. Just in case, he stuffed the Ruger into his belt and exited the car. He unlocked the padlock and opened the door. When he raised the trunk lid on the Impala, he looked both ways and saw that it was clear. "Boy! Here I am, still fretting over spooks. I'll unload the things into the unit and get out of here." He took both boxes in and hid them in a nonconspicuous place and started back out of the unit, but heard steps moving quickly. He looked out the doorway and saw a figure running in a direction away from the unit. "Hey!" Kevin yelled at the figure, but it kept running away. He quickly closed the door and locked it and jumped into the Impala and drove around the rows of units and past the one where he had seen the person. There was no one there.

Kevin drove to the gate and saw that the red Ford truck was gone. "So that means the guy at that unit was pretending to be opening a padlock when I went by. He followed me to see what unit I was using," he muttered. "Now, what am I going to do about that?" He turned around and went back to the storage unit and removed the boxes of files and floppies. As he watched, he didn't spot the red Ford pickup. "Maybe we have outsmarted that truck," he told the Impala.

Kevin drove back to Kyle Chevrolet and left the Impala. "I've gotta think about this," he told the salesman. He removed the boxes from the Impala and put them back into the rental car and left. He felt as though he had a hot potato and couldn't find a place to drop it, and it keeps getting hotter. He drove back to the house, pulled into the garage, and heard his phone ringing inside. He raced in and picked up the phone; it was his insurance agent. "They have found your Blazer, and it's burned to a crisp. That means you can find another car, if you wish," his agent told him.

He looked at his watch and headed for the Ford dealer. *Maybe I should get a totally different-looking vehicle*, he thought. The Ford salesman showed him vehicles, and he looked at cars and sports utility vehicles. He liked the Explorer and decided to buy a black one. He moved the boxes into the SUV after the paperwork was done and decided to go home. He had entirely forgotten about Frank Harley's offer to him but decided it didn't matter. The SUV would be a fit in any situation, he decided. He managed to sneak his Ruger into the driver's area and felt a sigh of relief.

Tomorrow it would be telephone installation time. He missed his car phone and wanted to call Carol or Cheryl and see if they were seeing the red Ford F150. That guy or those guys are staying busy. They are intent, and it is beginning to feel as though one needs a bodyguard.

He drove into his garage and ran the door down. The vehicle should be safe, and he would just leave the file box and the floppies in the Explorer for the night. "What to do with them when he was out is the question. They would be more vulnerable if he accidentally parked in a less exposed place that would tempt them to break in." *Actually*, he thought, *they are probably safer in the Explorer if one figures the odds. They know where the house is always, but the car will be relocating a lot.*

Kevin put together a snack and watched the news on TV. They were announcing the fire at Shady Valley in North Little Rock. The source of the fire had not been determined, and the cause of death was thought to be a heart attack, but an autopsy had been ordered. "Jim Hammons was a long-time appraiser in the Central Arkansas area for more than forty years," the announcer said.

I've got to find out what the autopsy report shows, Kevin thought. "But meanwhile, I'm assuming it was foul play, and that assumption is based on everything that's happening." He wondered about the files at Jim Hammons's house. The office had been neat when he was there, and he wondered if it had been ransacked. "If someone had been in the house when old Jim died, then it would have been intruders and they might have been after certain files," Kevin guessed.

Kevin sat down at his computer and started putting more files in from the floppies he retrieved from the back of the Explorer. He thought about the file cabinets at old Jim Hammons house. *If the office is a jumbled mess, I know Jim was murdered.* Kevin was guessing and stood up. *I've got to see that place before anybody moves things. I want to see how much different it looks,* Kevin kept thinking. He picked up the phone and called Carol. Cheryl had kids at home, and he didn't want to ask her. Carol answered, and he asked her if she wanted to meet him in North Little Rock on a risky mission.

CHAPTER 25

"Is this a date, Kevin?" she asked and he could see that grin on her face.

Kevin laughed. "If you like—we'll call it that. It may not be a fun date though," he said. "I want to visit old Jim Hammons house, and it will be a violation of the police yellow tape barrier, but I feel a strong need to see inside that house. I'll pick you up in a few minutes. Wear some dark clothes if you can and some strong shoes, not skimpy ones," he suggested. "We want to be as clandestine as possible. In other words, we don't want to be seen or caught."

"Gotcha," Carol said, "I have a dark outfit and some hiking boots, if that's what you mean. This sounds exciting, Kevin, I haven't had a date like this in a long time," she said and giggled a little.

Kevin laughed. "I am hesitant to invite you on this date, but I need someone to ride shotgun, and I think you are the person."

The black Ford Explorer was just the thing, Kevin thought as he pulled into Carol's driveway. *We might be a little less conspicuous in some places.*

Carol came running out, wearing that constant smile. She was also wearing some dark slacks, a black blouse, and a pair of brown hiking boots. She seemed excited. "Kevin," she said, "I haven't had a date this exciting since my junior year in college, and I see you have a new SUV. I like it. Am I your first date in this ride?" She laughed. "Let's go check that house."

"Good, Carol. I brought my camera. My plan is to get into the house and take some pictures of the office, at least." He was hesitant to tell her that he had been in the house two nights before Jim's death. "I have some high-capacity night film, and I want to try to take some shots without using a flash."

They were driving up Camp Robinson Road and passed the Hanson Ministorage. Kevin told Carol about his trip to the ministorage to put the floppies there. "The red Ford pickup was there and parked outside, but there was a guy inside who had sneaked through the small gap between the fence and the office building. I think he had passed me and somehow knew or guessed I was coming here. It was a close call."

Kevin kept the Explorer traveling up Camp Robinson and turned off onto Remount Drive for a short distance and parked on the side of the road. He reached into the door pocket and got his Ruger 9 mm pistol out and pushed the cartridge clip into the butt. He handed Carol a flashlight and grabbed one for himself. He swung the camera strap around his neck and locked the vehicle as Carol was coming around to his side. She was stuffing her Glock pistol into the belt of her slacks.

"Okay, Carol, we'll go through this undeveloped and wooded area and across that creek ahead. It will be rough traveling in the dark and maybe through some brushy area. We should wind up in the back side of Shady Valley Subdivision at old Jim Hammons's place. If we are lucky, we'll find a way in the back side of the house and take a look at his office. I have some rags in my pocket to use to avoid leaving fingerprints. Be very careful, please."

Carol was traveling closely behind him, and they were using their flashlights very sparingly and shining mostly toward the ground. They wanted to avoid having someone spot their lights. When they came to the creek, it was rough getting down the steep banks, and Carol slid once knocking Kevin down. "Sorry about that, Kevin, this is not exactly like a smooth basketball court." She grunted as they recovered.

"A basketball court!" Kevin whispered. "I remember now, you played basketball for the Lady Razorbacks when I was a senior at the university. You were quite a hotshot," Kevin said. I remember going to more games to watch you play. You were fresh out of high school, they said. I never saw you around otherwise. Why was that?" he whispered.

"Kevin, you were in a different crowd. I remember seeing you there and kept an eye out for you, but I didn't think you knew I existed. I was new to the campus, and you were on your way to graduation. Anyway, those were fun years on the basketball team," Carol remarked.

Kevin noted that she still moved with the agility of a skilled ball player. That came in handy in this rough terrain of this wooded area and traveling in the dark, he realized. They climbed back up the other bank across the creek, and through the wooded area, they could see a streetlight. "That may be old Jim's house," Kevin said. "Let's move on up carefully and be sure there is no one around." They moved up to the house. There was no backyard fence, and Kevin didn't know if the house was old Jim's. The house was dark and quiet. If it were occupied and people were asleep, they could get into trouble easily, especially if there were a dog.

Carol eased her pistol out and waited. She knew she wasn't going to shoot except to scare someone back while they ran. She watched Kevin easing up toward the house and around toward the front. He stopped and watched for a moment, then moved back toward her.

"It is old Jim's house," Kevin whispered, "let's see if we can ease up to the rear and find a way inside. The yellow tape is up in the front and all around the house. We'll have to cross the tape to get there." They moved on up to the house, and Kevin remembered that he hadn't seen a security alarm sign. "If there is an alarm, be ready to run back through these woods and toward that creek," Kevin whispered to Carol.

They crept up to the back door and found it locked. The streetlight out front made the front and sides more lighted so they got down on their hands and knees and crawled around to the garage end. Kevin carefully felt around the pedestrian door on the side of the garage and discovered it open. They were in luck. The police had missed that unlocked door.

"Kevin, are you sure we're not going to set off something? Let's keep these flashlights ready. If we set off something, I'm going to turn mine on and run like crazy through those woods," she declared and chuckled.

They slipped inside and closed the pedestrian door behind them and locked it. Kevin took his cloth and wiped the fingerprints off. He had to be careful. They eased along the garage and caught a glimpse of the blood on the floor. It would be Jim's blood. They moved on to the kitchen door and opened it carefully. There was a slight click; Kevin held his breath and held up his hand. Carol stopped breathing too. "Okay," Kevin whispered and moved on. He crept through the kitchen and into Jim's office. The blinds were open, and the window gave a view of the street in front. Just then, car lights were moving slowly down the street, which dead-ended there at Jim's house. A spotlight was trained on the house.

Kevin pushed Carol down toward the floor, and they remained there while the light illuminated the room. "*Sh*, it's the police," Kevin whispered. "Stay down and still!" The car lights were staying on the house, and they could hear the front door being shook. They were checking to see if it were still fastened. One policeman moved on around the other end of the house with his flashlight, checking and the first one went around to the pedestrian door of the garage. "Was that door left unlocked on purpose?" Kevin worried. He knew they had locked it behind them as they came in. He heard the two policemen walk back around to the front and stopped as they seemed to be talking. One walked over to the office window and shined his flashlight into the office. Kevin and Carol each flattened out, trying to be absorbed into the floor. The light beam flitted around and stopped near the file cabinets. Kevin had noticed that the office was in disarray. Was it like that this morning or was it like that after the police had left the scene.

The one policeman went back to the car, and they could hear the voices over the radio. "Was there a disturbance in the office this morning," the officer was asking.

"Let me check the report," the voice from the station said. Carol knew she could be seen if she moved, and she tried to melt into the floor. Her heart was pounding. She wanted to yell at them to hurry up and leave. The time seemed an eternity.

"Okay, Chuck," the officer at the car yelled. "It's okay. Let's go."

The flashlight went off and in a moment, the car lights swung around and moved down the street.

Kevin and Carol jumped up, and Kevin started taking pictures while Carol kept watch down the street. He took special note of the file cabinets with the drawers open and files strewn around on the floor. There had been a burglary and Kevin was virtually sure a murder.

"Let's go, Carol," he whispered as though there might still be someone around. They left out the back door, and Kevin wiped his fingerprints off the doorknobs. He turned the lock button on the inside and locked the door behind them.

"Kevin, did you know you stepped in that blood as we were leaving?" she asked.

"Oh cripes!" Kevin exclaimed. Now I have left a track, and there is no way to get back in the house and mar the track. Hopefully, it can't be identified, I hope…"

They made their way back through the wooded area and across the large creek again. When they were approaching the Explorer, there was a police car checking it out. He appeared to be calling in to identify the owner. "Uh-oh," Kevin said. "At the best, this could be embarrassing. Let's just wait here until he leaves. We are not parked illegally, but the vehicle raises some curiosity for that officer. He probably wonders if it had been stolen by someone and then abandoned there. I really don't wish to become involved with that policeman now, for obvious reasons. He'll wonder what we have been doing if we walk up there now." Finally, the officer finished his call, got back into his car and left. "Good, Carol," Kevin said with a sigh of relief. "Let's go."

"Yes, Kevin, he would have wondered what we had been doing. It would have looked a little obvious, wouldn't it?" she said and laughed. "And if he only knew! Kevin, I'm glad you asked me to go with you on this trip. It was scary but a little exciting and fun, in a way," she said.

Kevin looked at Carol and was feeling more and more at ease with her, the more they were together. It was beginning to be more than a business relationship. Yes, it was as though he wanted to be with her, just to be with her. "Actually, he could have made this trip by himself, but he supposed he wanted her to be with him. Yes, maybe to be with him," he was admitting. He shook himself a little. *Not yet, Kevin*, he thought. I did enjoy the shooting practice with her that Saturday. And she took care of me when those guys knocked the daylights out of me. She hung in there and took care of the lock at my storage unit and had the locks changed on my house. "Aw shoot!" he muttered.

"What's that, Kevin?" Carol asked and looked over at him. "What did you say?"

He pulled the Explorer in to the Dairy Queen and parked. "Carol, I said you are beautiful. There!" He couldn't help it.

Carol reached over across the console of the Explorer and kissed him on the cheek quickly and pulled back to her side immediately. "So there," she said. "I think we should get a milk shake and call it a day."

Kevin ordered two milk shakes and gave the server a generous tip, more than he usually tipped. *Hey, I guess I had better settle down,* he thought.

CHAPTER 26

The extra large hard drive would prove to be beneficial as Kevin restored the files to his new computer from floppy disks backups of his last year at Central Arkansas Workers Savings and Loan Association. As he looked at files regarding the Wemberly Warehouse Inc. loan application, he studied the record of the research he had done on that property. The effort to determine the ownership was interesting as he began to remember the complexity of the corporate filings. It was amazing to him how that sort of ambiguity would be permitted in a filing. Looking at his own records made him anxious to get into the records of old Jim Hammons. He knew those were full of gems.

The fax machine was ringing, and the printer started printing assignments. A mortgage company in North Little Rock was sending an assignment on a house in Jacksonville and one for a refinance in the same town. It started ringing again and this time an assignment for an appraisal in Little Rock. He was getting busy again, and this was going to cut down on his spare time for tackling the Wemberly Warehouse mystery, and he hadn't brought in the newspaper yet.

LONGTIME APPRAISER JIM HAMMONS DIES AT HIS HOME, the newspaper headline stated. "Cause of death thought to be a heart attack associated with a fire…" it read and continued to have the story of various possibilities of the cause of death. It told about the long history Jim had of appraisal work in the central Arkansas area. "There is, however, still crime scene tape surrounding the house, which prevents anyone from entering the house," the article continued.

The photos of Jim Hammons office that he and Carol had taken last night were still in his camera. They had to be developed. Kevin decided to finish the roll with appraisal work today so the film developers might not be as apt to see or notice those pictures. They might not be as conspicuous intermingled with those pictures of other houses.

The comparable sales looked good for the work in Jacksonville, and he set appointments for each in the afternoon of the same day. He left immediately for North Little Rock, where he wanted to get his license tag number changed over to his new Explorer. The tag was already mounted.

The lady at the revenue office recognized him and asked if he had heard about old Jim Hammons. "He was my neighbor," she said. "Last night, our little dog kept barking. I guess he was mourning old Jim's death. I looked out, and I thought I saw two figures in the dark, but my husband said I was crazy and imagining spooks—there was no car there," she said as she worked up his papers. She kept talking a mile a minute without stopping her work. "Nonetheless," she declared, "I called the police. They came and checked out everything real good but said they saw nothing. Our little dog was continuing to bark all the while they were there and for a while after they left. I guess it was spooks. His house is almost a block from ours, and I don't know how Scuffy thought he heard something. Can you imagine that?" she said and handed him his new tag and paperwork. "Next," she said without stopping. He was dismissed.

Kevin smiled and thanked his lucky stars. *I'll have to tell Carol*, he thought as headed for Jacksonville. It was nearing lunchtime, and he stopped at a popular pizza place to eat. He saw a couple of old S&L customers who wanted to talk about old Jim. He was well liked, both declared. "What do you think happened?" one asked.

"I think he was murdered. A heart attack doesn't make sense, because he was healthy as a horse. Murder! That's what it was."

Kevin had no comment other than to shake his head a little. He didn't want to get drawn into much conversation and act as though he was very familiar with the situation.

As he was driving into the subdivision with his first appointment, he realized he did not have a car phone. He had the urge to call Carol and chat a few minutes. *Carol is okay.* He felt. *She has really been there for me lately*, he was thinking. *Actually, she is more than okay.* He was remembering back at the university in his senior year when she was a freshman basketball player. Arkansas had a good team that year. He had graduated after that season and had not kept up with the girls' basketball after that. He and Marylyn had married, and life took on another interest.

Kevin finished the preliminaries of the appraisal by late afternoon and returned to Little Rock for the telephone installation in the Explorer. As soon as the phone was installed and he was driving home, the phone rang. It was Cheryl. "I have been trying to call you all day," Cheryl said. "Where have you been? I kept getting the message that your number was not a working number. Has something happened?"

"Oh, Cheryl, I'm sorry," Kevin said, "my Blazer was stolen, and they finally found it burned to a crisp, they said." I now have a new vehicle and just have gotten the phone installed. I have been busy. How have your days been?"

"Normal, I suppose," Cheryl said. "Mr. Harley has been asking about you and wants to talk with you as soon as you are available. He asked if you had said anything about his offer to you, and I told him I was unaware of the offer. He didn't volunteer to explain."

Kevin was not sure that he should go into details with anyone about Harley's offer. He was not sure why the offer and would want to know more details about what all it involved. "Cheryl, tell Mr. Harley that I am thinking about what he said and will try to talk to him some more about it."

"Kevin, strange things are going on, and I feel like I am more and more in the dark. Do you want to enlighten me or am I treading in private waters?" she said tenderly.

"I don't know to what extent he wants me to divulge our conversation. I feel I should let him provide that to you. I don't mean to be secretive, but I am not sure about the confidentiality," Kevin said. Now he was feeling she might be expecting him to reveal everything to her because of other things they had shared. He knew she was under undue stress because of the entire weird goings on and felt a little compassion for her at this moment, but he wasn't ready yet to confide all things with her.

"Okay…if that's the way you want it. I will give him your message," she said coolly. "Good-bye, Kevin."

Now what have I done. I like the close relationship we had going, but I can't share everything, Kevin was thinking. *Why did Harley even mention this to Cheryl? Surely, he knew it would pique her interest. Or maybe it's a test of my confidentiality in the event I accept his offer. And if it is a test, would Cheryl tell Harley his response? Well, we'll see what our relationship is now. I do want her as my friend*, he thought.

The phone works, I guess, Kevin thought. "Now to get these reports finished tomorrow. Tonight, I want to dig into those Wemberly Warehouse files." He drove home and parked in his garage, Explorer, new telephone and all.

He checked the house throughout to be sure he had not been invaded again. *This is a bad feeling,* he thought. I can't help but wonder if someone has been here every time I come home. Maybe I should think about a security system, but there goes another expense. Darn these crooks!" he declared.

Tonight, Kevin decided to look at the photos he had picked up. He had dropped the films off at the one-hour photoshop and picked them up after he had the telephone installed in the new Explorer. He was most interested in the photos of old Jim Hammons office taken when he and Carol were in there that night. He sat down at his desk and pulled out the first package that would include the photos of old Jim's office.

He had taken photos of the office when he visited old Jim, and now he compared them. The photos he had taken when he visited Jim showed a neat office. The file cabinets were all closed, and Kevin felt that Jim always kept them closed. The set of photos he had taken last night showed a couple drawers pulled out and a couple stacks of file folders lying on the desk. There were stacks in front of the chair and the chair was pushed over to the side of the desk.

Now, Kevin thought. *I know that old Jim was murdered, but how do I go about proving it to anyone and to whom do I want to prove it now? Why was he murdered? There is no doubt in my mind that he was murdered because of someone's desire to obtain these files of the Wemberly Warehouse Inc. to find out what work was done during appraisal process and what of that information is recorded in these files.* A little shudder came over Kevin as he thought about his risk now. Would they know that he had old Jim's files? Apparently someone thought he had something in his computer files. It had to be that they had some suspicion that he had files from work while at the S&L and that it might contain the information they wanted or that they didn't want someone else to see. "It has been a long day," he decided.

CHAPTER 27

Kevin wrapped up the reports on the two Jacksonville appraisals and took them to the mortgage company. The talk was about old Jim Hammons in the mortgage office. "What did Kevin think?" they asked.

"I think it was terrible. Have they determined the cause of death yet?" Kevin asked them.

"He had a bad heart, and when his roof caught on fire, he tried to climb into the attic to check on it and had a heart attack on the ladder," someone said. The others agreed. "He was old," someone said.

"Wow, appraisers make lots of money," the office manager said. "Kevin has a new Ford Explorer. We should get into the appraisal business. It's easy money! Isn't, it Kevin?"

"Sure, just look at old Jim," Kevin replied.

The Little Rock assignment was one for a larger house and was more complicated. It was for a new construction in southwest Little Rock and was to be built on several small lots where the surrounding houses were about 1,200 square feet of gross living area and no garages. The borrower wanted to build a 3,500 square foot house with a one-car garage. He wanted to borrow sixty-five dollars per square foot to construct the house. That would be financing $227,500 for the construction. The houses around it were selling for $40,000 to $50,000 each. What a mess. The applicant had family nearby in the neighborhood and wanted to build near them. There was no way that that project would appraise for what was needed. If he were to try to sell it once completed, he couldn't get anything near his money back. It was an assignment from First Trust Bank of Arkansas, Winston Kenwood's bank.

Kevin sat down at the computer and ran the comparable sales in the area and printed out the recent sales for the past twelve months. There was a small subdivision near the subject property where they were building some new two-thousand-square-foot houses for $120,000 to $130,000. Still, the data would not support a project in that neighborhood like the borrower wanted to build and get financing. Kevin took the assignment back to the bank and explained that to the originator. She was upset. "You don't know what you're doing," she said. "Jenny Lafferty was right. You are a deal killer. I think I can get Mr. Kenwood to put a stop to your ruining people's deals," she said. She was angry. "You'll see. You've had it."

Here we go again, Kevin thought. "If you're honest, they just won't accept it and strike you off their panel. If you go along with everything they want, you can't sleep at night. I may as well forget this client."

The next day, the originator took joy in calling Kevin and telling him she called another appraiser and had a full value appraisal in a half day. "He knows what he's doing," she said.

That afternoon, Winston Kenwood's assistant called Kevin. *Wow*, Kevin thought, *Mr. Big himself is calling me to try to get that appraisal done. He must not know the originator has already beaten him to the punch.*

"Mr. Henry, Mr. Kenwood would like for you to have lunch with him in the Top of the Arlington tomorrow if that's convenient with you."

"Ma'am, if it's about doing that appraisal on that house in southwest Little Rock at the value requested, tell him I cannot discuss that, and he can save his money on the lunch."

"I don't know what he wants to discuss with you, but I'll give him the message," she replied. "Thank you for your time, and you have a nice day."

"Thank me for my time," Kevin muttered. "I suppose I'll have more time now to do my research, if I can pay my bills," he lamented. Kenwood can put me out of business if he wants to."

Kevin was deep into Jim Hammons's files when the phone rang. It was Winston Kenwood on the phone, not his assistant. Seldom did an executive such as Kenwood dial his own telephone call. "Winston Kenwood here, Kevin. Good morning to you!" he bellowed with his booming voice. "Just a minute of your time, and I'll let you go. It's not about the appraisal for the 38th Street property. Don't worry about that weird piece of property, because you were right on with that. We'll handle that. We want that customer's business and will take a business risk. I have stopped the originator's gossiping—I think. I told her if she wants to continue here, she must give you another assignment and pronto. We are not in the business of ruining careers."

"Kevin…let's have lunch and talk. I want to talk about something that may be of interest to you and not on the telephone… how about noon tomorrow at the Top of the Arlington?"

"Well, good morning to you, Mr. Kenwood. Thank you for that support. Yes, noon tomorrow will be fine."

"Good, then I'll see you at noon tomorrow!" He boomed, and he was gone.

Now, that has me curious, Kevin thought. "What could Winston Kenwood want with me? I suppose I should have asked for an appraisal assignment for this appointment, hah!" he muttered aloud.

He dived back into Jim Hammons's Wemberly Warehouse files and was looking at some research Jim had done on the corporate filings in Arkansas when Carol called.

"Hey, Appraiser Man, I haven't heard from you in a couple days and wanted to be sure you were alive and not back in the hospital. I have a couple of appraisal assignments for you to pick up about five o'clock, if you have time."

"Good morning, Carol, it's good to hear from you. Yes, I'm alive and am plodding along on some research. You might want to see it sometime, but I have more digging to do. I may be about to find why so many people are worried about the Wemberly Warehouse history. But I'm not there yet and will let you know when I am." He didn't want to mention his luncheon appointment with Winston Kenwood. "I *will* come by and pick up those assignments…and thanks!"

Kevin went out to eat a quick lunch and came back to look at more of Jim Hammons's files. They were quite thick, as though Jim wanted to nail something down and be sure about it. The date of the files was at the second appraisal of the warehouse Jim did. He had gone out of town, even, to get some information.

The phone rang, and it was Cheryl this time. *Oh no*, Kevin thought, *is she going to bug me about what Frank Harley wanted?*

"Kevin…good afternoon. I have some appraisal work for you if you have time," she said. "It's here in Little Rock, and you should be able to whip it out quickly. Come by about five o'clock, and I'll have the assignments ready for you."

"Uh-oh, a conflict at five o'clock," Kevin said. "I have a previous appointment for five o'clock. Can I come by earlier and pick it up?" There was a moment of silence.

"I may not have this ready before then. Let me call you another time," she said and gently hung up the phone. Kevin wondered about this. *Was she irritated? She didn't slam the phone. No, of course not! That would not be like Cheryl.*

I may need to follow up on this and make sure where I stand. I can't afford to burn any bridges. Cheryl is Frank Harley's assistant, the closest one to him. I don't understand all the mysteries, and I need her help, if it is available, Kevin reasoned.

Kevin studied the Jim Hammons files and read through several pages of typed notes. They were quite detailed, but he felt he was missing some key points somewhere and went back over several pages. The owners of the various corporations seemed repetitious in places. A corporation owned a portion of another corporation, which was registered in part by a mother corporation that had previously been sold to a different corporation that owned some of the same parts. The principals were never named so far. There must be more information somewhere. The afternoon passed, and it was time to meet Carol Fleichman and pick up those assignments from her.

He closed all the folders and put them back in the box that old Jim had given him. They had to stay with him. He also placed the floppies from the last year at the S&L in a box and put both boxes back into the Explorer. He started backing out of the garage and changed his mind. He pulled back in, closed the garage door, and went back into the house. The computer would be at risk when he was gone, so he unhooked it and loaded it into the Explorer. He checked the Ruger in the console and made sure he had a loaded cartridge clip. Somehow, he felt, he must find a place to leave these things. Maybe it could be the storage unit except for the computer.

At precisely five o'clock, Kevin drove up to the New Home Mortgage Company, and Carol was at the door. "Come in, Kevin, I am just locking up. Everyone else is gone, and we'll have some privacy while we discuss the assignments. These two will be close, and I want you to look at them before you accept them. I don't want you to have to deal with some overpriced sales. I know they are close," she said.

"Thanks, friend, I don't need another blow here." He glanced at the locations and said they should be all right, but he couldn't guarantee it. "There should be enough leeway to work with. Is that really what you want to talk about, Carol?"

"Not really," she said. Frank Harley is still calling about the Wemberly Warehouse files. He said they should be here, that they were here when Kennon Foster died. I know they should have been, because our records show they should be here. But when I took over, they were missing, and Frank Harley had told the police that nothing was missing. I am not sure where I stand in this matter. I don't know if he is serious or not. He continues to give me praises for my management of this office, but then this constant pressing to locate the files gives me pause." Carol pushed her chair back and looked straight at Kevin.

"But I guess I can handle that, at least for now," she said. "What about your protection of the floppy disks? Have you decided where you want to keep them? I worry about all of this constant fear of the unknown, and I worry about your safety. How do you cope with this situation?

Kevin looked into Carol's eyes that had that constant smile and couldn't help but be distracted for a moment. He had to remind himself that they were still working in a business relationship. *There was a certain behavior expected, according to the norms of business protocol, but the norms be hanged*, he was thinking. "Carol, we have a certain amount of unfinished business that we should attend to. Will you have dinner with me tonight…say about six o'clock?" Kevin blurted out. *So there!* he followed.

Carol smiled and sat up straight. "Kevin, I agree, we have been negligent in some of these business matters, and I would love to have dinner with you," she replied. *So there, Kevin*, she followed. "But before we get carried away, we must remember the protocol of our business relationship and especially the circumstances of this Wemberly Warehouse situation. If we are seen in a too familiar relationship, it could bring down the wrath of my superiors," she said. "But, Kevin, I say we go. I'm not turning you down. Let's go somewhere."

"Good, meet me at the mall in North Little Rock, and I'll pick you up there. We'll drive up to Searcy and eat at a steak house restaurant. Maybe there'll be no one there that we'll know. I'll pick you up at six at Dillard's front door."

"Hey, Kevin!" Carol shouted as he was leaving. "I'm feeling like a school girl…"

"And you look like one too, Carol," he shouted back happily. This was the first date he'd even thought about since Marylyn died. It had been a long time.

Kevin raced home and showered and shaved quickly. *It's a great feeling*, he thought. *Man was not made to live alone. At least he was going to enjoy the company of a beautiful woman for this dinner date.* As he started out of his door, the phone started ringing. He thought he'd ignore it and let his answering machine take care of it. "Kevin, please answer." The voice sounded desperate. "This is Cheryl, please answer."

Kevin couldn't resist that plea and picked up the phone. "This is Kevin. What's wrong?"

"Kevin, that red Ford pickup is parked in my driveway, and the man is knocking on my door and ringing the doorbell. I'm as nervous as a cat, and I don't want to answer. Please come quickly."

"All right, Cheryl, get that pistol out, and be sure it's loaded. Don't let him in. If he forces his way in, shoot as soon as he enters the house. Don't wait. I'll be there in five minutes," Kevin said and ran out the door. He raced down the driveway and turned on St. Charles Boulevard toward Cheryl's house. His concentration was on getting there in time. "What on earth is that guy doing, going up to her house, even in broad daylight? In the past, it had been darkness when he was parked out by her house. Anyway, he can't be up to any good," he continued thinking and pressed harder on the gas pedal.

There was no policeman in sight, and luckily, the traffic was thin as he approached sixty miles an hour, then hit the brakes to slow for the turn onto Cheryl's street. As he approached her house, he saw a red Ford pickup driving away in a normal speed. It was not the pickup on which he had noted the license plate number. There was no pickup there at her house now. Kevin pulled around to the back of the house and dialed Cheryl's home number.

"Is that you, Kevin?" Cheryl answered. "He just left. Where are you?"

"I'm behind your house, in your driveway," Kevin answered. I saw the truck. It is a red pickup but I don't think it's the same one that we have had encounters with in the past." He was getting out as Cheryl was coming out of the house.

He could tell she had been really frightened. She still had the pistol in her hand and she hurried up to him and threw her arms around him. "Thank you for coming. I thought it was that crazy guy, and I didn't know what he was trying to do. I didn't get a look at his face but could see the red Ford pickup in the driveway. The kids weren't here, thank goodness," she said. "Are you sure that's not the same guy? I don't know anyone who has a red Ford pickup." She started trembling again, and he held her closely until she calmed down.

"Kevin, please don't leave. If that man returns, I would appreciate if you were here." She looked straight at him. "Please?" she said. Cheryl still had her bank clothes on including her earrings and high heels. She looked like the professional Cheryl who was ready to take a message from Frank Harley. "Please come in," she said and started for the door.

"Okay, okay," Kevin assured her. "I'll stay awhile and see if he returns. In the meantime, just get the feel of that pistol. He walked in behind her, and she locked the door.

"Kevin, I'm sorry to have bothered you like this, but I didn't know who else to call quickly. I think we don't want the police involved in this yet," she said. "You probably have something else you need to do, but while you're here, and if you don't mind, let me go in and change from these work clothes. I just want to get out of these after the work day is over."

"Okay, I'll wait." He didn't want to tell her. *Oh migosh*, he thought, *I've left Carol hanging. I am supposed to be over across the river in five minutes. I can't call her from here. This is embarrassing.* Cheryl was already in her bedroom changing. *Maybe she won't be long.* Kevin was hoping. He waited and looked at his watch again; it had been fifteen minutes. She finally came out of the bedroom in slacks and a cotton shirt. She had put on some low heel shoes.

"I'm sorry it took so long," she said. I put one outfit on and spilled some water all over me. I was so nervous. I had to change everything. I'm so sorry. Have you seen that truck again?"

The telephone started ringing. She let it ring, but they listened for the answering machine to pick up. "Cheryl, this is Frank Harley. I sent Eric Burley to bring you some fresh produce from the farm. I have had him to take all the employees of the local bank office some vegetables. We have an abundance of it this year on our East End farm, and we just wanted to share them. I hope you enjoy them. Eric will be driving a red Ford pickup. Do not tip him. I have already done so.

"Oh no! I'm so sorry. I had no idea, Kevin. All I could think of was the red Ford pickup. I am sorry, and I apologize for grabbing you when you arrived. I couldn't help but hug you when you came. I was so terrified."

Kevin smiled and told her that it's okay. "It's not every day I get hugged by a beautiful lady," he said.

Cheryl turned a little red but smiled. "At least I was hugging a handsome man," she retorted. "You are welcome to stay now, and I'll fix a burger for us. My kids are with my aunt for the night, and I am free."

Wow, am I lucky or am I unlucky? Kevin thought. *How can I tell her I have a date tonight with Carol Fleichman?* he pondered. "Cheryl, I must take a rain check if you will. I have a place I must be in just a few minutes. Now, if you'll please excuse me, I really must run." He left as she was waving 'bye and thanks.

As he drove away, he saw the red truck behind him. "I hope that's the same red truck with the veggies," Kevin muttered. He headed for North Little Rock. He picked up the phone and dialed the number for Carol's car. There was no answer. "She was expecting me at 6. It's now 6:20. Surely she'll wait." He said. The traffic was heavy all the way and travel was slow. When he got into the McCain Mall parking lot the time was 6:45. *This is a bad start,* Kevin was thinking. *She'll never want a date with me again.*

As he drove up to Dillard's front door, of all people, there was Winston Kenwood getting out of his Lincoln Town Car. He saw Kevin and yelled to him to wait. He went around and opened the door for a well-dressed lady. "Come meet Mrs. Kenwood," the banker said. "Margaret, this is Kevin Henry, one of the sharper appraisers and former finance officer. Kevin, this is Mrs. Kenwood. Kevin, I am looking forward to our meeting tomorrow." Mrs. Kenwood acknowledged Kevin, and they exchanged pleasantries.

Now the time was 6:55, and Kevin looked around for his date. She was nowhere to be seen, and he was becoming depressed. "Now what, she gave up and left," Kevin muttered. *What a predicament. I have not only stood up a beautiful date, but I have stood up one of my prime business customers. Is this a messed up day, or what?* he thought. He walked around in the store for a while and decided to go on home.

As soon as he got home, he called Carol on her home number. There was no answer. *I don't blame her,* Kevin thought, *she's madder than hops. No woman likes being stood up at a date. She won't talk to me now. There goes a good friend too.*

Kevin closed the door of the garage after he had driven in. He left the computer and the boxes in the Explorer and walked into the house. He started checking the house room by room, and when he reached the back door, the glass was broken, and he had been burglarized again. He went to his office and saw it had been ransacked again. They had been foiled again. Kevin almost laughed, but he felt almost desperate. *Is this going to happen constantly?* he thought. "Tomorrow, I must order a home security system."

The phone rang two rings before he could get to it and lift the receiver. "This is Kevin," he said quickly. He thought maybe it was Carol.

"Okay, Henry, now we'll make it easy for you. Here's what we want you to do: bring those floppy disks of your last year at your old S&L. To make your decision easy, we want you to know we have your sweetie with us. If you don't bring those to the foot of the Arkansas River Bridge at 1430 and drop them off in a bag at precisely midnight, your sweetie goes into the river below the dam. She's in a bag like a cat, and it's tied to keep the cat in the bag. Haw, haw, haw, git it? If those floppies are not the correct ones, she goes in the river after we check them. Be sure they're the right ones...and don't bring in the cops, or she gets her throat slit when they show up. Believe me, buddy, we know how to perform, and if you hang around after the drop, she goes into the river." He hung up.

Kevin had no chance to question. What about when and where they will release the woman and who is the woman they are talking about was his immediate question, but the caller had hung up.

"That must be the pock mark guy with the red Ford pickup," Kevin surmised. He tried to call Cheryl and got no answer. *She may have gone to get her kids. No, she said she was free tonight. Do they have her or do they have Carol? Should I call the police? What if they muff the job and "my sweetie" is no longer. I think they have already killed two people in this quest for records of the Wemberly Warehouse Inc. How will I know if they are releasing Carol as they say? I don't know how to call them back. He didn't leave time to try to negotiate.*

Apparently, they don't suspect that I have the Jim Hammons files. He pondered this dilemma for a moment. *And apparently, they don't know I have replaced the computer they stole. I have those floppies restored to the new computer. I have that information on the computer, so I don't need them.*

He tried calling both women again and got no answer. He got the floppies for the year they wanted and put them in a special box with identification of the year. There was no way to secure the woman's safety, and he had to hope they would be satisfied and release her. He checked his Ruger pistol again and made sure it was properly loaded. It was, and he stuffed it inside his belt and pulled his shirt over it. It was still two hours before the precise time.

Kevin's thoughts wandered back and forth over various questions. He couldn't reach Carol by phone. He knew she was probably mad at him for standing her up. He couldn't reach Cheryl. She had been home and said she was free tonight. "Has she gone somewhere for a night out?" he questioned. He thought about the call for help. That's when he left and probably when he was burglarized again. She said the red Ford pickup was in the driveway, and the man was ringing her doorbell and knocking on her door. He had seen the pickup driving away when he arrived. She had been frightened. She was shaking and hugged him genuinely when he got out of his vehicle. *Is she a good actress? Was all that for real? Gosh!* Kevin was reeling from all the thoughts and possibilities.

He tried to call Carol again. It was now 11:30, and he had to leave. Neither woman was answering the phone. Kevin took the box of floppies and backed the Explorer out of the driveway and onto St. Charles Boulevard. When he got to River Mountain Road, he stopped a moment to gather his wits. He laid the gun in the seat beside the console for quick access. He knew there would probably be a lookout to see when he dropped the box off at the foot of the bridge. He looked around for signs of someone but saw no one. He parked and with the gun in one hand and the box in the other hand; he walked down to the foot of the bridge and left the box. He turned the Explorer around and left.

Now what? How will I know when they release the prisoner? Do they have that much integrity? No, or is there a good reason for them to not hurt her and let her go. He drove back home and began to call both women's phone numbers—still no answer from either. Then 2:00 a.m. passed, and it was very frustrating. Then as daylight was lighting the landscape, Kevin got into the Explorer and drove down to the bridge again and checked where he had left the box. The box was gone. His fears were confirmed. They still had the woman or had done something to her. "What could I have done differently that would have saved her? These files of mine have caused this." He fretted.

"Should I report this to the police and get them involved, or would that endanger the prisoner if she is still alive?" Kevin continued to question himself at the office work time. He waited to call Carol's office until nine o'clock. The receptionist answered, and he asked for Carol. "I'm sorry Ms. Fleichman isn't in at this time. May I take a message?

"Has she been in today?" he asked the girl.

"I'm sorry, I will have Ms. Fleichman return your call when she is available," she replied.

That was maddening. He hung up the phone and then dialed Cheryl's office. "May I speak to Ms. Inmon please?" Kevin asked. He tried to keep his voice normal, but it was hard. "I'll transfer you. Hang on please.

"This is Cheryl."

Kevin felt relieved and angry. "Cheryl, this is Kevin, I have been trying to reach you at home all night and this morning. Why haven't you answered?" he said a little gruffly.

"Why, Kevin, I'm sorry. When you left, I went out to eat and then to a movie. When I got home, I was so exhausted. I took the phone off the hook and went sound asleep. I forgot to put the phone back on the hook until just before I left. How was your night?" she asked. "I thank you for what you did for me last night. I was terrified. Can I help you with anything?"

"Never mind, I wanted to be sure you were safe. Now that I know you are, I will move on." He didn't stop to explain. Maybe she would think he was concerned about another visit from the red pickup truck.

Carol is missing, and the search must go on. Kevin drove to her house in North Little Rock and went to the front door. He knocked on the door and rang the doorbell. There was no answer. He waited ten minutes to give her time to dress and come to the door. Finally, he got back in the SUV and called her home number. He called her car phone. There still was no answer. The police would be the normal response, but he was afraid they would jeopardize Carol. They are holding her somewhere for some other blackmail, or worse yet, they have done away with her. *How have we gotten into this mess? What could I have done differently?*

Maybe I'll go to the police, he mused. *If I do, they'll want to know what they said, what I did, why they wanted me to do it, etcetera, etcetera, and then…* The phone rang.

"This is Winston Kenwood's office reminding you of the luncheon appointment," the lady said. "Will you be there?"

It was now 11:30 a.m., and he hadn't shaved or bathed since late yesterday and had been up all night, *But why not, I may as well mess up this too,* he thought. "Yes, yes, of course. I will be there," Kevin said politely.

CHAPTER 28

Winston Kenwood was waiting in the lobby of the Arlington building, and they rode up together. He started apologizing to his host for his appearance. "Please pardon my appearance. I have been up all night trying to help a friend and still into this morning and haven't had a chance to go home to cleanup. I don't mean to disrespect you like this," Kevin explained as best as he could improvise.

"I see, Kevin, I'm sorry your friend had problems. I hope she is good looking," he laughed knowingly and whacked Kevin on the shoulder.

Kevin smiled at the gesture. "I wish that were the issue. I don't know whether my friend will overcome this difficulty, and when we are finished today, I'll be back to help," he responded. He knew this would bring questions. "It's a rather confidential thing and will require me to be discreet." He stumbled with more response. He was trying to avoid the conversation.

They arrived at the Top of the Arlington and were escorted to a private room for the lunch. "Very well, Kevin, I'll get down to why I wanted to have this visit. I know you have various talents and experience. I know you have been involved in more than appraisal business and have worked in the finance business for several years." The waiter served their orders and left.

Winston Kenwood continued, "I am looking for someone to work for me who will give me absolute loyalty and support. I want someone to be watching my backside, if you will. I will pay you well, more than you probably expect. You will have freedom of time and movement to operate to my advantage. You will be an employee of First Trust Bank of Arkansas, and I will probably get you appointed to some kind of position on the state banking committee on which I serve. I want you close to me and involved, business-wise, as much as possible. You will not necessarily be my physical bodyguard, but I want you to guard my wellbeing. How does something like that appeal to you?" he asked pointedly.

Kevin picked up his drink and took a sip slowly. *This is strange,* he thought, *this is the same approach as Frank Harley a few days ago. These men have relatively same positions. They are apparently well acquainted with each other and are making the same proposition to me.*

"Mr. Kenwood, that is certainly an offer that is flattering, and I respect that. You know that my appraisal business provides me a measure of independence, though maybe not as financially rewarding. I will definitely keep this in mind, but I want to think it over for a few days before I make any decision, if you don't mind. I do have a question, though."

"I thought you might," Kenwood said. "Go ahead. I know this is an unusual job assignment, and you should ask.

"What has prompted this need for that sort of job? I'm, sure you don't want to spend that money for no good reason."

"Kevin, the money is not important. The bank can well afford it, and your position at the state banking committee will be paid by the bank and will be a contribution to the state. I will go ahead and tell you that some strange and unusual things are happening in central Arkansas at this time. It may involve other banks before it is resolved. I want to be sure we are up on things. I need to spot irregularities and see who is involved before it gets out of hand. I need you to not only watch out for my bank but for me personally. That's about all the details I can offer at this time."

"Another question, what if your concerns are resolved and you no longer have concerns to this extent? I will have given up a career, and it will be rather costly to start over," Kevin asked.

"I will give you a five-year contract in which you would have the option to withdraw at any time you become unhappy with your job. I do want to protect you and your livelihood, Kevin. I can tell you that at the end of the five-year contract, if we no longer have a need for that position, if you are in good standing with the bank, there would always be a place for you. I will include in your pay, stock bonuses," Kenwood said and smiled.

Kevin thought about this quietly for a moment. This offer was far exceeding what Harley had offered though he hadn't gone into detail. "Mr. Kenwood, that appears to be a great opportunity, and I do appreciate your confidence. My judgment is to give it some time and thought to roll around in my mind. So if you don't mind, I want to give this some thought, and I'll get back with you shortly."

"That's good, Kevin. I'll look forward to hearing from you soon," Kenwood said.

CHAPTER

29

The time was one o'clock when the meeting was over with Kenwood, and Kevin felt time was of the essence. He must locate Carol, but where to start? *I'm glad he didn't ask for a quick decision,* Kevin thought, *because I would have been forced to turn him down. I've got to find Carol. That is first priority.* He left the Arlington parking lot and headed straight for home. That was where they had contacted him before. On the way, his eyes kept searching for the red Ford F150 pickup truck.

As he neared the house, he thought about how insecure it was and that a security system was of necessity. He drove into the driveway and pushed the button on the remote garage door opener. He watched the door go up and started to doze as it seemed to take forever. He shook himself and parked inside the garage. He picked up the Ruger 9 mm pistol and stuffed it in his waistline as he exited the Explorer. "That rear door will need repaired too," he remembered.

He walked through the kitchen from the garage and started checking the house. He had just finished when the doorbell rang. He opened the door, and there was a man with a baseball cap pulled down low on his forehead, and he needed a shave more than Kevin. *Whiskers,* Kevin thought. That guy shall be known as

Whiskers, if no other name. "Mr. Henry, I have a message for you from Carol Fleischman if you'll let me come in for a moment."

Kevin's first reaction was of some relief. Maybe he could find out something about Carol. "Where is she?" he said immediately.

"You'll know soon enough if you cooperate. First, I must come in, or I'll leave with the message." Kevin looked in the driveway and saw the red Ford pickup.

"Come in," Kevin said. *Maybe this mystery is about to unravel*, he was thinking. He turned and walked back into his foyer and turned back around. That was a mistake. The man had pulled a gun.

"All right, friend," he said, "the message is she is safe and wants you to cooperate with us. What do you know about Jim Hammons's files?"

Uh-oh, Kevin thought, *now I've got to convince them of my ignorance, but play along until I can get information about Carol*. "I don't know what you're talking about. I suppose they are in his office—maybe in his house. Why ask me?"

"We know you had lunch with Hammons and had other contacts with him at the party last Saturday," Whiskers declared. "We know he was considering the appraisal of the Wemberly Warehouse property, and we know he had appraised that property several times. He must have had files. Carol Fleichman has admitted that he was asked to appraise that property again. What did he tell you about that property when you talked?"

"Look," Kevin said, "I don't know about the files you want, but I'll see if I can help you find them if you release Carol. I've got to know she's all right." Kevin was thinking about the box in his Explorer. *If this guy keeps probing, he may start searching again and think about my vehicle.*

"If you want that woman alive, you better help us find those files. I think you know more than you're admitting. We'll give you twenty-four hours. Then it's curtains for your sweetie. And one more thing, buster, if you call in the police, we'll call off the offer, and your sweetie will exist no more. I'm leaving now, and don't try anything. If I don't return in the next few minutes, she's a dead cat. The cat's in the bag. Haw, haw, haw, git it?" He laughed.

"How or where can I reach you if I find something," Kevin asked.

"You can't reach us. We'll reach you," the visitor said and turned and walked slowly out the front door and toward his red truck. He had never discovered the pistol in Kevin's waist under his shirt, but Kevin felt helpless. It would be counterproductive to shoot the guy, but he grabbed a camera that was in his office and ran to the window. He snapped pictures as the guy was leaving and also got some shots of the truck. When the truck backed out and turned down the street, Kevin got the license number. It was a different number than what he had remembered, but he had this one now.

Are there two red Ford F150 pickup trucks they are using? It makes sense, he was thinking. The pickup he saw driving away from Cheryl's house yesterday was not the one with the license number he had memorized. *Could it have been this one? That makes sense*, he thought again.

Kevin was pondering his next move when the phone rang. "This is Kevin Henry Appraisals," he answered.

"Mr. Henry…Mr. Harley would like to speak to you," the voice said very formally. It was Cheryl's voice.

"Yes," Kevin said.

"One moment please," she said.

"Kevin!" Harley's voice boomed out on the phone. "I have been hoping to hear from you. Can you come by today?" he said. "I would like to talk."

Kevin was tempted to solicit Harley's help, but at this point, he didn't know whom to trust. *Harley? Maybe and maybe not*, he thought. "All right, I'll come by there in about an hour if that's good for you," Kevin suggested.

"Please come," he said. "I'll set aside time for you. We need to talk," Harley said and hung up.

I'm not ready to talk about his proposal, Kevin thought as he started shaving. "This is just not the time, but I should go by there. He sounded urgent." Kevin rushed through his shower and changed clothes. He felt refreshed and headed for the New Pulaski Bank. He dropped off the film on the way. They said he could pick up the photos in an hour.

He walked into the bank and was greeted by the receptionist. "Hello, Mr. Henry…Mr. Harley is expecting you." She rose from her desk and escorted him to Harley's office. He did not see Cheryl. *Maybe she was out*, he wondered.

"Kevin! Come in and sit down at the round table," Harley stated and moved over to the table. He reached out and shook Kevin's hand robustly. "How have you been son," Harley said warmly but was lowering his voice.

Kevin responded in a low tone also.

"I've asked you to come over here, rather urgently I realize, but, Kevin, it is urgent. You may know that Carol Fleichman at our mortgage branch in North Little Rock has not been to the office today. She cannot be reached on the phone, and we are very concerned. Rachel, one of her assistants, said she remembered Carol had asked you to come by and pick up some appraisal assignments. That was the last time anyone there had seen her. They said they were just leaving when you arrived. Do you have any idea of what she may have been planning after her meeting with you?" Harley asked him. "It's not like Carol to be absent from work. She has worked for me for twelve years and never has been late for work, neither has she ever been sick."

Kevin was torn between telling Harley everything and keeping everything to himself. There were so many weird things happening. He knew Harley seemed to care about his employees. He had just had a party at his estate and invited all employees, even the janitors.

As Kevin hesitated in his response, Harley continued, "I have hoped you would have an answer to my offer by now. I wish you were on board already at a time like this. Too many things are happening. Kevin, you just don't know, and I can't tell you all of it," Harley said in a lower voice.

"Mr. Harley, I don't have any idea where Carol might be," he told him truthfully. I have not seen her since I met with her yesterday at the mortgage company office." He watched Harley's face and saw some disappointment. "I'm sorry, sir," Kevin said.

"Well, Kevin, I suppose that makes it even more desirous to have you on board with us," Harley stated. "I need you to be able to work here and be observant of not only the business matters but also the extra happenings that may affect this bank and even me personally. I will pay you an ample salary, and you can feel secure at this bank for as long as you are loyal and reasonable. I know you are familiar with the banking laws and lending laws. Kevin, I need your help."

Kevin was feeling sorry and sympathetic for Harley, but then, he started thinking about the insistence on getting the Wemberly Warehouse appraised for an offbeat value. Even Cheryl had been assigned to coerce him into taking that assignment. "Plus," he remembered, "Carol had been assigned to get old Jim Hammons to complete an appraisal on that property for value well exceeding the actual value. If he were to go to work for Harley, would pressure be put on him to perform like that? Also, Winston Kenwood had made him a similar offer with a guarantee," he was remembering.

"Mr. Harley, I too have a lot going on with me at this time, and I must not make that kind of decision yet. If you can't hold the offer open, I will understand. I must be going now because of some urgency of my own."

"No, no. Leave if you must, but let's leave this thing open for now. Get back with me as soon as you can," Harley told him.

Kevin thanked him and left immediately. He was beginning to develop a headache and remembered he hadn't slept since 6:00 a.m. yesterday. He stopped by the Sportsman First Stop store and went in to the specialty department. "Do you have shoulder holsters here to fit a Ruger pistol? They brought out a couple, and one fit perfectly. He purchased that and left. There was no registration needed.

The shadows were falling when he drove into his driveway. He drove into the garage and closed the door. He had stopped at the lumber company and gotten a piece of plywood cut to fit the glass on the back door. Kevin took screws and mounted the plywood on the door and secured it with extra screws. *There, they will have to go to a lot of trouble to get that door open, and they won't be able to see what's on the other side before they start to enter*, Kevin thought.

He went to the Explorer and retrieved the box with old Jim Hammons files and began to research some more. The headache was subsiding after he had taken three aspirins. He was reading fast when he found some key information that really gave him pause. *This is what they want*, Kevin thought. *They are willing to kill for this. I know what they want. I don't want them to have this, but I must get Carol free. This needs to be developed*, he thought.

The copy machine was operating nicely, and he was getting good crisp copies of these key documents provided by old Jim Hammons. Kevin copied about three dozen papers and stuffed them in a separate set of folders. He found an empty box and placed the old folders and files in it. Then, he took the new copies and folders and went to the garage. He had been afraid to hide anything there because they might look there anyway. But now, he carried the folders up to the attic and went a few feet from the entry and lifted the rolled insulation up carefully, placing a folder under the roll, placing it back down, and repeating this until all folders were hidden. When he looked out across the attic, he could see no signs of the work he had done. In fact, he might have to hunt a while to find them.

Now he was ready when they called. He was exhausted. He had just crawled into the bed for a nap at midnight, and the phone rang two hours later. It was the intruder. "All right, Henry, have you got those documents? Time is running out," the caller stated.

"I'm working on it, but I must have a little more time, and you gave me twenty-four hours," Kevin reminded the caller. I must do a little more searching. Please give me some time. Is the woman okay? She must be all right or the deal is off," he said strongly.

"Yeah, yeah, she's still alive," he replied. "If you don't come through that's more than you can say later. When the twenty-four hours is up, we're coming for the files."

"All right," Kevin replied, "I'll do my best to have what you want." He was ready but wanted to stall as long as possible so he could think of what to do. He was tempted to call for police help but was afraid they might trigger Carol's death. He left all the papers in Jim Hammons's file folders except four key sheets. That was his ace if they didn't deliver Carol.

At precisely 8:00 a.m., there was a knocking on the door. Kevin went to the door and spoke through the closed door. He could see the red Ford pickup in the driveway. *He is bold now*, Kevin thought. Daylight, and no doubt he has a gun. "All right, who's there?" Kevin asked.

"You know who. Open up, and deliver if you know what's good for you," the man said in a low voice. He didn't want to rouse the neighborhood. Neither did Kevin.

"Come in with your hands in the front of you. No gun showing," Kevin instructed.

"Okay, no gun," the man said. "I'll have my hands out like you say," the man said.

Kevin opened the door, and the man walked through with his hands in front of his body as Kevin had instructed. He moved inside, and Kevin held the Ruger pointed at him. Turn around, and hold those hands high in the air. When he turned around, Kevin frisked him and pulled the gun out of his inside holster.

Just as he tossed the gun down, a second intruder with a pocked face barged in with a pistol pointed at Kevin, but Kevin shoved the one he called *whiskers* into the *pock-faced* man and knocked the gun out of his hand. "Get those hands in the air now. "Now!" Kevin yelled, "Or I'll blow your head off, and don't think I won't." He meant it. He wasn't sure Carol was all right. "Down on the floor, and crawl over with your head against that wall, and put your hands behind your head," he ordered. Don't move them, or I'll shoot. And be very careful, because I am very nervous. Just give me an excuse," he said. They hit the floor and did what he said.

Kevin picked up both guns and tossed them aside and frisked them again for more weapons. He wanted some heavy cord he had in the closet nearby. "Hold it there, gents, while I retrieve a little something. Don't move," he ordered as he backed toward a bedroom. The pockmarked one jerked his hands down and flipped over ready to jump. Kevin fired a shot near him, and it hit the wall nearby. "Flip back over, and put those hands behind your head or the next shot hits home. You won't move again," Kevin shouted.

The guy quickly flipped back over and kept his hands behind his head. Kevin retrieved his material. He tied the pockmarked one's hands behind him with the cord and blindfolded him with two cotton balls over each eye and a strip of tape around his head to secure them to his eyes. Then he placed a pillowcase over his head.

"Now, boys, we are going to retrieve your prisoner. How many are keeping her?" Kevin asked them.

"Ain't nobody," Whiskers replied. "She's secure in a bag."

"You had better hope she's in good shape if you want to live," Kevin admonished them. "Whiskers, you are going to take your red pickup and lead the way after you tell me where we're going. If you stray, your buddy here gets the bullet square dab between his eyes." Kevin threatened.

Whiskers looked at his blindfolded buddy and asked, "Jocko, what we gonna do? Cain't you do somethin'? I ain't gonna lead him out there. That's the only security we got, and we ain't gonna get no pay if we don't deliver that stuff," he said.

"Shut up, stupid. You're gonna lead the way, and you better not forget the way. If you run off or lose the way, I will kill you as soon as I get loose from this here entrapment," he said through the bed pillow.

"So your name is *Stupid*," Kevin said.

"It ain't neither," he said. "It's Fred Walker"

"You're stupid," Jocko yelled.

"All right, where is she being held? I want to get there, and she had better be okay," Kevin told them.

"You tell him, Jocko, I don't remember the name of that place."

"It's Gruntington's Island, stupid. You know the way. Just lead him to it, and don't get lost."

"Okay, Fred," Kevin said. "I want you to lead Jocko out to my SUV and help him into the passenger side, and then I want you to put a seat belt around him, including his arms and secure it tightly. Then when I raise the garage door, you can get into your pickup and lead the way. If you get too far ahead, I'll just shoot Jocko and then chase you down. This Explorer runs pretty fast, and we'll have a good race. Then I'll just shoot you, because you can't outrun me."

They got Jocko secured, and Kevin raised the garage door. Fred looked back at Kevin and seemed doubtful as to what he might do. "Now go rip your car phone out and bring it to me," Kevin said.

"There ain't no phone," Fred said.

"Just get the phone, Fred," Jocko yelled.

Fred ripped the phone out and brought it to Kevin who threw it on the floor of the garage.

The entourage backed out onto St. Charles Boulevard and headed toward the river. Kevin had heard of Gruntington's Island.

He had read something about it in the history of the development of Wemberly Warehouse. He remembered that was where Harold Wemberly disappeared during that hunting trip. *That is a huge island, and it might be tricky getting to somewhere on that island with these two men*, Kevin was thinking.

They drove southeastward several miles along Highway 65, then turned south through farming country for several miles to a levee that protected the farmland from floodwaters when the Arkansas River overflowed. They crossed the levee and traveled a narrow roadway with water on each side and then across a bridge that crossed a narrow channel of the Arkansas River. Meeting another vehicle and passing would be prohibitive until they drove onto the island and arrived at a cabin. This island was used only for hunting and was privately owned by a couple of corporations and managed by a couple of hunting clubs. There were two nice cabins for the hunters with one on each end of the island.

On this end of the island, there was a cabin built of solid logs, sealed with a honey colored seal, and chinked with concrete. It had a large porch in the front and six windows in front, he could see. Though deep in the woods, electric wire had been run to the cabin, and running water was provided with a well and a pump with an electric motor. It was even cooled with window air conditioners. Tall trees lined the perimeter of the house site and near the cabin. Several large oaks loaded with acorns provided food for squirrels. The house was on a site that showed to be above the flood level.

As they neared the cabin, Kevin motioned for Fred to stop. He could see the other red Ford F150 pickup truck parked at the cabin. He motioned for Fred to walk back to his Explorer. "Is Carol in that cabin?" he asked Fred.

"Oh yeah, she's tied up in there," Fred said. "She's in there by herself. We can just go in and git her."

Kevin could see tracks leading around to the back of the cabin, and he eased his Explorer around Fred's truck and toward the end of the cabin where he could see behind it. "Aha, just as I expected, Jocko, there are others there." He reached over and checked the seat belt on Jocko to be sure it was fastened securely and then leaned out the window to call Fred to him. "I want you to go in and bring the lady out."

"Bring her out, Fred," Jocko yelled through his pillowcase hood.

Fred walked into the cabin and stayed for a couple minutes and returned to the Explorer. "I can't bring her out. She can't come with me," Fred said. "They said you are to send those files into the cabin, and they'll release her."

Kevin tapped Jocko on the shoulder. "Who are they, Jocko?" Kevin asked. "Who are you working for?

"We don't know. They just call him the Big Man. We never see him," Jocko answered through the pillowcase that was over his head. "Those are some of my buddies."

"Fred, tell them I have Jocko here, and if I don' get the lady, Jocko goes to the police to tell all he knows," Kevin said. "Then he'll be charged with kidnapping, and we'll come after the whole bunch of you. He turned to Jocko. "Tell him, Jocko, do you want to just go to the police and forget about the lady?"

"Go get that woman, Fred, or you'll have me to deal with and tell the others their names will be recorded for sure," Jocko shouted at him. "Those bastards better send her out. They don't want me going to the police."

Fred went back into the cabin and came out again with a message. "They said send Jocko and the files in first."

Kevin knew he had to get Carol out first and might have to bluff some. "All right, guys, I've decided Jocko needs to go in and talk to the police. We are leaving in two minutes if the lady isn't out here. If she comes to me in two minutes, we'll release Jocko." He started his motor.

Fred ran into the cabin again. Kevin heard a loud noise ensuing as though there was a fight going on, but in the middle of that, Carol came running out as Fred was untying her. She ran to Kevin's arms. Fred was getting Jocko out, and Kevin let them go. They were at the end of the cabin, which had no windows and hidden from the view of anyone inside. Kevin hurried Carol into the front seat and jumped back in. He could hear the banging and crashing going on inside.

Kevin threw the Explorer into gear and spun off while Fred was unwrapping Jocko. They crossed the bridge and raced for the levee at a fast clip and turned onto the farm road. Carol had started laughing hard, and Kevin wondered if she were suffering a little hysteria from the capture. She slowed her laughter and told Kevin why she was laughing.

"Those goons in that cabin are pretty stupid. I don't know why they are there with the other two. I suppose just to guard me while they went for you. When you were bargaining, they were arguing whether to release me in exchange for Jocko. They started having a knock-down-drag-out fight, and Fred got me out of there. He said if I didn't get out of there, Jocko would kill him. Jocko doesn't want to see the police. That would put him under pressure he doesn't want. He is afraid of the big guy, I think."

"How did you wind up in their captivity?" Kevin asked her.

"I was in the foyer at Dillards, waiting for you to pick me up, and they walked up to me and stuck a gun in my ribs and told me I was going with them or else," Carol said. "I thought I would be able to wiggle my way out somehow and went along with them. They told me they had captured you and would wipe you out if I didn't go with them. They immediately took me out to that camp house and have held me there since. I knew somehow that you would find me. I became anxious at times, but I never lost hope."

Oh my gosh, Kevin thought. *If she only knew how inefficient I felt.* They drove awhile, and Kevin reached over and took her hand. "Carol, I'm sorry I was late for our date," he said and smiled.

"I wondered where you were and was about to go to my car and call you. Did you stand me up, Kevin?" Carol said and smiled back.

They drove to the Dillard's parking lot and found Carol's car still there. "Kevin, please follow me home. I would feel better. I'll even cook us some brunch at my house. You can park in the garage beside my car. There is room," Carol said.

"It's a deal," Kevin said. "At some point, we need to report your return. Harley is sincerely worried about you. You may need to make a very good excuse. He said you had never been late or missed a day from sickness. They have been looking for you, I think."

"Yes, I'll call as soon as we finish our brunch. First, I'll stop and get some eggs and bacon. I know I am out," Carol told Kevin.

"Let me get that for you. You go ahead, and I'll pick those things up and join you," Kevin quickly told her. "I'll see you soon."

The time was almost noon when Kevin got back into the Explorer with the groceries. He was looking forward to time with Carol. Just as he sat down in the car, his phone rang; he picked it up, and Carol was urgent. "Kevin, hold up! It's Frank Harley driving up to my house. I don't know what I want to say to him. Let's play this cool, if we can. I'll call you later."

"Darn it." Kevin was disappointed. "How did Harley happen to be Johnny-on-the-spot just as Carol got home? How did he know?

CHAPTER 30

The next day was booked for continuing education class. Appraisers were required to attend fourteen hours of continuing education each year, and this was a chance to attend a local class.

The CE class was attended by appraisers from several parts of the state. There were appraisers of all ages. It was noted that the average age of appraisers was predicted to become older and older. The average age in Arkansas was now over sixty years. It would be more difficult for young people to break into the appraisal business. More women were predicted to enter the appraisal work because of the time to break into the industry. More education was required, and fewer men who must provide the family's income could afford the financial pain of getting started. "Be glad you have a license and a start in the business," the speaker declared.

Kevin was lost in thought for a moment as he thought about whether he wanted to add an appraiser to his business. He presently had his office at home. If he added an appraiser apprentice, he would need to acquire an outside office. It would be taking time for the training and checking the apprentice's work. That was not very appealing. He thought about the offers that Kenwood and Harley had made him. If he knew more about the issues they were concerned about, he would go for one of them. "Should I discuss this with Carol or Cheryl? They are more closely connected to Harley and the New Bank of Pulaski. What about the First Trust Bank of Arkansas? Hey, Cheryl formerly worked at that bank. Should I talk with her? Well, I don't' know." He worried with the issue.

Back in the class, the instructor was explaining what appraisers should expect. "Now that the laws are changing, a new appraiser must work under an experienced and fully licensed appraiser for at least a year to gain the experience and must have enough cases within that period, and in most cases, it will take two years for him to gain that history. Few fully licensed appraisers can afford to share their business to sustain the new appraiser who must support a family that long…and the requirements will continue to increase," he continued. "So…guys, safeguard your licenses, do a good job, cover your backsides, and don't screw up. There will be pressure to conform to someone's numbers. Use your heads, and be fair, but do things right."

At break times, several appraisers were discussing old Jim Hammons's absence and his death. What happened to him was the question. Jim was a good guy and was always willing to share information and help someone who had a problem, and there were always problems, they admitted. Jim had been at it so long, he had experienced many situations, but he lived on the edge when it came to risks. He took chances a lot. There was always pressure, and he seemed to thrive on it. When the Feds came down on him lately, he would smile and challenge the application of their rules. He was smart and knew the business after forty or so years.

Back in session after the last break, the issue of fees came up. "We can't discuss fees," the instructor stated, "but remember to do your job right and charge justifiable fees. There can be no price setting. No price fixing. No further discussion of prices."

"Well, I'm going broke," one attendee stated.

"These mortgage companies and banks are afraid to charge the fees to their customers, and the secondary market like Fannie Mae want more and more work done on each appraisal," an old timer stated, and others agreed. One appraiser in the class pointed out that Fannie Mae and Freddie Mac would change the forms for new requirements. They would add required items to the pages but just make the blanks smaller so they could keep things to two pages as previous.

"Hah!" he scoffed.

Kevin knew that appraisers could make a good living if they worked hard and continued to promote themselves in the finance world. He also knew that apprentices who trained and obtained the required experience would probably leave and start their own business. That was the way it usually worked, so he had no desire to go that route.

Well, should he accept one of the offers? His independence was a nice thing, but security and greater income was nice also. How peaceful would the job be with either of the two?

—⚏—

As he stepped out from the class and into the open air, Kevin could hear his car phone ringing. It was Carol. "I have two appraisal assignments for you if you want to come by at five o'clock. I thought you might like some work that pays money after being out of circulation for a few days."

It was good to hear her voice, Kevin realized. How glad he was that he could hear that voice under normal circumstances. "Yes, I'll be there at five," he told her.

Immediately after hanging up the phone, it rang again. "This is the Secretary of State's office, Mr. Henry, with the information you asked about. You can pick it up any time tomorrow or later," the speaker told him.

The corporate filings information of several years ago had taken some searching of the archives to bring up what he wanted, but it was done. Kevin looked forward to reviewing those records to bring to light a little better knowledge of the ownership of the Wemberly Warehouse Inc.

Carol was waiting when he arrived. The door was already locked, and everyone had left except her. He pecked on the glass, and she came to let him in. "Kevin, I just wanted to talk in addition to the two appraisal assignments," she said and smiled. "You know I got cheated out of that date, and I didn't call you yesterday after I finished talking with Mr. Harley. I knew you were exhausted, and I felt you should rest."

"You guessed right, Carol, I went to sleep on the couch and woke up at midnight at which time I went on to bed. What did Harley have to say about your absence? Did you have a story for him, or did you have to tell him the facts?"

"I fabricated a story that was a little absurd, but I tried to convince him," Carol said. "I am not sure where I stand with Mr. Harley, and there are so many inconsistencies in his behavior and statements. I told him I had buckled under the pressure of everything with the disappearance of the Wemberly Warehouse files in our office. I couldn't find them and that I felt under pressure until I could. Harley said he felt there must be more and asked me if I had been out of town looking for another job. I told him no, and when I asked why he would think that, he said he knew I wouldn't just stay home without notifying my office," she continued. "I told him he would just have to accept that, and he backed off and told me to never mind about those files, that maybe they will turn up somewhere. He said he wanted to take the pressure off."

"Do you think he accepted that or did he just decide to not push it, or do you think he knew something about your disappearance? It's all a little muddy, don't you think? He appeared at your house just as you returned," Kevin said thoughtfully.

"Kevin, I waited at Dillard's for a half hour before those goons grabbed me." Carol asked, "Where were you?"

Carol still had that constant smile on her face and in her eyes. Kevin felt he had to level with her and hoped it was the right thing to do. "Carol, just as I was ready to go out the door, Cheryl called me with desperation in her voice and frightened. She said there was a man knocking on her door and ringing the doorbell, and there was a red Ford pickup in her driveway. You know about the red Ford F150 truck that was following you that Saturday. It made sense to me that it was the guy with the pockmarked face, and I rushed there to help. The pickup was driving away, and I saw it had a different license number than the one I had memorized.

Cheryl seemed traumatized by the ordeal, and I had assured her it was not the pockmarked man and maybe the man was there for another purpose. "That appeared to be a life-threatening emergency to me, but now I wonder. I left to join you as soon as I could. It was during that time that you were kidnapped. Was it one man or two men who grabbed you?"

"It was Jocko and another one of his goons who were at the cabin," Carol said. "Those other guys seem to be a comedy act, but Jocko and Fred, I think would do you in, in a minute. They had you in mind all the time. They told me you would be joining them soon."

"I think Jocko and Fred must work together, but Jocko seems to be the leader," Kevin said. I don't know who their boss is, but I'm sure they are working for someone else."

Carol looked at Kevin and, with her constant smile, told him he still owed her that date. "Somehow, we've got to do this differently. I don't know if Mr. Harley knows that you and I talk about anything other than appraisal assignments. He implied yesterday that he thought you should have known what had happened to me when I disappeared. I told him you weren't privy to my personal life. I disappeared so I could get some relaxation immediately. I think he reluctantly backed off in his questioning and told me I could take more time off if I felt I needed to. But I was ready to get back here in the office. I want to get a handle on all this stuff, Kevin."

Kevin watched Carol as she talked and with that enduring and endearing smile. *She certainly has an appeal*, he thought. He was beginning to not hear what she was saying as much as the date he owed her. "Carol, we were cheated out of that date. Is tonight at seven o'clock a good time, or do you need to get caught up some more?"

"Let's go for it, Kevin. I'll see you at seven o'clock."

Kevin got into the Explorer with spring in his step, looking forward to the date with Carol. This was going to be great. They were meeting at Walmart in Sherwood. They still thought they should be discreet.

He turned into his driveway, and his car phone was ringing. "It's Cheryl, I had to call. The vault room behind Mr. Harley's room is left open. He is gone for the day. If you will come by now, we can search for those files you were interested in. Now would be the best time," Cheryl said.

"The Wemberly Warehouse files! What do those files hold? Those must be loaded with delicate and significant information," Kevin surmised. "Blast it!" he said. *Carol is waiting for our date, and that is important*, he thought. *If I hurry, I can get back and make the date on time.*

"Kevin, this may be the only opportunity we have in a long, long time. Hurry now," she pleaded. "Don't miss this. I have a key to his office door but not the code to the vault room. We should check this while it's open."

"Okay, if we make it quick, I must be somewhere else shortly," Kevin said and hung up. He tried to call Carol, but she had left the office and was between the office and her car. He decided to call her in a moment. He drove hurriedly to the New Bank of Pulaski. The lot was vacant except for a couple cars that perhaps belonged to one of the bank's tenants. He tried to call Carol once more but got no answer. "Well, he would have to hurry this effort," he decided.

Cheryl was at the bank door and let him in. "Hurry!" she said. We must get this done before anyone shows up. I don't want anyone seeing us in that vault room." They moved into Frank Harley's office and then the vault room. Cheryl said the Wemberly Warehouse file was probably in the second row of *W*s, and he could check it out.

Kevin looked at her and questioned whether he should be the one searching. He pulled out a handkerchief and worked the drawer open and looked in the Wem folder area and came to Wemberly Warehouse, Inc. "*Sh*," Cheryl whispered. "There's someone coming. Let's close this vault door quickly." Kevin helped her close the door and wiped it clean of fingerprints.

"What's up, Cheryl?" Kevin asked her. "I thought everyone was gone. If we're caught in here, there goes your job and probably my career as well as charges against us both."

"Just be quiet, I think they can hear through this wall. It's fireproof but not soundproof," Cheryl said. "Just listen."

Kevin listened, and the voices were entering Harley's office. "Blast it," they heard Harley say. "I left my office door open. I could have sworn I closed it. Oh well, at least I didn't leave the vault room open. Hah!" Harley said. "I guess I'm getting a little absentminded in my old age."

Then a voice that Kevin recognized as Winston Kenwood. "Frank, you need to use some attention sharpener," he said jokingly.

Then the thin and gravelly voice weighed in. "Frank, you'd better get someone lined up to cover your back side. There is too much at stake. What about your assistant? Can you depend on her?" The thin voice asked.

Harley's voice boomed out. "Shelton, my help is the best. They watch out for me. You should know everything's covered here."

"It had better be. There have been some screwups lately, and I don't like it. Let's see what we are faced with before we can close this deal. You don't have an appraisal on this property yet. Neither one of you have been able to get near the figure it will take for our deal to close. What's wrong? When are you going to find an appraiser to handle that for us? You need one that is credible and experienced. What about that guy you said would do the job some time ago?"

"You mean Kevin Henry?" It was Frank Harley's big voice. "He has turned it down twice for us. He would be the most likely one to do the job if he wanted to. There may be a way for us to get it done. I'm working on that, and maybe we'll get it closed soon. Give me time," Harley declared.

All right, gentlemen, whatever you do, it can't smell of any improper moves, or it'll set off investigations to high heaven. I can't afford that. Keep it clean. I'm nervous about some things that have happened, and it better not have been caused by our group. Understand?" Winston Kenwood stated strongly.

The thin gravelly voice piped up. "Men, we've got to have some efficiency and get the job done. Excuses don't make success. Action does. Look at your task, get the tools you need to do the job, and get it done. I mean business. If he gets back here and starts cleaning things up, it will be havoc for all of us, and y'all may wish you had handled things differently. Don't leave yourselves open and keep my name out of anything that happens. That's your assignment. Meeting adjourned," the thin gravelly voice commanded.

The group left, and they could hear the lock turning in the office door. Kevin cringed. "Cheryl, what now?" Kevin asked. "Are we locked in now? Can we get out of this vault?" He was feeling a little pressure now. *What have we got ourselves into?* he was thinking again.

"We can get out of this vault, but getting out of the office is going to be a problem," Cheryl responded. "Do you want these files while we're in here?" she asked Kevin. You have your chance to take them now."

"What do you think would happen when Harley discovered those files were gone? Is there a copy machine in Harley's office?" he asked Cheryl. "We could make some copies and put the originals back, and he wouldn't know they had been violated."

"No, there is no copy machine. We make all copies that are necessary for him. Let's get out of here now. We can open this door from the inside with the safety mechanism," Cheryl explained. She began to turn some knobs and work the release. They pulled the door open and peeked out.

"I hope no one passes by in the hallway. They might see us in this office. It appears to be all clear," Kevin stated. He wiped his fingerprints off again. "Cheryl, what's the solution? You have been around here several months now."

"Well, there is one possibility," she said. "I remember his putting a spare set of keys in his lap drawer. If we can get the drawer open, maybe we can find a key. Hopefully, he left it unlocked."

They went to the desk and tried the drawer. It was locked solid. Cheryl sat down on the floor and blew out a long breath of air. "There's no way to get that open unless you're a locksmith," she said.

Kevin looked at his watch; it was now 6:30. He was to meet Carol at 7:00 p.m. at Walmart in Sherwood, across the river. That was a half-hour drive unless you could speed a lot, and he hadn't freshened up after sitting in that classroom all day. *I don't want to be late anymore*, he thought. "Cheryl was the cause of his being late before. But this couldn't be suspicious though. This is too real. We are in a mess," he told himself

They heard a sound of someone whistling from the hall. "It's the janitor. He always whistles as he walks alone. He says that drives off the spooks," Cheryl explained. "He's coming in here I know. Get down behind this desk. They watched around the corner of the desk as the janitor started vacuuming in the corner of the office. He moved chairs and vacuumed around the round table, then started dusting the bookcase, and they eased around the end of the desk. The man was oblivious to anything else in the room as he continued to whistle and dust in a fast and vigorous way. As he had his back to them, they eased out the open door and down the hall to Cheryl's office.

"Whew, that was close," Kevin said. "We could have been locked in that place all night and then been caught red-handed. And still, we don't have copies of those files. That vault room door is still unlocked, and Harley is going to discover that. How will he respond to discovering the room was not locked?"

"That's a good question," Cheryl said. "I think we had better leave now. It's unusual for me to be in here this late, and I should go. We can get out ok while the janitor is in Mr. Harley's office."

They exited the bank, and Cheryl locked the door behind them. When they walked out of the building, she said, "Kevin, my kids are over at my aunt's tonight. Come home with me, and I'll make us some dinner, and we can visit. You can park in the garage again. I want to discuss some of the things Mr. Harley has been working on that you should know about, for your sake. I think you would want to know. Tonight's the only night I can have you over, so please say yes."

Kevin was surprised at Cheryl, and though he was unhappy with her for not answering his phone calls a couple nights ago, she was still a very attractive woman. She would grace any man's side. But tonight, this is the date with Carol. He had to make a good excuse to Cheryl. He wasn't ready for a very good one. *Maybe she does have an interest in his wellbeing*, he thought. *So here goes for the excuse.* "Oh, that would be wonderful, Cheryl, but I have another meeting tonight that I must attend. Please give me a rain check."

Cheryl looked disappointed, and he wasn't sure he handled this just right. "We'll see," *was all she said.*

"*Cheryl, be safe. I really must hurry now, or I will be late or miss the meeting." He wasn't sure Carol would wait this time.*

CHAPTER

31

Kevin left Cheryl and drove near the speed limit, taking advantage of every move on the interstate highways. As luck would have it, there was a traffic stop. "Probably a drug stop," he grumbled, and he had to drive onto the next exit. He turned back toward Walmart and saw the red Ford F150 pickup. "Now what?" Kevin grumbled louder this time. He was behind the truck but didn't want to engage that at this time. He wanted to meet with Carol before she got mad and left.

The pickup truck pulled into the Walmart parking lot, and the driver got out and walked toward the store entry. Kevin found another parking place and parked. He went back to the pickup and wanted to disable it. Apparently, they were intent on following her and looking for another chance for ransoming the Wemberly Warehouse files. This guy would probably follow Carol and him wherever they went on their date. So Kevin pulled out his pocketknife and stabbed two tires. That should hold him up for a while. He hadn't had time to go home and dress as he normally would, so he couldn't wear his shoulder holster. He stuffed the pistol in the front pocket of his trousers and headed for the store entry. He saw the guy standing in the foyer of the store. It was Jocko who was looking through the glass doors, no doubt looking for Carol.

Kevin walked up to Jocko who jumped when he recognized him. "Are you looking for someone? Try me," Kevin said.

"Naw, I was just waiting before I go in," Jocko said.

"Where is Fred?" Kevin asked him. I know he is surely here, and you two have been playing the tag method of following her. Well, for now you're tagged, and you must stay here. If I catch you following one of us, I'll finish the game for you. Do you understand that?"

At that time, Carol came through the door and saw Jocko and Kevin. She hesitated a moment and walked on past them. Behind her was Fred. Kevin stuck his foot out and tripped Fred who piled up on the floor of the foyer.

"Fred, you're stupid," Jocko said quickly. I don't see how you ever walk upright.

"Go back into the store, both of you," Kevin told them. "If I catch either one of you near either one of us, I may just open fire on you," Kevin said and patted the pistol in his pocket.

He stepped out of the store, and Carol was waiting for him.

"You're late," Carol said, but her eye and those lips still had that constant smile. "I had decided you weren't coming, but I see you were engaging our friends. Kevin, I think we must stop meeting like this. From now on, you can come to my house and to heck with the bank. This is tricky and tiring besides dangerous. I need a life."

"First, let's move your car. I want to escape those two for tonight," Kevin told her. I have incapacitated Jocko's pickup truck, and he will be mad as hops. They have Fred's pickup out here somewhere to follow, but let's move yours to the mall and leave it or, better yet, take it to your house and leave it in the garage."

"Okay, I like the idea of my house. I think the clandestine meetings may be passé now. I think even Harley knows we have had extra interaction together. Anyhow, let's go," Carol said.

Kevin picked Carol up at her house, and they headed for Searcy, forty miles away. "Carol, I didn't want to leave your car there because they might decide to do something to it. I disabled Jocko's pickup with two flat tires. I didn't want him to follow. I didn't know Fred was also there."

They headed to the freeway and toward Searcy, thinking maybe that would be out of sight for most people they know, and they could have a night of peace from the goons. "Those goons are getting bolder," Carol said. "We may have to take more stringent action."

"I think you're right, Carol, this is a tricky life we're in now. I suppose we could bring the police into this situation, but I'm afraid things would be more likely to be muddled at this point. Somewhere there is financial and political power to override some of these things unless there is enough evidence to prove malfeasance. I think Kennon Foster was murdered, and I think old Jim Hammons was murdered.

They arrived in Searcy and found a steak house. The evening was quiet except for their light conversation. It drifted to other things besides the latest stressful things. Kevin studied her face and marveled at the constant smile on that face, the relaxed look all the while when she was in dangerous circumstances. He thought about Cheryl who had called upon him at times for help, and the terrified look she had when she was under scary circumstances. He wasn't sure about Cheryl and where her loyalty would be. He liked Cheryl's poise and intellect. She had taken a chance by going into the vault room. But he wasn't sure.

Carol bounced back into his thoughts with what they should do about the Wemberly Warehouse situation and the constant focus on that. "What is going on, Kevin? Why do they want those files and who are they? Why have they been insistent on someone appraising that Wemberly Warehouse property for that high value?"

Kevin's thoughts went to the conversation they overheard in Frank Harley's office. He remembered the statement one of the men made about not completing the deal until the appraisal was made. He needed to find out more about the deal. *What kind of deal?* he wondered.

There may be some answers in the files of old Jim Hammons, Kevin was thinking. *Should I share all this information with Carol? She is an employee of Frank Harley. Would her ultimate loyalty and trust lie with him if I take her into my absolute confidence? Cheryl? She took a great risk this evening at the bank, going into that vault room. I need some allies if I see this thing through*, Kevin decided.

"Carol, there are some characters involved in this mystery, about which I don't know what to believe. They come together quite frequently, and I am wondering if they have a mutual fear of something that they want handled or if there is just a large amount of money they want to put into the hands of whatever corporation owns that property." Kevin ventured.

"The loan application was in the files in our office, and now that is missing," Carol said. "I wonder if it is now in Mr. Harley's office or maybe in the vault. If we could get access to that vault and check the files in there, maybe they would provide a lead to this mystery."

Kevin looked at Carol and wanted so much to take her into his full confidence, but would that be premature? She has been there for him in many ways and has been subjected to some ruthless guys who may be hired killers. She is tough, she is beautiful, she is smart, and she may be loyal, but yet, she could be loyal to someone else and just lead me on. He felt he must be cautious and get a little more information.

They finished their meal and drove back to Sherwood. He drove into the driveway and got out to let Carol out and walk her to the door. He supposed that was still the way dates did. It had been a long time. It was awkward until Kevin's car phone started ringing. "Carol, it was great but not long enough. Let's do it again."

He ran back to the car and picked up the phone as he was backing out. It was Cheryl. "What's up, Cheryl?" he asked her. *What could she want this time of night?* he asked himself.

"Kevin, Mr. Harley called me to ask if anyone had been in the vault room. He said the office door had been left open and had I seen anyone in the office. Did you move anything? I reminded him that it was the night for the janitor. Maybe the janitor moved something to clean. He seemed satisfied with that. But boy is he paranoid about that vault room? Kevin, I know it's late, but I have some more information for you that I think is urgent for you. Would you like to come over now and let me go over that with you? I don't want to discuss it over the phone. I have been calling your house, and I assumed you were still in the meeting. I'll be here if you want to come over." She hung up.

"Well…" Kevin pondered what was going on. "Cheryl had wanted me to come over earlier tonight and said then she had something to tell me," he remembered. "Maybe it is urgent, and I shouldn't let my imagination blind me—I'll go."

Kevin drove into the driveway behind Cheryl's house, and he called her to open the garage. "Oh, Kevin, I assumed you weren't coming, and I am dressed in my sleep clothes. If you don't mind, I suppose it won't take that long, and you can come in if you won't think I'm too risqué. I will change back if you wish. I have pajamas on." She was opening the garage.

Oh well, Kevin thought, *I am a grown man, and we both have been married before.* He drove into the garage, and Cheryl closed the garage door behind him. He walked in and saw her in her silk robe and pajamas. He couldn't help but comment. "Cheryl, I thought maybe I would have to hide my eyes. You look decent," he said. "You look very decent, and it could be said you look… well…" He smiled and his voice trailed off. Cheryl smiled and offered him a seat at the kitchen table.

"Let me make a pot of coffee, and I have some cinnamon rolls." She rose and started the coffee. He watched as she got around the kitchen. *Gosh, she is a beautiful woman, and I'll have to be on my best behavior or lose my status as a gentleman*, Kevin was thinking as he watched her move about. She got the cinnamon rolls out while the coffee was making and placed one in a plate and set it in front of him. The temptation was there to reach his arm around her and draw her to him. The setting was almost too much.

"Kevin, I wanted to tell you about Mr. Harley's conversation I heard with someone on the phone a few days ago. I don't know who the other party was, but he told that party he was near hiring a man who would take care of things and handle these problems. He said the man was the ideal person for the job and could assume some of this liability. I have heard enough and observed enough of his conversations that I have suspected the man to be you. I am afraid the liabilities might be something to do with the Wemberly Warehouse case. I know that case involves some very suspicious happenings."

"You know," she went on, "I wonder about the Kennon Foster death and the Jim Hammons death. Kevin…" she paused as she served his cup of coffee. "I don't want to see you get tangled up in that. Mr. Harley could do it. I don't know if he would be that kind of man, but he is in a position financially and politically to put you in jeopardy."

Kevin looked up at her as she was standing beside him when she set his cup down. He saw tears in her eyes as she said that. *She really cares*, Kevin thought. He felt drawn to put his arm around her trim waist and pull her down to his lap. She put her arms around his neck and laid her head on his shoulder. He held her tightly against him and she felt good. That was his first embrace with a woman since Marylyn died. Cheryl felt so tender. She drew back and looked in his face. "Don't let anything happen to you. I have already lost one whom I cared about." She was within a couple inches of his face, and Kevin pulled her head to him and felt her lips touch his; she withdrew and quickly rose.

She blushed. "Now about Mr. Harley," she said. "I think there is danger. Those three men who were meeting in his office the other night are worried about something. I hate to see you get drawn into whatever the problem is. It seems gigantic."

CHAPTER
32

Kevin rose early in the morning and set his itinerary for the day. He thought about a day of relaxation, but these things were building up, and he couldn't wait, so he tackled the two appraisals Carol had given him yesterday. He researched both of them and set the appointments for the fieldwork. That would be done Monday.

Then he gathered the Jim Hammons files of the Wemberly Warehouse work Jim had done. Jim had some good details recorded of his research. *This stuff is powerful*, Kevin thought as he read these records. The research old Jim had done coincided with what Kevin had asked for from the Secretary of State's records and some work he had done when he was with the S&L. The registration showed the principals of the corporations who owned the corporations that had organized the Wemberly Warehouse, Inc. *Strange*, Kevin thought. But there were some gaps that left some questions as to who can control Wemberly Warehouse operations and involvement in financial obligations and distribution of funds. He started the methodical tracing of the corporate filings.

"Do these records provide some information that, coupled with information that others have, tell a story that someone doesn't want told?" Kevin wondered. Some of his research he had done when he was associated with Central Arkansas Workers Savings and Loan Association showed evidence of Harold Wemberly having control when the project began. He disappeared when it was almost complete. The hunting trip on Gruntington's Island resulted in a change that left a chain of ties to the ultimate control. It may lead to other states before one could determine the current ownership and control. *But first*, he thought, *I must take care of some security around here. I'm too vulnerable.*

Kevin called the security alarm people, and they agreed to install a system that day. That was none too soon for him. They came out with a crew and started to work. The system would provide motion detectors even outside when set for that. It would provide an alarm when someone broke a glass in the door as had happened before. The alarm was loud and would also be registered at a control center. The control center would call police immediately. They assured him it was foolproof and virtually impenetrable. *Yeah, yeah*, Kevin thought, *just wait until someone outsmarts this*. But it beats nothing, and he let them secure his computer also.

A wire cable was attached to the case of the computer, coupled with another cable, and then anchored to the wall. The coupling was secured with a padlock. At least it would slow down someone who was not expecting that and didn't have something to cut the cable. He wanted to leave the computer hooked up where he had it installed and not have to carry it with him all the time.

He had those copies of the Jim Hammons files that he had taken to trade for Carol. He had avoided having to give the files to those goons. He had removed the critical part of the files from the copies so they wouldn't have gotten the key information. Their boss would have been infuriated when he got that if they had succeeded in obtaining them. He still didn't know who that boss is.

Gruntington's Island

Kevin searched the pages of Jim Hammons's files and came to the special pages he had extracted when he was to exchange the files for Carol Fleichman. "Wow! Catch this," he told himself. He read awhile and folded the folder and placed it away. This called for some investigation on Gruntington's Island and around that area on the Arkansas River.

He turned off the highway and down the gravel road toward Gruntington's Island. There were still a few old farmhouses with farm workers who had lived there for many years. Kevin noticed a person moving at a house at the end of a short lane. He turned down that plain dirt lane and stopped at the house. An old, gray-haired black man was on the porch when Kevin drove up, and he raised a hand to wave him in. "Stop and sit awhile," he invited. The house was about a half mile from the river. "You must be lookin' for someone, mister. Ain't no one come this way 'ceptin' they's lost or lookin' for someone," he said and smiled a hearty welcome.

"Thank you," Kevin said and stepped onto the porch and introduced himself. "My name is Kevin Henry," he told him.

"Name's Rufe, suh," the old man said simply. "Ain't never knowed no one named Kevin," he said and smiled an almost toothless smile. He had his two front teeth in the top and three front teeth on the lower right, Kevin noticed. He liked Rufe immediately.

"Have you lived here long?" Kevin asked.

"Yes, suh, a considerable while. I come here with my pappy and mammy. They done gone long ago," he explained and grinned. "I reckon I done chopped cotton on all this land 'round heah. I knowed 'purt near everone who been heah."

"Rufe, did you ever go hunting on the Gruntington's Island?" Kevin asked.

"Oh yes, suh…we hunted that Island for many a year. It 'purt near fed my family 'til the big shots come and took it over. They stopped us from goin' out there when they knowed it," Rufe said and grinned widely. "When they wasn't there, it made no matter. It wasn't right for them to stop us from gettin' our meat out there," he said seriously.

"Some of us used to load barges that docked at the island. They would come with big fleets of empty barges, and we'd load bales of cotton from the warehouses north of heah and truck loads of soybeans. That was before they built that big warehouse up the river."

"Was that the Wemberly Warehouse, Rufe?" Kevin asked him.

"Yes, suh," Rufe said. "I knowed that Mr. Wemberly what done disappeared back then. He hunted there and used to get me and RC to show him where to hunt. Then he'd give us tips if he did good. And he allus did good," Rufe said and grinned widely again. "We knowed where to get the game."

"When Mr. Wemberly disappeared, did you have any idea what might have happened to him?" Kevin asked.

"Well." Rufe looked around and scratched his chin. "That was back in '86, a long time ago. I reckon I can talk 'bout it now," he said slowly and thoughtfully. "Me and my brother, RC, was helpin' Mr. Wemberly hunt, and he give us a big tip and swore us to never tell no one whut he done did. Me and RC was both raised to keep our mouth shut when we wuz supposed to," Rufe said very seriously.

Kevin looked into the old eyes with the red rims that had a little teardrop in one of them. Honor for their promise was what many of the old timers held dear to their principles and values. To many of the poor country farm workers, that value was big when they had little.

"Mr. Wemberly...he...he said, 'Rufe, I want you to go with me to the barge and leave me right there, and I want you to take my truck down to that bluff on the Island where the river makes a curve and drive this truck over the edge of the bluff into that deep water.' Mr. Kevin, you ain't never to tell no one 'bout that." Kevin didn't respond to his request, but Rufe continued on, "Mr. Wemberly…he…he had a pocket full of money with big bills." Rufe paused a moment as though savoring the memory. "Mr. Kevin, he pulled several of them big bills off one of them bunches, and he give me some of 'em, and he give RC one later. He told us we could have his rifle and his shotgun out of his truck and keep them but never tell no one 'bout that, 'cause they might know who they belonged to and think I kilt him."

Rufe walked into the back room of his house and came back with a twelve-gauge Remington automatic shotgun. "This is Mr. Wemberly's shotgun. See, it's done got his name engraved in it. Well, suh, we took that truck and drove it off that bluff and come back. Mr. Wemberly wuz gone, and I ain't never seen him no more." Rufe shook his head sadly. We helped hunt and hunt for him, for a long time, me and RC, with everone else, 'til everone give up," he said. "Ain't no one never come ask me about him in this whole time. Wouldn't have made no difference though," Rufe declared as he looked down toward the ground. "I kept my word like ol' RC. RC done dead now though. I reckon he kept his word the whole time."

"Rufe, you're a good man. This is very interesting." He gave Rufe a bill. "I would like to know anything about those days that you can remember," Kevin told him.

"Mr. Kevin, they's more, but now ain't the time," he said and looked around both ways, thoughtfully, then shook his head. "Naw…maybe someday."

Kevin got back into his Explorer and drove slowly down to the river and across the small roadway and bridge across the channel of river and on to the island. The overflows of the river had cut a channel through the land many years ago and created the island.

Instead of going right toward the cabin where the goons had held Carol, he turned left on the trail toward the other cabin that the other corporation group had built. He passed a well-built cabin and kept going. The slight trail wound its way around the whole island.

As he came full on the main riverside, he could see a tugboat with a fleet of barges. He came to a steep bluff and stopped. He got out and walked to the edge and wondered how deeply submerged Harold Wemberly's pickup truck might be. *Might his remains still be in that truck? Might old Rufe be lying?* The water was murky, and it was difficult to see very far down. He thought about bringing a swimsuit some day and diving to see if he could find the truck.

"Was this the whole truth about the disappearance of Harold Wemberly?" Kevin wondered. "Did he get on that barge or is he in the truck that may be below where I'm standing? *Someone should dive for that truck and check it out,* he thought.

Kevin watched the tugboat slowly push the fleet of barges down the river as it flowed toward the Mississippi River. He knew the barges would eventually wind up in New Orleans, and the cargo would be transferred to ocean going freighters. One like that could have carried Harold Wemberly toward an island in the pacific...but why?"

The sun was going down in the west, and Kevin got back into his Explorer and drove the rest of the way around the island past the other cabin. There were no cars or trucks there now. He wondered who controlled that cabin. It was almost dark when he completed the trip around the island and drove back across the river channel to the farmland and passed old Rufe's house. He was probably inside, and Kevin thought about trying to get him to tell him the rest of the story.

It had been six years since the disappearance of Harold Wemberly. They had decided he was dead. He and his wife had already divorced, and she had remarried. His estate could not be determined. She had wanted to reconcile, but he would have no part of that. She had their home and decided she was lucky to have that. She knew he had sunk a lot of their money in the warehouse venture and that there had been a lot of manipulating for larger stakes. What he had done was not discernible, and she was glad to be rid of him, she said. They had been fussing before he disappeared, and she hated him.

CHAPTER 33

Kevin was almost home when his car phone started ringing. He picked it up, and it was Carol. He was glad to hear her voice. He wanted to share what he had learned today but decided now was not the time. He had to learn more and not chance revealing his source yet. He just hoped that no one else happened to stop and question old Rufe.

"Carol, it's good to hear your voice," Kevin told her.

"Where have you been? I have been trying to reach you all afternoon," she said. Mr. Harley has been pressing me again for those Wemberly Warehouse files, and I know he must have taken them. I just wonder if he is trying to set up something to pin the disappearance on me. Why does he keep pestering me with that? I know they should be here, but they are not, and I have never had them under my custody and control. "Do you want to hold my hand while I feel sorry for myself?" She chuckled. Kevin could imagine the smile on her face as she asked that.

He decided he would like to see that smile. "Carol, let's run away to Russellville and eat. I'll buy dinner. I assume you are home. I'll swing over and pick you up. Okay?"

"You're on," she said.

Kevin swung around and crossed back over the river and back to Carol's house. She was watching and came out the door as soon as he drove into the driveway. She had her hair in the usual ponytail and some flats on. She was wearing a freshly starched and ironed pink cotton blouse with a pocket on the left side. She had put on a dark-green skirt that looked great on her. But he was thinking, *Anything looks great on her. Well, let's face it, she is just downright good looking."*

Look at me, he thought. *Maybe all women are looking good to me.* He thought of Cheryl and how attractive she is.

He had to say it. "Carol, you look gorgeous tonight!"

"You're just saying that," she said. "But I needed that. It hasn't been often that a handsome man has said that to me in a while. Just say that any time you want," she said and laughed. "Kevin, what have you been doing? I know you have some appraisal work to do, but I mean have you thought about this mess with Mr. Harley. It seems he won't relent on the Wemberly Warehouse thing. Like it's constantly on his mind."

"I'm trying to figure things out," Kevin said. "I have some more research to do, and maybe things will make more sense. Have you seen either one of those red Ford pickup trucks in the last day or so?"

"No, I haven't noticed it. I don't want to either, I feel like taking a potshot at it if he starts following me again," Carol blustered. "Maybe they'll lie low for a while, at least."

"Do you have your gun with you tonight?" he asked.

"No, Kevin, I am totally relying on my date tonight to protect me." She laughed and placed her hand on the console of the Explorer.

Kevin put his hand on hers, and it felt good. *Strange*, he thought. *Such a thing as holding hands, I have missed since Marylyn died. I like this.*

They drove in silence and held hands for a long way...until Kevin lifted her hand up and looked at it. It was a strong hand to be so slender. He held it to his lips and pressed them against it. He glanced at her eyes, and they were closed.

"Thanks for being there for me, Carol. You've been a good sidekick," Kevin said. They pulled in to a Chinese food restaurant and went inside. The attendant showed them to an enclosed cubbyhole. That provided them the privacy they wanted. Although they were from out of town, they were not ready for the bank to see their associating with each other and start restricting their contact.

Carol laughed and said she remembered sneaking out as a teenager to go with a boyfriend sometimes. "It was fun then," she said. "Here I am thirty-one years old, and it's kinda fun now." They talked about college days and relaxed for a while.

Kevin took her hand and looked at her. "Carol, I can't imagine that guys have let you stay single without remarrying, but I'm glad," he said.

"What about you, Kevin?" she asked him.

"We'd better go," he said quickly. *Gosh*, he thought. "I'm about to get myself into a situation that might be difficult for the time. I think I'm getting vulnerable."

They drove home with lighthearted chatter, laughing and bantering with each other. The old days at the university were brought up and gleaned of conversation bits. "It was fun," Kevin said as he pulled into Carol's driveway. "Maybe we had a good time without the bank seeing us."

"But if they did, so what?" Carol said. "I think I'm tired of hiding. Bring it on."

Kevin got out and walked her to the door. She unlocked the door and stood there a moment. He took her in his arms and pulled her next him and brought her to a full embrace and a long kiss. How he had missed these and had actually longed for that with Carol, he realized, but had not allowed himself to yield to the desire. She put her arms around his neck and held him tight while she laid her head against his. "Kevin," she said, whispering quietly. "I have had a good time. Let's not let it be so long again. Now go before…"

Kevin ran down the steps and to his Explorer. It was time to go. He drove across town and felt the world was good again.

He entered his house and found everything okay. He laughed and thought about those goons. He wondered if they had noticed the sign in the yard and didn't want to challenge the security system.

The day had been full, and he lay in bed that night, thinking about the day's events and the things he had learned. He wanted to get back into those files and the papers he had gotten from the Secretary of State's records.

If he could trace the principals of the corporations sufficiently, maybe he could tell who actually owned this property. *There must be a story there*, Kevin thought.

Sleep came, and it was sound until he was awakened by the telephone.

CHAPTER 34

Kevin answered the phone, and the loud booming voice jarred him out of the bed. He had overslept until 7:00 a.m. It was Frank Harley. "Good Morning, Kevin!" He boomed. "I wanted to catch you before you got gone on some appraisal. I hope you have thought over my proposal. Can you meet with me in the next couple days and let us see if we can conclude something that will be of mutual benefit to us both?" He was jovial and upbeat in tone.

"Well, good morning to you, Mr. Harley," Kevin sounded back. "It's a good day for something. I haven't concluded my thoughts on your proposal. I will need to let you know later. I am thinking about it but am not quite ready to make a decision."

"I see, Kevin, just don't forget about it. Try to get with me soon," he said cheerfully and hung up.

Gosh, he is persistent, Kevin thought. *I wonder what he was hoping to shove over to my responsibility that Cheryl was concerned about. I guess I should find out.*

The fieldwork had to be completed for the two appraisals, and he loaded up his camera and attaché case. He headed north toward North Little Rock and crossed the Arkansas River. His thoughts turned to old Rufe and the Gruntington's Island. He thought about that island and wondered about its history. *What was the ownership through the years?*

Kevin took the pictures, measured the houses, and sketched the floor plan as he inspected them, then hurried and photographed the comparable sales and made adjustments for the differences. He completed the fieldwork for the two appraisal assignments and went home to his office.

He drove into his driveway and got out of his Explorer in the driveway because he could hear the security alarm going off. He grabbed his pistol from the console and ran to the rear of the house. He could see the backs of two men as they jumped the fence and ran through the neighbor's yard. *Ah yes!* Kevin thought. "Fred and Jocko, and I'll bet if I headed for Gruntington's Island, I could catch those two driving in at that cabin?" But he heard the police coming and knew he should wait for them. He ran to the Explorer and hurriedly ejected the cartridge clip and placed the pistol in the console. If they happened to search the vehicle, at least he didn't have a loaded pistol in it. *If it were not for having to explain everything to the police about why I needed to carry a concealed weapon, I would apply for a permit*, he thought.

He had just closed and locked the door of the Explorer when the two patrol officers rolled into his driveway with their sirens blasting. They jumped from their car with guns out and yelled for him to raise his hands. He raised them high and greeted the officers. "It's my house," Kevin yelled, but one officer held the gun on him and the other frisked him and cuffed him. "Wait, wait," he pleaded. "I just saw the burglars run from the back of my house as I drove up. My name is Kevin Henry. Please check with the security people."

One officer got on his radio, checked and came back to Kevin. "We are sorry, sir, would you please show some identification?"

Kevin quickly showed his ID and asked them to go with him to the rear to check the house. They went to the back door and saw where the glass had been broken. That was what set off the alarm and caused them to run before they opened the door. *Well, at least it worked that time*, Kevin thought. He unlocked the door and they walked inside. There was no disturbance and the officers wrote their report and left.

Kevin called for someone to come and repair the glass in the door. He supposed he could install a solid door, but then, they would kick the door in if they wanted in badly enough. *Hopefully they won't try again, now that they know there is an alarm system. They were dumb enough that they did not read the sign about the alarm system*, Kevin mused.

CHAPTER
35

The fieldwork was transferred to his computer, and the reports were printed out and assembled into the three copies for the mortgage company and one for his files. They were packaged in the envelope for delivery and labeled just as the telephone rang.

"Good afternoon, Kevin." It was James Carpenter. "I just got into town and would like to buy your dinner if you have time," he said. "I have some information for you that you might want to have, and we also can reminisce a little. You know, just talk about old times."

"Sure, James, tell me where, and we can meet about six o'clock," Kevin said.

"Let's eat in Conway at the fish house," James suggested.

Kevin thought a minute. "Let's meet closer by, like the Western Sizzlin'. I have work I need to do, and I want to return before too late," he stated.

"Okay," James agreed, "that will do."

James is my friend and my former boss. I really think he wants the best for me, but I remember the last time we ate together, my house was burglarized. It may be coincidence, but I want to be sure I'm not far away, Kevin was thinking.

Kevin and James met in Western Sizzlin', and they shook hands and slapped each other on the shoulder as men do. "It's always good to see you James," Kevin told him. "How are you doing in your new position? I think about you a lot," he said.

They walked the line and ordered their food, and James paid the tab. They both ordered steaks and were told they would be brought to their table so they found a booth in the corner and sat with some limited privacy. James scooted around close to Kevin to talk.

"Kevin, there is something going on here in Little Rock that I'm getting some scuttlebutt on. Are you under any pressure on this stuff?" James asked.

Kevin wondered what James knew about these happenings. He had tried to not let too many people know about the happenings, and even with Cheryl and Carol, who were more involved, he had not been passing information to them very freely and didn't discuss things with them except the things he knew they knew about. "What stuff are you referring to, James? Actually, there are a lot of weird things going on here."

James leaned forward and almost in a whisper said, "Wemberly Warehouse. I am aware of some things but not all. You know we worked on a deal with that property when we were together at the Central Arkansas Workers S&L. We decided to leave it alone because of some things we discovered. You were in the thick of it. I remember most of that. I am still in the S&L circles and attended a meeting last week with Shelton McKinley.

Shelton is the head of one of the largest S&Ls in the country, now defunct, but that has nothing to do with what I'm about to tell you. He has some concerns about what is going on up here regarding the Wemberly Warehouse properties. I don't know what all of his concerns are, but he asked me to do him a favor and see if you would meet him at his office in Plano, Texas. He said he wants to meet you entirely outside of Little Rock and wants the meeting to be absolutely a secret. He doubted you would meet him if he approached you directly and asked me to be a go between because of our friendship. He and I have some current dealings with each other." James leaned back in his seat and smiled as he waited for Kevin to digest this.

This is strange, Kevin first thought. He knew that McKinley had been in Little Rock at different times recently and had contact with Frank Harley and Winston Kenwood. But it had never been clear what connection they had if any.

"James, you know I trust you," Kevin said. "Is there anything else you know about this, man? I'll tell you, I met him at Frank Harley's cookout party only a couple weeks ago or less. I don't know why, but Frank Harley wanted to introduce me to him."

"It sounds as though you have had more formal introduction than I have," James said. "My feeling is that I would go down to meet with him. I would call him and talk first and let him know your time is valuable and ask if he would expect to pay the tab. I feel he would. He invited you, and your time is the way you earn your living. Here…he said if you showed interest, to give you this private contact number. It will put you straight through without secretaries, etcetera. Call him Kevin."

"James, did you drive all the way from Oklahoma to talk to me about that?" Kevin asked.

"Yes, mostly, and I am on the tab. I will bill him just for this. He wants this to be confidential, and he trusts me to keep it that way," James told him. "I do have one other appointment while I am here. It is to be confidential also. I can't share that information."

"All right, give me the number, and I'll set up the meeting," Kevin said.

James paid the bill and told Kevin he would honor his needs to do something else and would let him go. "Thanks for meeting me, Kevin," James said, and they shook hands and left.

Kevin went straight home and drove into the garage. He got the Ruger out of the console of the Explorer and popped the clip into the butt of the pistol and went inside. He checked the house because he knew the door glass had not yet been repaired and the alarm was not reset. He checked the office and was sickened. The computer had been pulled out a little but not gone. The cable attached to the computer tower was intact and had stopped the theft of the computer.

He was sick because his friend James had betrayed him. *It had to be*, he thought. "This is the second time I have been burglarized while I was meeting with James, and he even wanted to go all the way to Conway—that would have given them more time. Why? What would he gain? Maybe he was paid to set this up? At least they have not been able to take anything. Was I a sucker? Did James help set me up for this?"

"James I hope you get paid a lot for that," Kevin muttered. "Why would he turn on me or betray his former principles and integrity? But should I contact Shelton McKinley?" He pulled out his note with the contact numbers and looked at them for a moment; put it back in his pocket and turned his thoughts back to the goons who had broken in and tried to get his computer again. He thought about them and laughed. He imagined their trying to grab the computer and run. *Guys, that was another two thousand bucks saved. At least something worked*, Kevin thought.

CHAPTER
36

Kevin rose early and got started on some chores. He called the glass company to repair the glass in the back door again so he could reset his alarm properly. He wanted to be sure to set the motion detector for the outside also. He drove across the river to McCain Mall to buy a new outfit of clothes. He was beginning to feel a need to dress for some dates now.

He had headed back to Little Rock when the telephone rang, and it was Carol. "Good morning, Kevin. I called to tell you that I have seen the red F150 Ford pickup truck, or one of them, I think. I saw one yesterday and one today. Of course it could be anyone, I suppose, but I can't help but think of them when I see one of those pickups. Have you seen them?" she asked.

"Hah," he said. "I saw them once when they tried to break in and then I felt them once when they got in and tried to get my computer." He explained his security system and how it was circumvented before he had the glass repaired. "Carol, I want you to be extremely careful. I don't want to frighten you but be aware of your surroundings at all times. If they try something and you have a chance, take that pistol out and fire a couple of shots in their direction. That may give them second thoughts." Kevin was getting angry at the thoughts of those guys capturing her again. He suspected they would try it again just to get these files. "He had to do something to head these guys off. *But what?* he thought.

He had just put the phone down, and it rang. "Kevin speaking."

"Mr. Henry, this is Winston Kenwood's office," the speaker said. Mr. Kenwood would like to speak to you. Please hold."

Winston Kenwood immediately picked up the phone. "Kevin, I have been anxious for your thoughts on my proposal to you. I hope you've had time to give good consideration for a favorable answer." Kenwood's powerful voice came across. "I want you to know that Mrs. Kenwood, also, has been anxious for you to come aboard. We both want you working here." Mrs. Kenwood was a silent stockholder in the bank.

Kevin had been hoping Kenwood would not be getting back with him yet. *Several things had happened in Kevin's life that he felt Kenwood didn't know about, or was it possible that he was aware of much of it?* he wondered.

"Winston." Kevin remembered that Kenwood wanted their discussions to be on an informal conversational basis. "Thank you for still having an interest in me. Actually, I have had such a hectic involvement recently, I haven't had time to give your proposal due consideration. I would like to defer a decision until a little while later, if you will. I promise to try my best to properly weigh this and reach a decision," Kevin said.

"Yes, yes, Kevin, I don't want you to make a rash decision. That is a long-term commitment I am asking for, and I know you should give it your best judgment," Winston said. "Please try to get back with me within the next week. Mrs. Kenwood and I are anxious for you to come on board." He hung up abruptly.

Kevin had just turned off the I430 freeway when his phone rang again. It was the security company. "Mr. Henry, your alarm system has just been activated, and we have notified the police. They should be there promptly. Will you be able to respond now also?" the caller asked.

"I'm about two miles away, and I'll go directly there," Kevin told them. Two miles and two red lights later, Kevin drove up to his house and joined the police who had just arrived and were in his driveway with lights flashing. An officer had run around the house to the rear and another had checked the other side and was returning to the front. He motioned for Kevin to stop there, and Kevin got out and told him he was the owner. The alarm horns were blaring when the other office returned from the back. "Everything is intact there," he said. "If you're the owner, you can enter and turn off the alarm. We'll check the inside for you."

Kevin entered and turned off the alarm and let the police do their thing. Everything was still secure and they left. *At last*, Kevin was thinking, *this time it worked, and maybe they'll give up. Man, are they persistent. They must be watching when I leave and decided to try one more time before I returned.*

"They must be watching!" That thought reverberated in his mind with a rattle almost. *They must be watching, and I wonder if they had been watching when James Carpenter and I went to dinner*, Kevin was wondering hopefully. James was not only his old boss but he considered him a loyal friend. Now, he still had some reservation but was feeling a little better about James. "I hope he's still my loyal friend," Kevin muttered. "I hope he had nothing to do with that break-in."

His note pad had several pages of handwritten notes and copy pages he had slipped into the tablet. Kevin set it down on his desk and was about to pick up the phone to call Carol when it started ringing.

"Mr. Kevin Henry, please," the lady requested.

"This is Kevin Henry," he responded.

"Can you take an important phone call from Mr. Shelton McKinley?" she asked.

"Shelton McKinley!" Kevin's mind was jarred a little. *I wonder what brings this call?* he quickly thought. "Yes, I'll accept the call."

"Good afternoon, Mr. Henry," the gravelly voice said. "I hope you a have few minutes. I want to invite you to Plano, Texas, for a private conference. Before you ask, I know you are self-employed and time is money. Be assured you will be well compensated for your time."

"Mr. McKinley, what does this visit concern?" Kevin asked.

"That is the reason I would prefer to visit with you in private and not on the telephone. I assure you it will be relevant, and it won't be a waste of time for you. I will just ask you to take that risk," McKinley responded.

Kevin was beginning to have a good idea of what McKinley was interested in. "Yes sir," he answered. "I will meet with you. Tomorrow is out because of a previous commitment that I must keep."

"The next day will work for me. I will have my plane meet you at the airport in Little Rock at 8:30, and we should be able to meet for lunch in my office at noon," McKinley said and hung up abruptly.

Boy, the bigwigs don't waste much time. When they are finished, they are gone, Kevin thought. He had met McKinley and remembered his slight body that went with the gravelly voice. He knew that could be deceiving because the man was extremely smart.

Kevin continued to think about McKinley's call and wonder about the purpose. He had just had a call from Winston Kenwood who had been asking him to join him at the bank and work closely with him personally and to watch his back. Also, Frank Harley was pressing for a similar deal. He thought of these three men as a trio. He wondered if McKinley was going to approach him with something similar. "We'll see," Kevin muttered. "We'll see."

Kevin called Carol to confirm their trip they had planned to see the island tomorrow. "What's up, Appraiser Man?" Carol said as she answered the phone. "I'm glad you called. I have a surprise for you," she said and waited.

"Well, you sound extra cheerful today," Kevin responded. "Have you just inherited a great aunt's fortune? I called to see if we should have a clandestine meeting tomorrow morning. Should I pick you up somewhere besides your house?"

"No…I want to invite you to dinner tonight at my house. You can park in the driveway, and I will meet you at the front door," she laughed as she said that. "I'll see you at 6:00 p.m.…okay?"

"Okay, 6:00 p.m."

He gently laid his phone back in the cradle and began to think about things. *What brought that on?* Kevin wondered. *We have always tried to keep our contacts discreet to avoid the familiarity appearance. Now she apparently wants it to be known. Dinner at 6:00 p.m. That sounds great. Life is good*, Kevin was thinking. He felt like his feet were lighter now. *Good things are happening.*

He sat down at his desk and began to lay out the papers from his research today. He also got the papers from the Secretary of State's office and started to correlate the purchases with the filing at the state office. He had documents that showed the filings of the application for incorporating the various companies. He picked up the filing for Wemberly Warehouse Inc. The principals of that corporation showed Harold Wemberly, president and owning five hundred shares of the one thousand shares. The secretary, treasure owned ten shares. The other shares were owned by various corporations. Some were out of state corporations. *That was a strange thing*, Kevin thought.

CHAPTER
37

He continued to study the transfers of the property until time to get ready for his date with Carol Fleichman. He shaved again and jumped in for a quick shower. He was feeling young again.

Kevin set the security alarm and backed out of the driveway. There was a red Ford pickup coming his way, and it triggered an alarm in his head. He had to wait until it passed. It was neither of the goons, he decided. *Now I am getting paranoid*, he thought. *Here I am suspicious of every red Ford pickup truck. I'm wondering about my old friends and sometimes my new friends. I've got to figure this thing out and get rid of these suspicions and the paranoia.*

Carol is now a special friend, but he still felt he must use precaution to not disclose everything to her or any of the others. How he would like to take her into his complete confidence. She seems to be an A-one gal, and I really enjoy her company. I hate holding back on things with her. Yet she is employed by Frank Harley, and I'm not sure how much of her loyalty would be toward him and how much toward me, whom she has known for a short while, Kevin was thinking as he drove to Carol's house.

—⁂—

Kevin turned the Explorer into Carol's driveway and parked. Carol had purchased a nice brick home on Illinois Bayou Drive in the corner of Sherwood, a nice neighborhood, just across the city line from North Little Rock. He walked to the front door and rang the doorbell. It felt good. Carol opened the door and said, "Come in, Appraiser Man, I am so glad you could come on such a short notice. I haven't had a man guest in a long, long while." She took his arm and led him into her living room and to a chair. "Sit here while I finish putting things together and on the table."

"Oh, let me help you, Carol. I'm not a stranger in the kitchen—may I?" Kevin asked.

Carol motioned for him to come on in with her, and he joined her. This felt good. He wanted to be near to her and visit. She smiled and directed him in carrying some dishes to the table. The table was set with one setting at one end and one setting at the other. Carol filled their plates, and Kevin filled their glasses with their drink. This looked like his kind of dinner. It was plain Southern eating prepared with elegance. Kevin remembered that he was a guest with a lady and held her chair. She looked up at him and smiled. They sat and starting eating.

The conversation was kept at a light vein and about days of the past in the finance business. "Carol, I think I remember you have said you have worked for New Bank of Pulaski since college. You graduated college three years behind me. So you have been there ten years?" Kevin asked.

"Yeah, ten years and a quite a lot has happened during that ten years. Mr. Harley bought the bank or controlling stock in the bank and took over two years after I started there. He made me his assistant then, and I worked at that for eight years. We know each other fairly well, and he tells me much of what goes on. I think he has taken me into his confidence many times, but I am not sure about now. There is an awful lot going on that I have no idea about why and what.

Now…let's go into the kitchen and sit down in the little booth, and I'll pour some coffee. I want to share with you the reason I invited you for dinner so abruptly tonight. I would have liked to have done that long ago, but I didn't want Mr. Harley or others to think that we were getting too personal and drag you into this quagmire that has developed. But now Mr. Harley said he wants me to help him in something he needs at this time. This is to be confidential with the three of us. Kevin, I am leveling with you," Carol said. "I am not sure why he has given me this assignment, but he told me about his request to you and that he would like for me to see if I could persuade you to accept his request. He didn't make me privy to what he has asked you to do, though I can put my imagination to work and do some guessing."

Kevin watched as Carol made the pot of fresh coffee. He was always drawn to her beauty and her ease of motion as she moved about. *She must have really been great as her basketball career had progressed at the university*, he thought. He wished he had been there to see her play. She had her hair put up in the ever-present ponytail, which he liked. It brought out the beauty of her face and those compelling and enchanting eyes. He could well understand why Harley had selected her for the assignment.

Carol continued on as she got up to pour the coffee. "Kevin, I think you are aware of the danger that is present now, maybe more than I. I suspect that the job Mr. Harley has for you might involve this danger and put you more in jeopardy. I want you to know that my worry is for your safety, and whatever I say to influence you should be carefully weighed in view of that danger. I will say to you that Mr. Harley has always kept his word in everything he has promised me. I will also say that I have wondered about something he has done, though I have not ever had reason to know of anything out of order, just enough there to raise suspicion."

The coffee was ready, and she poured a cup for each and set the sugar and cream on the table. "I know," she said, "I have wondered about his insistence on the Wemberly Warehouse files being at the mortgage company office when I think they may be with him."

Carol sat down in front of Kevin in the little kitchen booth, and he looked into her eyes. *My, how I want to tell her everything and confide in her.* he felt. "Carol, my beautiful hostess and my friend, we haven't known each other closely very long, although I remember you back in college, but we have been through some things together. I want you for my friend," he told her. He thought he could sense a little disappointment in those eyes, though they never lost that constant smile. *Had she expected him to say more?* he wondered.

"Let's go into the great room where we can relax," Carol suggested and led the way. "Kevin, I can understand your apprehension. I understand that I have been employed with Mr. Harley much longer than I have been working with you lately. I will assure you that whatever you tell me in confidence will be kept in confidence between us," she said and took his hand as they walked into the next room. They sat down on a nice curved sofa. Carol guided him to the middle, and she sat close.

"I'm sold," Kevin told himself. *I must trust this girl…or woman! Yes, she's quite a woman*, he thought.

He set out to tell her about what he had learned so far about the research on the Wemberly Warehouse property and its ownership. "I don't really know who owns it. I know it is owned by the Wemberly Warehouse Inc. Who is signing the loan application? That may be confidential but I think it's important for us to know if we are to understand or determine what is taking place. Can you tell me who is signing the application?" he asked Carol.

"That is something I can't tell you because I don't know, Kevin," Carol told him. "The loan originated in the bank's office…probably through Mr. Harley. Of course, through our connection, we sometimes work on a sizable loan together. That application is probably in Mr. Harley's vault room. He guards that almost with his life. For a long time, I could go in and out of the vault room any time, but for the last couple years I was there, it became off limits. I think I still know the combination, but I would not have access, and my presence there would stick out like a sore thumb. Maybe Cheryl could get in there if she would."

Kevin thought about telling Carol about the experience he and Cheryl had but felt it was not the time to have the two employees to become intertwined in the activity if they would or even could. He thought about whether to tell Carol about why he was late to pick her up when she was kidnapped and taken to the island but felt quite sure that would be counterproductive. *It wasn't the time to bring all this information together and share it between the two*, he thought. He didn't know what Carol's reaction would be if she were given the full story.

"Tomorrow, I want to go to the courthouse for Gruntington's Island and try to find who owns that land. I know there are two cabins on the property—one on each end," Kevin told her. I went for a ride out on that island, just recently, and drove all around it. It takes a little while to get around and there is a lot to see. Part of the island is bordered on a narrow river channel, and the rest is bordered on the larger river side of the Arkansas River. The tugboats are escorting large fleets of barges with freight. Those barges will go all the way to New Orleans going south and all the way to Tulsa Oklahoma going north, maybe farther," Kevin said. "Are you still game to see the rest of the island?" he asked.

"You betcha, Kevin," she said. I only saw the one cabin and not much else while I was there. Those goons were afraid to let me see the outside. I would like to see the island for what it has on it. I know there are five thousand acres there and a lot of wild game. But I don't think there is much hunting that takes place on it from what I've heard. I guess you've heard the story about the hunting trip when Harold Wemberly disappeared. He was never located. They don't know if he got lost and died. Some say he might have got on a barge and just went away. He and Mrs.

Wemberly didn't get along very well. In fact, they were already divorced," Carol told him.

"Yes, I've heard that, Carol." He told her about his trip to the island a few days ago and meeting old Rufe near the island. "I don't know if I was getting the facts," Kevin said. "I don't think there was any reason for him to lie unless he was a pathological liar, and I don't think that's the case. Rufe told me there was more to the story that he could tell me but not that day. I would like to get the rest of it now if he will tell us."

"Then let's try to see him tomorrow, Kevin. That's very interesting. That mystery has been hanging a long time," Carol said excitedly.

"Sounds good, I hope he'll tell us then," Kevin said. "I suppose I should go and be ready for tomorrow," he said as he rose to go.

"Oh, don't go so soon, Kevin. The time is early, and you're not that old yet," she laughed. "What should I tell Mr. Harley if he should call me? He'll ask me if I did any good. He didn't know I was going to contact you so quickly, but you never know Mr. Harley. It would be like him to think I would make a move quickly. I usually don't put things off, and he knows that." Carol had that smile and watched him closely.

Kevin was standing at the door, and Carol was near. "Carol, tell him I really enjoyed the dinner and…and…" He looked into those eyes that he decided were the most beautiful and attractive eyes he had seen in a long time. He put his arms around her and pulled her close to him and she tilted her head back a little. Her lips were full, and he couldn't help but draw her head toward him as she placed her arms around him for a lingering kiss. "Tell Harley you will have to work on me some more—that I'm too reserved for you to tell," Kevin said with a smirk and gave her another full kiss. "Now, Carol, I must go or…well…I shouldn't be hanging around," he said and went quickly through the door.

"But…but…good night, Kevin." He was gone.

CHAPTER 38

Kevin backed out to the street from Carol's house and headed for home. Just ahead a red Ford pickup was turning onto North Hills Boulevard and sped hurriedly down the street. He couldn't see the license plate to determine if it were one of the goons. "But it could be those sorry no good..." he trailed off. "I think both of them stay busy keeping up with where I am or one of these bank people," he muttered. He wondered about Frank Harley. "He is very persistent about getting me on board with him. I don't want to keep him hanging on, but there is something about this whole mess that worries me. Why are he and Winston Kenwood offering me the same or similar deals for similar reasons, so they state?" he questioned as he drove on home to Little Rock.

He drove into his driveway and wondered what he would find in his house this time. The garage door opened, and it seemed okay there. He opened the door to the house and reset the alarm quickly. He found no problems and wondered if those goons had given up.

Day after tomorrow, he was to meet with Shelton McKinley. Maybe he and Carol would find some information in the county records about Gruntington's Island that would shed some light on some corporations and partnerships. There were four hunters on that ill-fated hunting trip. Three still had communications after these many years. *Of course, that might not mean anything*, Kevin thought.

The date tonight, Kevin reflected. *I enjoyed the date—maybe too much. I have been too long a single and Carol too*, Kevin thought.

The alarm rang, and Kevin rose, shaved, and showered quickly. Breakfast was simple and didn't take long. He was looking forward to the day and what it might reveal. A day with Carol would be the icing on the cake. He enjoyed her presence. She was sharp also and maybe the two of them could sort out some of these mysteries.

He had decided to pick Carol up and drive back across the river because of the goons circulating in town. He called her as he started toward her house to tell her he was on his way. "Good morning, Kevin. I'm glad you called, but let me tell you about some visitors. It's the red Ford pickup truck, and it has two men in it, and I'm quite sure it's Fred and Jocko. They drove by once about a half hour ago and again maybe five minutes ago," she said.

"Okay, I'll tell you what I'll do. I'll come to your house from the back way and turn onto Seminole Drive to Little Creek Drive and to Illinois Bayou Drive from that direction. I'll drive into your driveway, and you can get into the Explorer then, and we'll leave from there. If they see us leave, we'll think of something. Be sure you have that pistol and cartridges with you. You'll need that for your target practice anyway. Hopefully, we won't need it for defense," Kevin told her. He laid his Ruger in the seat to have it handy. *Those guys can be murderous*, he was thinking.

Kevin pulled into Carol's driveway, and she locked her house door and hurriedly came to the Explorer and entered. Kevin moved the Ruger back to the console. "I haven't seen them since I came into the neighborhood the back way," he told her. "Have you seen them?"

"No," Carol said, "I almost wish I could see them. I don't think they want me except to get at you and get those files. Appraiser Man, let's ride! I am anxious to check those courthouse records and then see that island. Can we see Rufe while we're out there? My curiosity is up now. I would like to hear the rest of that story."

Kevin was driving with his eyes watching the rearview mirror. They headed southeasterly and got onto Highway 65. They both kept an eye out for the red Ford pickup and never spotted them. After a forty-five-minute drive, they came to the Jefferson County courthouse and entered the Circuit Clerks office. The assistant showed them the records, and the search was on. Carol was quite efficient at the search. She and Kevin buried themselves in the job and didn't look up for four hours. Kevin stopped and looked around and saw Carol had just finished the records she was working on. It was long after lunchtime, and they had searched through several books and several deeds, and both had pads of records.

The land had been owned by several people back in the early days, but it had been purchased by corporations along the way. They found that the corporate ownership was disguised by stock held by other corporations. It was the same technique as the Wemberly Warehouse. It would make one believe that the owners might be the same. Apparently, the cabins may be owned by two separate entities, but it's not clear who owned the entities. "Let's go eat," Kevin said. "I'm hungry. Let's get outta here."

They grabbed a sandwich and drink at Dairy Queen and headed for Gruntington's Island. Carol was anxious to see Rufe and see if he would tell the rest of what happened to Harold Wemberly.

Kevin got his map out again and found a route from Pine Bluff to the farm side of the island. It would be a shortcut to Rufe's house. Carol had her purse open and was reworking her makeup. He looked at her and her ponytail. She had lost all her lipstick and was just natural. She looked wholesome and ready to play a game of basketball. Her starched shirt still looked fresh even after the grueling hours at the courthouse.

Kevin turned down the lane that went to Rufe's house and drove more slowly. The dust was thick, and the road needed a rain. He turned to Carol. "You are going to like Rufe a lot," he said. He grows on you." He turned the Explorer into the front yard of old Rufe's house and let the dust blow by before they got out. Kevin got out and let Carol out as she grabbed her purse.

"Hey, Rufe!" Kevin yelled toward the house. There was no answer, so he yelled several times as he walked up to the house and onto the porch. He knocked on the door several times. Finally, they heard a noise inside, and Kevin opened the front door. There was Rufe flat on the floor, face down and groaning weakly. "*Oh, oh,*" he moaned. Kevin knelt down and started to turn him over. He noticed the blood on the back of Rufe's head and a puddle on the floor by him.

"Wait," Carol said, "I'll find some water and a cloth." She found a pail of water in the kitchen and a towel hanging on a nail. She grabbed the towel and wet it in the pan of water from the pail. She ran back to the front room and started washing the wound on the back of Rufe's head. "What happened to you, Rufe?" Carol asked. "*Oh,*" Rufe groaned as they gently turned him over.

Rufe looked up at Kevin. "Oh, it's Mr. Kevin. They got me good, Mr. Kevin, suh. They's mean," he said weakly. "They come in heah and said they's gone sell my house and I best leave. I told them I'd had this place for sixty years since Mr. Gruntington done give it to me. They said he ain't owned this farm in many a year and he ain't around no more. I said I knowed that, but Mr. Gruntington said it would allus be mine, he said. They looked around my house like they done own it. They come outta the back room with that shotgun that Mr. Wemberly done give me long time ago. I said it's mine. They said no it ain't 'cause his name is done on it. They took it Mr. Kevin, suh. *Oh,* my head sho' do hurt."

They helped Rufe to his couch, and he sat his long body down gently and leaned his head back. Carol dipped the towel into the pan of water again and squeezed it out. "Here, Rufe, let me bathe your face. You had better let us take you to the doctor. They should take an X-ray to see if you have damage that should be cared for."

"No, ma'am, I ain't goin' to no X-ray place. My old daddy did that once, and he died," Rufe declared strongly. "Besides that, I be all right." He rose up a little from where his head was resting on the back of the old couch. He looked at Carol. "Mr. Kevin, this here's a fine-lookin' woman you done got here."

"Rufe, this is Carol. She is a good friend of mine, and yes, she is a fine-looking woman, Rufe."

"Mr. Kevin, suh, I wuz gonna tell you the next time you come. I seed him. He wuz heah," Rufe declared. He suddenly got sick, and Carol grabbed the pan she had been using and held it while old Rufe vomited into it. He turned pale and leaned over to the side. Kevin caught him and helped him lie down on the couch. His long legs were hanging off onto the floor, so Carol picked them up and laid them on the arms of the couch. "Thank you, Ms. Carol," Rufe said weakly. "I ain't feelin' quite up to par, but I be a gettin' better. Ya'll don't need be worryin' 'bout me none."

He looked at Kevin and then slowly turned and stared at the ceiling. A pleasant expression came over his face, and he stopped breathing.

Carol felt his pulse and said, "Kevin, Rufe is gone. He couldn't make it. What do we do now?" she asked as she started crying.

Kevin tried CPR as best as he knew how but could get no response from Rufe. He gently closed Rufe's eyelids. "I suppose we should take him in to the hospital and tell them what happened," Kevin mused. "No, we might be doing wrong by removing a dead body from a crime scene. Maybe we should go to the sheriff's office and report this. They would want to investigate the crime scene. Let's do that. I don't want to send you by yourself or

I would stay here while you went for the sheriff. I hate to leave Rufe here alone…but let's lock up and go find the sheriff," Kevin finally decided.

They covered Rufe with one of the sheets from his bed. "We've got to find out who did this," Kevin said. "It will take some luck."

"Carol, did you notice what he said? 'He wuz heah,' he said. He was here—who was here? My first thought would be someone besides his assailants today, because he said he was gonna tell me the next time he saw me. Could Wemberly have reappeared? That is eerie, don't you think? Could he have done this? I don't think so," Kevin answered his own question.

"It's been six years, Kevin. No one has heard of him since, but I suppose he could still be alive, and now that adds to this mystery of who is digging into his affairs, that is if he's the one Rufe was referring to. Who else could it be?" Carol said.

"At this time, we can only speculate, and I think I'll not say anything to anyone about that statement—yet," Kevin replied.

—∞—

They drove back the route to the county seat, and it was getting dark when they drove up to the sheriff's office. The sign over the front door said: "Sheriff Robert Benefield." He was just leaving but stopped. "What can I do for you folk today?" he asked them.

"Sheriff, we have just left a man who has been beaten. We happened on him and tried to help him, but he died as we tried," Kevin started telling him.

"Who, where is he?" the sheriff started firing questions and called out for his deputies.

Kevin told him where the house is and that it was Rufe. "That's the only name I know," Kevin said. We had to leave him. My car phone had no service in that area.

"I know Rufe," the sheriff said. "He voted for me every time I have run for office. He's an old friend. Let's go, men. Mr. Henry, I'm going to ask that you two go back with me," he said. The sheriff led the way, and two deputies followed in a van to bring the body back. Kevin and Carol fell in behind them.

"Kevin, are we in a precarious situation here? When we get there and they find Rufe dead and it shows that he was killed by a blunt blow to the head, what's to keep them from accusing us if they want to?" Carol said.

"I know what you mean, Carol, but we have driven in here with the information. Unless they just want to have someone to throw into the jail, surely they won't try to put this onto us." They drove in silence for a while.

The entourage left the pavement and traveled down the gravel road toward Gruntington's Island. After a distance, they turned the corner at Rufe's lane and down toward Rufe's house. They stopped at Rufe's house and saw that the front door was open. The deputies told Kevin and Carol to wait outside while they went inside to investigate the scene. "Ya'll wait out here. We've got to put up a yellow tape."

In a moment, the sheriff came out and approached Kevin's side of the Explorer. "Mr. Henry, are you playing a game here?" the sheriff said. He was a big guy and wore his badge on his civilian shirt. "There is no body in this house. What kind of story do you have now?"

"May we go inside with you, Sheriff?" Kevin asked. "Maybe we can see something of evidence of what we're telling you."

"Very well, see what you can do. This looks a little fishy though," the sheriff said with a scowl.

They all went back into the house, and Kevin looked at the floor where Rufe was lying when they arrived. There had been blood on the linoleum floor covering. It had been cleaned, and there was no sign. He looked at the couch where they had laid him. There had been blood on the couch. He looked closely and could see where the blood had been washed off the best they could, but he could detect some residue, and it was still damp. "Sheriff here is a spot that shows a slight stain where Rufe was lying when he died. Someone has washed the blood off, and if you feel, you can tell it is still wet," Kevin explained.

"How do we know that Rufe hasn't just gone somewhere after he has tried to clean up a spill," the sheriff said. "You may be for real, but we don't know." He seemed to ponder for a while then turned to them. "Give us your contact information. We'll do our investigation and may need you later." He directed the deputies to take the crime scene tape down.

Kevin and Carol left their information with Sheriff Benefield, who left in a hurry.

"There goes our pistol practice," Carol said. "Kevin, I still want to see that Island. I just wonder if those goons are there now."

"They might be there, but we wouldn't know if they killed Rufe or if someone else did," Kevin said. "It's dark now. One thing that causes me to doubt that it was the goons is that they were talking about selling that land. If that was for real, or if someone is selling that land, we have more information to get. But first, I want to get my camera and take some photos of this house and of the interior. I also want a photo of the couch where Rufe lay. I think the bloodstain on the couch will show in a close-up. Kevin took the photos and said, "lets go."

"Let's go on to my place," Kevin suggested to Carol. "I want to get to my computer and see if we can find out if that land has been listed for sale in the Little Rock MLS. It may be in the Pine Bluff MLS. If so, I'll call a friend tomorrow. Go with me, and I'll order us a pizza."

"Sounds like a winner," Carol said and smiled. "I'm too wound up to go home now. That man's death has my dander up. I want us to find the killers. We know he was murdered whether or not Sheriff Benefield believes that. Besides, I am supposed to be persuading you to accept Mr. Harley's offer. Have you thought about it anymore, Kevin?" She smiled and looked at Kevin. "Has he made you an attractive offer?"

"Yes, it is an attractive offer," he answered. Kevin was tempted to tell her the offer but felt that things were a little uncertain to bring all that to the open. He dialed his favorite pizza place and ordered a large pizza delivered.

They drove into Kevin's driveway, and he had the garage door going up. He closed the door down before they got out of the Explorer. "How's that for being discreet. They won't know we're both here, if they are on stake out."

They went straight to the computer after Kevin shut off the alarm and reset it. No one had breached the system. Kevin opened the MLS system on his computer and checked on Pine Bluff listings. Sometimes Pine Bluff properties would be listed in the Little Rock MLS. Carol watched with him as the computer searched through the Pine Bluff Properties. It did not show. He searched for farmland in the Little Rock area. Sometimes agents will list a property in Little Rock to make sure Little Rock agents found it. They watched as the Little Rock land search continued. There was no listing for that property. "Maybe someone wants to sell it but doesn't have a Realtor yet," Kevin declared.

Carol was looking over Kevin's shoulders at the computer when the search was finished. "Who owns the property now? Maybe we can find out," Carol said. "Maybe these papers we have found will give us a clue."

The doorbell rang and the pizza delivery was there. They took the pizza and sat at the kitchen table and ate. "It's been a long day," Kevin said. "It was not what I had expected it to be and I'm sorry Carol. I wanted it to be fun, but you've been great. I hesitate to end the day, but I have a trip to make tomorrow and I suppose I must get ready for that trip. Later, I will tell you about that trip."

Carol finished her pizza and walked around to put her arms around Kevin's neck as he sat there. "You still owe me a trip to Gruntington's Island," and she kissed him on the cheek. "You can take me home now, Appraiser Man."

Kevin returned from taking Carol home and checked his messages on the telephone answering machine. There were three from Cheryl. "Where are you?" she said. "Call me when you come in. I have been trying to call you on your car phone, to no avail. Please call me as soon as you return. I may have work for you."

It was late, but Kevin picked up the phone and returned her call. Cheryl's answering machine picked up the call and said to leave a message. "This is Kevin returning your call. I'll call you later," Kevin said to the recorder and hung up.

In a moment, his phone rang. It was Cheryl. "Kevin, where have you been?" she asked. I have been trying to reach you all day. Why didn't you answer? I called you several times on your car phone."

"I'm sorry, Cheryl, but I went out to look at some land and was out of the signal range," he told her. It was the truth but not the whole truth. "I couldn't even get any kind of signal. What's up? Are you okay?" Kevin asked.

"Yes, I'm all right, but I was going to invite you for dinner. I haven't talked to you for too long. There are several things I want to talk to you about, and I thought dinner would be a good time to do it. Can you come tomorrow night?" Cheryl said. "I promise to be dressed," she said and laughed.

"I can't promise you that I'll be there, so I don't want you to prepare something, and I don't show up. I have to make a trip out of town, and I don't know what time I'll return. So don't look for me. By the way, do you feel comfortable with the possibility of someone seeing us together like that. Might it create suspicion by Mr. Harley?" Kevin cautioned.

"Kevin, I'll explain later, but I wish you would try to come tomorrow night. That is Friday night, and my kids will be at my aunt's for the night...please try," Cheryl pleaded.

This is not supposed to be, Kevin was thinking. *Cheryl is a very attractive woman, and I am not turned off by her. I would be glad to be a part of a dinner engagement with her, if the circumstances were right. I am surprised though that she is pushing in that way. It's not like her to push like that*, he thought. He decided to try to get back with her after he returned from Texas.

CHAPTER

39

The phone rang at 6:45 a.m. "Good morning, Mr. Henry, this is the pilot for Mr. Shelton McKinley's private jet plane. We are leaving Love Field at this moment and should arrive at the Little Rock Airport at 8:00 a.m. If you are ready, we will depart immediately for Love Field."

"Thank you. I'll be ready." He hung up and finished his breakfast. *This should be an interesting day*, he thought.

Kevin arrived at the airport and was looking around at surroundings he hadn't seen in a while. There in large, bold letters and a more than life-size picture was an advertising sign showing an image of Jenny Lafferty. "Number 1 Realtor with Bristol Realty," it stated. Kevin had to admit. She was a knockout. "I Can Help!" the sign said.

The plane arrived on time, and Kevin was ushered onto the jet. He was immediately offered breakfast or drinks by an attractive attendant. He was the only passenger on the plane, and he started mentally wondering what this trip was costing Shelton McKinley. Kevin declined the offerings and sat back to enjoy the trip. The plane took off in a fast assent, and they were on their way.

He watched the forests go by and then town after town. Texarkana was below, and Kevin thought about the Franklin S&L that had been based there. It had gone under also, with a scandal. He remembered how Shelton McKinley had come close to being indicted. It would have meant prison time, but his congressman came to his rescue. *I wonder how many campaign dollars that cost McKinley*, Kevin thought. *Oh well, that's the way the world goes around, it seems, and it will probably continue to go around that way as long as there are super wealthy people.*

The attendant came around again and offered drinks of his choice. Kevin was a teetotaler, but he would have declined anyway. This meeting would require his full alertness, he suspected. He didn't want any alcohol to dim his wits. Some thought a few drinks would sharpen their wits, but he decided to not try. He knew McKinley was a very sharp character.

The plane arrived at 9:15 a.m., and a limousine was waiting. They ushered Kevin into the limo and made the drive to McKinley's office. The driver parked in the parking garage of the twenty-seven-story office building. He asked the driver if Mr. McKinley owned this building. He was told quietly that he had owned it at one time, but it had been sold.

Kevin was met at the garage and escorted to McKinley's office on the seventeenth floor. They entered the reception room of the office, and he was greeted by the personal secretary. He was offered coffee or Coke, but he declined. "Mr. McKinley will be with you in a moment," she assured him. "He is in a meeting at this time but should be finished shortly. Please come into his sitting room while you wait. This is also where lunch will be served."

Kevin waited about a half hour and was beginning to be a little impatient. He had been told by McKinley that he would probably arrive in time for lunch. *Oh well, I suppose I shouldn't be impatient as long as he is paying well*, Kevin thought. Finally, the secretary came in and said, "Mr. McKinley will see you now, sir," and showed him in.

McKinley came from around his desk with his usual limp from the bad leg and motioned Kevin toward the round table and four chairs. "This is better for close talking," he said. "How are you, Kevin?" he asked with a smile and the gravelly voice. "I have asked you to come visit me because I need your help, and I want to work out a favorable arrangement with you."

"What is the need you have, Mr. McKinley?" Kevin asked directly. "That is important first."

"All right, I have interests in Texas and Arkansas. Some of these interests have been weakened lately by my fight with Office of Thrift and Supervision—OTS. They took my S&L as you probably know. I had to pay those bastards five million dollars to get free from that thing. Now they want to get part of my other assets. I have interests in some banks and warehouses in Texas and a few in Arkansas. I need help to protect my interests in these banks. I can take care of the land assets. You have done consulting for banks and S&Ls, and you know your way around. I understand you are very sharp in that field. I need an expert."

"I know Harley and Kenwood are trying to hire you," he said. "I know they want you to watch out for their interests. I want to hire you and have you to devote your energies to my interests. I will pay you double what they offer you and give you a severance guarantee. If we terminate your employment, you will have a healthy severance check. It will more than pay what you will earn in appraisal work for the next thirty years. You will not be taking a chance," he declared.

Kevin was thinking all they while that McKinley was building up the grand offer. *If his fears are realized, there would be no way for him to make good on his contract. Is his ship sinking? I don't think I want to be part of a sinking ship, but I'll listen.*

"What are your thoughts on this, Kevin? Can you make a fast decision?"

"That sounds like a very generous offer you are proposing, Mr. McKinley. I'm not sure that I'm as good as you are portraying me to be. I don't know how hot the fire is that your irons are in. I may not be strong enough to pull them out," Kevin responded. "No, I can't make a fast decision without knowing more of the facts. I don't like to walk into a jungle with a blindfold on. What are the interests that I would be charged with protecting? What are the problems attached to those interests?" Kevin stated further while looking McKinley straight in the eye and trying to keep a smile on his face.

"I own controlling interest in several banks here in Texas and some in Arkansas. I own interests in some banks but not controlling interests. I own several warehouses in Texas and part interest in some in Arkansas. I have corporations that own part interest in assets in Arkansas. I know that some of my properties have not been operated properly and some that are being abused. I want these properties straightened out and operated according to the law and those properties that I don't own controlling interest in, I may want to acquire control. That would be your job to straighten out the mess," McKinley elaborated.

That explains the meetings that McKinley has been having with Harley and Kenwood in Little Rock, Kevin was thinking, so he decided to get bold and ask him. "Do you own part of the New Bank of Pulaski and the First Trust Bank of Arkansas?" Kevin asked him.

McKinley's eyelids narrowed, and his voice raised a half pitch. "Why do you ask about those banks? What do you know about them?" he asked.

"You probably remember I was at the cookout party given by Mr. Harley, and I was introduced to you at that time. From what you have said today, it would make me think you might have an interest in those banks," Kevin responded. He was not going to let McKinley know he and Cheryl were hearing them from the vault room when he had the meeting with those men.

"*Ah* yes, I suppose you would wonder about them. No, I am not saying anything about my interest there. I am a long-time friend of those two men. We do have some common interests. You would be made privy to those interests if you come aboard," McKinley said.

McKinley's assistant buzzed him and told him their dinner was served in his private dining room.

"Kevin, let's take a break and eat some lunch. We have had a selection brought in, and I hope there will be something for your taste," McKinley said

They entered the private dining room and were seated at a lavish meal served buffet-style with all the foods of elegant living. Kevin marveled at the lavish setting and display of opulence.

They selected their choices, and their plates were brought to the table. After eating awhile, Kevin asked McKinley what he did with the food that was left over. "That seemed enough to feed many people," Kevin commented.

"That's a good observation, Kevin," McKinley said. We don't waste it, but it is served to our employees on these days. We have a lunch room upstairs for our employees. They eat free. That is cost-effective because they are more productive when they don't have to fight their way from the building and back every day."

Lunch was over, and they returned to the private office and the round table. "Kevin, I can tell you that you would not be asked to take part in any illegal activity or anything that would be questionable. You would have a legal staff available to you at all times who would guide you in things that may have a narrow definition of the legality. There are those who challenge me or my corporations a lot because of our size. That goes with the territory. When they get tough, we get tough, and when their complaint is frivolous or ridiculous, we can cause them to wish they had not traveled that journey. I don't like for people to raise issues just to see if they can get a free ride. We don't pay to stop a lawsuit just to not have the lawsuit. Even the attorneys they use will regret their action."

They discussed the business of McKinley's enterprises with the intricate details still obscure to Kevin. McKinley apparently considered the discussion revealing enough. Kevin felt he didn't want to make a decision yet.

"Mr. McKinley, your offer is generous and is challenging. It probably is an offer that one would normally jump at, but I wonder how you know about the proposals made to me by Mr. Harley and Mr. Kenwood," Kevin said.

"Harley and Kenwood have common interests with me, as I have said. I have pushed them to tighten up their ships because of things that have happened and the possibility of insidious and serious things that can happen and could affect me also. You will not know these interests until you come on board with me," McKinley said and sat back in his chair with a finality motion.

"Mr. McKinley, I think I will not make any decision at this time. If you feel a decision must be made now, then I would have to decline," Kevin said with a smile and stood. "Thank you for inviting me here and for the elegant lunch."

McKinley reached into a drawer and retrieved a previously written check. "Thank you for coming, Kevin. Here is the promised reimbursement for your time and consideration today. My pilots will return you to Little Rock. Good day!" That was it.

The return flight was simple, and they landed at Little Rock at four o'clock. He thanked the pilots for a nice flight and returned home. It seemed it had been more than an eight-hour trip. He was compensated for what he might expect to earn in two months. Everything McKinley did was with a flare and was costly to him.

When he walked into his office and checked his messages on his answering machine, there was one from the security alarm company. "Mr. Henry, there was breach of security on the exterior. The alarm was set off, and we sent police to check. There was no sign of entry to the house and we turned off the alarm. If you find a breach of the interior, please let us know so we can follow up." Kevin walked around in the interior and found no entry. "This is good," he muttered. "There must have been intruders, and the alarm scared them away. Bravo, security guys!"

CHAPTER
40

There was a message from Cheryl. "Kevin, if you return before office hours are up, please call me at the office. If you return after hours, go ahead and call me at home. I must talk with you," she said.

Kevin felt she sounded very urgent and decided to call her back. He called Cheryl's direct number and got the message that she was out on an errand and would not return today. This was Friday, so Kevin called her car phone. "Hello, this is Cheryl, the voice said pleasantly and professionally. "Please leave a message. If I don't return your call soon, please call me at my office," she said and gave the bank's number. He left a message for her to return his call.

The offer of employment for special duty by three men was intriguing Kevin though. Shelton McKinley's offer would put him into a league that he had never imagined being. He would hobnob with people of the very wealthy class. Would that be a happy lifestyle for him was one question? Would he enjoy working for McKinley? Winston Kenwood's offer would put him at home among people he felt comfortable with. He felt like Kenwood had integrity; although, he had at first implied that he needed a certain price on the appraisal. That might have been a test. Maybe so, Kevin assumed. Then Frank Harley, who is he really? He has wanted an unrealistic value for that warehouse property. Why? Is he ordering that appraisal for himself or for the corporation? McKinley had referred to a "deal" that maybe hinged on the appraisal.

The phone rang. It was Cheryl. "Hello, Kevin, I'm so glad you are back. I must talk to you, and I am inviting you to my house for dinner. I have just picked up some things to prepare if you will come," she said.

"Cheryl, I'm glad I made it back. Yes, I'll be glad to have dinner with you, but let me take you to dinner, and we'll go to a steak house in Conway. Do you like steak?" Kevin asked.

"Oh, Kevin, are you asking me for a date? I accept," she said hurriedly. "I really must visit with you about something. Can we probably dine in private?

"How about Chinese food? If you like Chinese food, there is a nice place in Conway with some small private rooms. We can talk all you want. We can also talk on the way there and back. How about that?" he asked.

"Kevin, I love Chinese food, and I haven't eaten in Conway since I became a widow. I must admit my dates are few and far between. I suppose I just don't fit anymore," she said and laughed.

Kevin knew better than what she had suggested. *She probably had few dates because men were so in awe of her. They assumed it was no use to ask. She is a beautiful and attractive woman. She can walk by my side any time*, he thought.

"You do fit, Cheryl, and I am looking forward to your being my date tonight. You are some gal. I will pick you up at six if that's okay!"

"Kevin, you are being so sweet. You can park out in the driveway and pick me up at the front door. We don't need to be secretive anymore. I'll see you at six," she said and hung up.

"Tonight can be a fun night or it can be serious night. I have a feeling that it may be some of both," Kevin was speculating. He continued on with his messages and checked his faxes. There was a message to pick up an assignment by one of the other banks to appraise a house in Sherwood near old Jim Hammons' house. *I'll drive by Jim's house and see if the crime scene tape is still up*, Kevin thought.

Kevin finished checking his messages and decided to take a moment to call Carol. *She should be home now.* She answered quickly.

"Oh, Kevin, how was your trip? Can you tell me tonight? I have been wondering if you have heard any more from Sheriff Benefield. I am very curious as to what happened to old Rufe's body. Something very strange is going on there. Why would anyone want a body? My guess is it's the ones who killed him," Carol said.

"I am very curious too, Carol. I think you are right about who took the body. I would speculate they came back to make sure he was dead then decided to get rid of any evidence. Let's go tomorrow and see the island. How about eight in the morning? I'll pick you up. I'll tell you about the trip tomorrow."

"Okay, it's a deal," she said. I'll have my pistol ready," she said and laughed.

Kevin hurried and showered and shaved again to be fresh for the date with Cheryl. How have I gotten into this dating thing with two women at my age? I haven't intended to be in the romantic stage, but some of this has been necessary for this mysterious thing attached to this bank, now these banks and that mysterious warehouse, the island and now the land near the island. But I must admit the two women are first rate, in my view. Now tonight I think I may find out more about some of these things, Kevin mused.

Kevin carefully set his security alarm and left in his Explorer. He wondered if the red Ford F150s were covering his activity.

He watched his rearview mirror to see if he saw either of them. There was no sign. He drove the short distance to Cheryl's house and parked in her driveway. She apparently was watching and stepped out the door. She was in a skirt and blouse and low heels. Far different from her business dress, and he thought she looked more like the girl next door. Before he could get out to open the car door for her, she opened it and jumped in.

"Kevin, I'm so excited. You don't know what this means to me. My first date in three years," she said. "My aunt and uncle will invite the kids to spend the weekend with them periodically to give me a little personal time, and this is one of those weekends. It is such a rest. Although my kids are a lot of fun. Have you ever had children?" she asked.

"No, we never got around to children before Marylyn developed the brain tumor. We had planned to try that year and were so disappointed. We were afraid the pregnancy would exacerbate the tumor and afraid the treatment might damage a fetus," Kevin said.

"I'm so sorry, Kevin," she said.

They drove for a while in silence, and Kevin thought about this date being so exciting for her. He wanted her to enjoy the evening and wanted it to be fun for her, but it was also an evening in which she was to talk about something very important. He continued to chat lightheartedly during the drive to Conway and arrived at the Chinese restaurant.

Cheryl jumped out of the SUV and joined Kevin. She took his arm and walked close as they entered the restaurant. Kevin had made reservations, and they were escorted to one of the private enclosed cubicles. A server took their orders and left them alone. Cheryl became more serious then.

"Kevin, I do have a mission tonight as I told you. Mr. Harley has been pressing me more about whether anyone ever enters the vault room somehow. I told him he usually locks it, and it would take a Philadelphia locksmith to get in there. He seems worried and under a lot of pressure. He approached me yesterday and told me about making you an offer to work for him, and he very earnestly wants you to accept the offer. He didn't give details but didn't hide the fact that he is hoping you come aboard. He said he needs you and your knowledge and abilities. He asked me to talk to you and see if I can persuade you.

"I do like Mr. Harley in spite of the pressure he puts on me at times," Cheryl continued. "I think he needs you, and will you please consider helping him? I have the sense that he's a good man and is pressured sometimes to do some things he shouldn't do. Will you consider and come on board soon?" she said seriously.

"Are you aware that there are other offers to me in this industry?" Kevin said. "There is something going on that has created this strange thing. We might have been close to some answers when we got into that vault and almost got caught. I will consider his offer and try to make a decision within the next few days. Tell him I am not stalling to be hard to get, but there are some things I must do before making that decision. He may know there are other offers to me and he may not. I don't know."

They continued on in a more lighthearted way and finished the meal with a little banter between them. Kevin asked her if she ever got to practice her revolver and was told she hadn't had a chance. Would he teach her sometime, she asked.

They drove home to her house, and Cheryl let him open the car door for her when they arrived at her house. He walked her to her door, and she thanked him for a good time. He could tell she was waiting for a good night kiss. He remembered the last kiss that was almost. He embraced her and told her how attractive she is and how he was amazed more men hadn't been trying to date her. "You are beautiful, Cheryl," he said and saw tears in her eyes. He said nothing else but kissed her lightly and said good night.

He drove home and gave some thought to the two women and how they appealed to him. They both had strong appeal but, but…

Kevin drove home with deep thought about the day and about the past several days. His first offer to assist a president of a bank was from Frank Harley who surprised him with that sort of thing. He had to find out more about these concerns; it seems that fears are driving these men to make such extreme offers. Maybe the next few days he can uncover something if he can do it in time. He knew he had to study the information that he and Carol had obtained from the Jefferson County records, and he decided to do more research in Little Rock in Pulaski County.

CHAPTER
41

The alarm went off early that Saturday morning, and Kevin rose quickly and ate a quick breakfast. Today was to be a fun day as they visited the Gruntington's Island and did a little target practice. He knew they had to be careful because of the goons in that first cabin—if they are there. The county records showed ownership to be in a corporation's name. He felt sure those guys didn't own it. Did they have permission to be there?

Carol was ready and answered the door with her pistol in a little case. They headed out of town immediately. "How was your trip, Appraiser Man?" she asked.

"You wouldn't believe it, Carol. I have known that there are those who live in extreme opulence, but I had never been exposed to such as I was yesterday. He described the plane that was sent for him and with no one else on board but him, the two pilots, and an attendant. "I think the privacy and expediency was important to Shelton McKinley as well to let me know he had money to burn. He told me about his interest in several banks in Texas and some in Arkansas. That makes me wonder if he has an interest in the New Bank of Pulaski and the First Trust Bank of Arkansas, but he skirted around the questions I asked."

Carol thought about that a moment. "I don't know. I have never seen anything formal about that, and when I worked in the main bank, I never saw anything addressed to him, but I know that he occasionally met with the two presidents in Mr. Harley's office. I don't know if they met at other places.

Kevin drove in silence for a while and decided to share some more of his inner thoughts. "Carol, I have given a lot of thought to why these three men are so intent on finding someone to help them and all of them at the same time. Something has occurred that has stirred this feeling and this need for someone to help them protect themselves and their personal interests. A common denominator could be if Harold Wemberly has been sighted, and they fear some problems if he were to return to the present scene. Could it have something to do with the Wemberly Warehouse and maybe more?"

They traveled down the highway until the turnoff toward Gruntington's Island. That was the beginning of the 640 acres for sale by Bristol Real Estate. Jenny Lafferty was shown to be the contact agent. The gravel road had been freshly graded and was smooth riding. Acres of cotton and soybeans were growing on this rich and fertile land. Kevin picked up his car phone and dialed the number shown on the sign.

"Bristol Real Estate," the voice said. "How may I direct you?"

"May I speak to Jenny Lafferty?" Kevin asked.

"Jenny is out of town at this time. May I take a number and have her call you?"

They lost connection then, and Kevin found they had gone into a no signal area. There would be no telephone service now while they were traveling in this area.

They were approaching the lane to old Rufe's house, and Carol asked if they could just drive down to see the house again and Kevin turned down the dusty road. As they approached where the house had been, they saw a burned out pile of ashes. Very little of the wooden structure was still existing. Only a little chicken house and an outdoor toilet several yards from the house site and a garden site were left to show old Rufe's former existence.

Kevin stared at the pile of ashes and thought of the cruelty that was exhibited there. A poor and old black man had been bludgeoned and left for dead. Then someone had stolen the body and done something with it. *How sad*, he thought. He looked across at Carol who was fighting tears; her constant smile had changed to sadness. He reached back to the floor of the backseat and brought forth the camera he always had with him for his appraisal work and snapped a few pictures of the scene. "I don't know why, but I just think I want a picture of all this," he told Carol.

He turned around and headed for the Island. "Carol, get your pistol out and I'm getting mine out in the event those goons are in that cabin and spot us as we go by," Kevin told her. "I want to see if they are here now." They passed in front of the cabin and went on around the island trail. There was no one there now and Kevin stopped and snapped a picture of the cabin. Maybe we won't have any contact with them today, but we should keep an eye out," Kevin suggested.

This was a hunting forest, rich with live game of various kinds. It was five thousand acres of rare, undisturbed forest with nature's natural habitat. Large oak trees, ash, hickory and sweet gum were abundant here with an abundance of cypress along the lowland portion. When the river was flooded, much of the land was covered with water for a while. Wild life scampered away as they drove slowly observing the scenery. After driving about three miles, Kevin stopped and told Carol they could do some shooting here with their pistols. We shouldn't attract any one hearing the shots.

The Body

They were near the main channel of the river, and there was an occasional tugboat pushing a fleet of barges. "Walk over here, Carol. There is a deep hole at this bluff. According to old

Rufe's story, this is where he and his brother, RC, drove Harold Wemberly's truck over the edge and into that hole. If the story is true, there should be an old rusty truck at the bottom. They walked over to the edge of the bluff.

"*Oh.*" Carol almost screamed. "Look, Kevin—it's a body. Look!" she said.

They both walked closer to the edge of the cliff and looked more closely. "Could it be? Oh, Kevin…" Carol said. "Could that be old Rufe's body? Oh that poor man!"

"Yes, it could be. I'll get my camera and try to take a photo for now," Kevin said and went to the Explorer and retrieved his camera. He eased over as close to the edge of the cliff as he could safely get and used the telephoto lens to get a close up shot of the body. It was lodged in a tree top that had fallen into the water from the edge of the bank. He thought he might need a good picture later and took some extra shots. He also took a few shots of the scenery around where they were standing for site identification.

Carol walked over to Kevin and put her arm in his. "What do we do now?" she asked. "We probably don't have a telephone signal here, but if we did and called Sheriff Benefield, what is he going to say with the message coming from us?"

"I think he will have to check out what we tell him. We'll drive back toward town until we get a signal, and I'll call him," Kevin told her.

They drove a little way and drove around a slough where there was water and some cypress trees. Kevin noticed snakes in the water and stopped. "While we're here, we might as well shoot a couple snakes," he said. "Take your pistol, and see if you can pop a snake," he suggested. He wanted Carol to have some pleasure from the trip instead of the sighting of the body.

Carol loaded a clip into her Glock pistol and took aim at a water moccasin. She fired one shot and he submerged. "You got close," Kevin consoled her. "Try another—there are several down there."

There was another water moccasin moving toward them. Carol held the pistol in both hands to steady it and gave a little lead, aiming it at the head of the snake. She pulled the trigger and the gun bellowed. The snake turned upside down and jerked its tail rapidly.

"You got that snake in the head," Kevin told her. "You are good!"

They took a few more shots and left for Little Rock. As they passed the big cabin on the east end of the island, they noticed some vehicles, but none were red Ford F150 pickup trucks. There was no sign of individuals, and they assumed they were hunters out in the woods.

They went on out of the island and traveled until they could get a telephone signal. Kevin called the sheriff's office and told him about the body they had seen in the river lodged in a tree top at the bend of the river. "Sheriff, I think that is old Rufe. It is a black man." I think you should be able to see the treetop at the bend of the river, but if you need my help, I will be glad to help," Kevin told him.

"Henry, if this is another wild goose chase you are gonna answer to me. I have enough to do without that sort of business," the sheriff grumbled.

"There's one more thing, Sheriff," Kevin said. Old Rufe's house has been burned flat to the ground. We drove by on the way to the island today. These are vicious persons we're dealing with. Rufe was telling the truth. You can call me," Kevin said and hung up.

CHAPTER 42

They drove on into Little Rock and straight to Kevin's house. "Help me decipher some things, Carol," he asked her. I think we might figure out what's going on if we dig deep enough into what we have. Are you game?" he asked her.

"Appraiser Man, I so want to get to the bottom of this. I was hoping you would let me help you work on it. Let's get with it," she declared.

"All right," Kevin said, "I'll get files out from my old S&L, the research at the Secretary of State's office, and the research at Jefferson County, and we'll see if things will connect. There must be a link in my old S&L computer files that will tie some things together, and that's why the goons were trying so hard to get them. Someone wants that badly. I would like to know why.

"First, let's look at the Pulaski County tax records and see where the tax bill is mailed to and who pays the bill," Kevin said. "That normally would show an owner, but this shows a tax service company who receives the bill and pays. It is a general servicing company who is sworn to confidentiality. That didn't help much. We might have to get a court order to help there, and that will bring in the police. Let's hold up on that for now.

"Secondly, let's review the Secretary of State's records of these corporations. He put the paperwork out onto the kitchen table, and they started to work on the layers of corporations and stockholders. Most of the stock in Wemberly Warehouse Inc. was owned by other corporations, which Kevin had obtained a list but he didn't yet know who owned those corporations. He would still have to get that information from the states where they were incorporated. They marked "More Info Needed."

"I wonder if there is more information about that in the Wemberly Warehouse file we had in our office," Carol said, "and did that disappear when Kennon Foster was murdered, if he were murdered?" There could be a connecting piece of information in that file. Whoever killed Kennon, wanted that information, but Mr. Harley said nothing was missing. Does he have that file?"

Kevin decided to tell Carol about when he and Cheryl tried to check on that file in the vault room. "We almost got caught," he told her. "That was a close, close call." He told her about the meeting of the three men while he and Cheryl were closed up in the vault room. That was a serious meeting, and I think it might have been about more than the Wemberly Warehouse files." There are some files in that vault room that must be critical, but we came out empty handed. We were almost caught by the janitor.

Carol's eyes took on a little more of a smile and she laughed. "You are a busy man." She laughed. "Is there more to tell?"

"Well, yes," Kevin answered. "I'm going to tell you more about when you were abducted and carried off to the Gruntington's Island. I think now that it was set up by the two goons to draw me away and take advantage to abduct you. How they knew I was going to meet you is another question. Cheryl called me, desperate about a man in a red Ford F150 pickup truck. There had been one of those trucks by her house before. She sounded terrified, and I ran to the rescue. A red Ford F150 was parked in her driveway and a man knocking on her door. When I arrived, the truck was going down the street, and I knew it was a different license number, so I figured it was a false alarm. Now I know there are two of those pickup trucks and two goons. That's why I was late to pick you up."

"Okay, okay." Carol laughed. "So I have competition."

Kevin stopped and looked up at her as she stood there. He thought about how she had come to his rescue when he was cold-cocked at the Harley's cookout party and how she got him to the emergency room and raced to his house and the ministorage unit to secure it. She was a trooper. He liked that. She liked sports, and he liked sports. She liked to shoot some pistols. She is a can-do girl, he had decided. But he was not ready to hasten the relationship to a serious point yet, he thought. *But I feel like jumping up and throwing my arms around her. She is so darned attractive*, he thought. He got up and went to her and pulled her tightly to him. "Carol, don't quit competing," he said. "You are one beautiful girl and one great competitor. Am I lucky or what?" Kevin laughed and went back to work.

The 640 acres showed to be owned by the GSORWR Holding LLC. It had been deeded from RWR Holding LLC and filed in Jefferson County, Arkansas? That transfer was from HW Corporation. That corporation was an Arkansas corporation filed in Little Rock. Each transfer had been by quitclaim deed.

The property had been sold to Harold Wemberly by F. W. Gruntington and Mary E. Gruntington. It was sold to HW Corporation for five hundred dollars per acre in 1975. The deed from HW Corporation to RWR Holding LLC provided a condition that the property would belong to the RWR Holding LLC as long as RW Rudlow shall live, but if his death should precede that of the grantor, the property would revert to the grantor. That would be Harold Wemberly's Corporation. It was stated that the condition would run with the land. Each transfer showed the same condition.

Kevin was following the trail of holdings in Wemberly Warehouse Inc., which was owned and acquired similarly. He found that a large percentage of the warehouse stock was now owned by GSORWR Holding LLC. Other corporations owned the rest of the warehouse, and the warehouse was operated by a designated representative of the owners. Revenue of the warehouse was distributed by the management to the corporations. Taxes were paid into the tax servicing agency, which billed the management. A report of income and expenses was sent to each corporation.

The names of stockholders of each corporation were available at the Secretary of State's office in each state except that for the GSORWR Holding LLC and a court order was required to obtain the names. Their tax notification and payment was through the tax service agency. Revenues from the property were sent to a receiving agency. All those files were sealed. The transactions transferring the ownership of the shares of the warehouse, and also the land, from Harold Wemberly was made in 1986, the year he disappeared. That had never been known until now when Kevin and Carol had dug up the information.

These requirements of court orders had made it hard for anyone to obtain the names of those entities, so the hunt had gone to other methods; some of which were definitely desperate and costly in life.

This explains why they are desperately trying to get my files and old Jim Hammons's files. There is some information in them that leads to the current owners. People are paying a terrible price for the greed of others, Kevin thought.

Somehow, someone had learned or had been told that he had some key information in his files. Kevin remembered the loan application that had been made with the Central Arkansas Workers Savings and Loan where he worked at that time. James Carpenter knew about Kevin having that information. Would James be in on this? Kevin was getting sick again.

He moved over to the computer and brought up the S&L files of that year. Now to find the loan application for a loan to Wemberly Warehouse Inc. He scanned through and found the file. Check with Jim Hammons the notation said. He knows the identity of the corporation names. It said that Jim Hammons has information regarding the ownership of the warehouse. "Go see Jim Hammons about this," the notation read. There was nothing further in the file except to say to decline the loan. There was nothing else there.

Jim Hammons's files showed the ownership identity of the corporate names, but Kevin wondered, *Why had someone been trying so hard to get my computer and the backup floppy disks? Why did they think I had this information? I know why those files were key but who else would know why?* He was getting sick again. He had a fear of finding the answer. *It all points to James Carpenter, but he's my friend. I just can't think that James would do this. There must be an explanation! But is he working for these people?*

Carol came over to him and put her hand on his shoulders and massaged them a little. "Appraiser Man, how about I order some pizza delivered. It's getting late, and it looks like we have a lot more work to do?" she said.

"That's good, would you take care of that," Kevin said and handed her a bill. He went back to work.

When the pizza arrived, they took a break to eat. Kevin pondered whether to share his fear of what he felt about who had leaked information to someone that had made him a target. He had more work to do and didn't want to stop yet until he dug deeper in the records they had on hand.

Kevin went into the garage and climbed to the attic. He lifted the layer of insulation and lifted up the Jim Hammons files and took them down to the kitchen table. They were the files that Jim had told him would be of interest to him. He read the notes of information Jim had written down. There were pages and pages in the files. Jim had talked to Harold Wemberly when they were building the warehouse. Harold had told Jim about an incident that he had never told anyone about. Jim had recorded the very personal information. A powerful bit of information was there, and it was leading Kevin to a strong theory in this mystery.

Kevin's research had been intense, and he had lost awareness of the hour. The hour was late, and he looked for Carol. She was exhausted, and he found her asleep on the couch. It was three o'clock in the morning. He got a blanket and covered her. He looked down at that beautiful face and kissed her lightly. She never woke.

CHAPTER

43

Sunday Morning

Carol woke to the smell of bacon frying and the aroma of coffee brewing. Her clothes were wrinkled, and she felt wrinkled. She walked to the kitchen where Kevin was preparing breakfast.

"Good morning, sleepy head," Kevin said. "Would you like a quick shower before breakfast to feel better?"

"That would be great, but I didn't bring my clothes. I didn't know I was spending the weekend," she said and laughed.

"There are some clothes still in Marylyn's closet that I have never disposed of. If you don't mind wearing those, you are welcome to them. I don't know how you might feel about that…or you can wear my bathrobe…your choice, but hurry, breakfast is almost ready." Kevin told her.

"Okay, I'll find my way," Carol said. She rushed to Kevin's shower and was out quickly. The bathroom had two separate sinks and vanities. Marylyn's vanity was still fully stocked. She found the hair brush and quickly had her hair back in a ponytail. She looked in the larger closet and found several things that looked her size. *Marylyn must have been a woman about my size. I wonder what she looked like*, she was thinking when she saw the picture on the night stand beside his bed. She moved closer and picked the picture up and saw a beautiful image. She had a soft but strong face. *I'll bet they were a good pair. I wonder if she would be competition now?* Carol selected a pair of jeans and a blouse and clean under things and was surprised how well they fit. *Oh, how will Kevin feel about this?* she thought but rushed out to the kitchen.

Kevin looked at Carol as she came into the kitchen. For a moment, he stood and looked at her. "You are beautiful, Carol," he said and a few tears could be seen in his eyes as he observed her. He opened his arms, and she came to him. He folded his arms around her without saying anything. She laid her head on his shoulder and said nothing also. It was not necessary. "Breakfast is ready, and let's eat," he said softly.

Kevin served the breakfast, and they ate a relaxed meal. "It was a long day yesterday, wasn't it?" Kevin said. "I'm sorry I wore you out, but thanks for your work. We accomplished a lot."

"Yes, it was a long day and a short night," she said and laughed. "Sorry I conked out on you. I don't know when I went to sleep except I remember lying down on the couch for just a short rest—I thought. The next thing I knew was when I woke up this morning. You should have wakened me to help."

"No, you had done enough, and I appreciate that. I think we are close to solving this mystery. Do you still think I should sign with Frank Harley? I'm not for certain that Frank is totally innocent of everything in all this mess. There is still more information needed," Kevin noted.

"Kevin, do you remember what old Rufe was saying just before he died?" Carol asked. "Remember? He was saying 'I seed him. He was heah,' and then he got sick and never recovered. Who was heah?"

"My gosh!" Kevin responded. "I'm thinking that could have been Harold Wemberly. He had told me about when Harold Wemberly left—when he disappeared and everyone was searching for him for days. Rufe said he and RC took Wemberly to the barge and left him. So he disappeared for some reason, and now, maybe he has reappeared for some reason. Why?" Kevin said.

"We have work to do," Kevin stated. I wonder if these three bankers were on that hunting trip when Wemberly disappeared. Let's go to the newspaper archives.

They were lucky and found someone working in the archives that morning. They were shown the records of the story on the disappearance of Harold Wemberly. "They could never find him," the record showed. "His pickup truck was still where he had entered the woods when they went in for the hunt. It was left there for days as they continued the hunt and even after they discontinued the hunt. After he was declared missing and assumed lost in the woods or maybe had drowned in the river, his truck disappeared. An all-points bulletin was issued, but it was never found. It was assumed to have been stolen. Among the hunters who were on the hunting trip were prominent bankers Frank Harley, Winston Kenwood, and visiting bank mogul, Shelton McKinley of Plano, Texas." The file continued on about the all-out search that failed to find him or the pickup truck.

Kevin and Carol left the newspaper office and went back to Kevin's house and sat down at the table with some fresh coffee. "Carol, I think I should accept Frank Harley's offer. What do you think?"

"I think that with your association with him, you might find more information that will help solve these mysteries. Go for it," Carol said. "I know you will be working more closely with Cheryl, but remember old Carol," she said and laughed. "She will have competition that will not give up." That constant smile was on her face.

CHAPTER

44

Kevin caught up with his appraisal work and called to speak to Frank Harley. "Good morning, Kevin." Harley's big voice boomed. "It's good to hear from you. I hope you have some good news for me," he said cheerfully.

"Mr. Harley, I want to work out something with you. Maybe we can meet for a private lunch somewhere."

"Well, how about a meeting this evening here in my office? The staff will be gone, and we'll have a chance to talk as plain and open as we want. Say…6:00 p.m. tonight, here?"

"I'll be there," Kevin replied. He sat back in his office chair and formulated a plan for his discussion with Frank Harley.

―⚏―

It was six o'clock, and Kevin walked into the bank lobby. Frank Harley was there to greet him and led him back into the bank and to his office.

"Kevin, I am so glad you have decided to come aboard. Let's get started and iron out any issues we may have. I think you know what I want you to do," Harley stated.

"One thing I want to know first," Kevin said. "Why are you ordering the appraisal for the Wemberly Warehouse property to be so high and who is the applicant?"

"That is a good question, and it's time I leveled with you on that. I am sorry to have used two of my trusted employees in this quest, but I needed their skills and appeal. Ever since you left the Central Arkansas Workers S&L, I have considered hiring you for this bank. I have posed this high value appraisal on that property to see if you could be bought. I have used Cheryl, who as you know is an attractive person to appeal to you and send my offer of the high appraisal fee, and I even used poor old Jim Hammons to see if he could drag you into working with him for that high value. Part of the scheme was to have Carol hire old Jim. I talked privately to Jim. Carol did not know about that," Harley said and smiled slightly. "You resisted. I now know you have a high integrity and have decided to bring you aboard if you would accept. Unfortunately, I have told the other two men about your value and my plans, and I think they are trying to undercut me."

"Yes, you are right. Mr. Kenwood has made a very attractive offer, and I think it would be good to be associated with him. Shelton McKinley seemed to have been determined to bring me on with him, but I have a strong sense of doubt about that man," Kevin said.

"Now, Kevin…" Harley paused a moment and looked straight at Kevin. "I will tell you now that it is almost certain that a large factory will be built on the sixty acres of the Wemberly Warehouse acreage. Shelton McKinley wants to buy all of the property. We don't know all the ownership yet. Shelton McKinley said he would handle finding the ownership and has made an offer of the amount we have asked for in the appraisal. Kenwood and I have told him to wait for the seven years to be up, and we might get the courts to help before we can close. Much depends on the final outcome of the ownership. The courts will want to determine if there are heirs involved. Kenwood and I have urged McKinley to wait, but I know he is in a hurry.

"Now, I would like more details about what you would expect from me. I know you want me to watch out for your back side and look out for your personal interests. We have not detailed what my income will be, so let's go ahead and deal with that," Kevin suggested.

"Here is a copy of the agreement I had planned to present to you if you decided to come with me. It shows that you will receive a salary of 250,000 dollars per year with insurance paid. You will be furnished a car of your choice with all expenses paid and unlimited use of the automobile. You will be furnished an office here in the main bank, and your time will be your determination.

"I am asking you to watch for unusual happening in the bank activity and for you to be aware of anything that may be a threat to me or Mrs. Harley personally. I would like for you to do discreet inspections of all the branches and recommend any improvements for me to make. You will not have the responsibility of personally supervising employees. Any questions?" he said and paused.

"Of course, the first and immediate assignment is protecting my interest in the Wemberly Warehouse property and the Gruntington's Island property."

He had handed Kevin the copy of the agreement, which he scanned quickly. "Mr. Harley, I accept these terms of employment, and I'll go ahead and sign now," Kevin said.

Harley signed the agreement and smiled big and seemed to relax as he rose from the round table and reached out to shake hands with Kevin.

"Now, I want to get to work on some things that I think are of personal interest to you. A lot has been happening lately, such as your request for the excessively high appraisal value on the Wemberly Warehouse property. Several things have happened that seem to be related to that property. I will tell you that I have gained a lot of knowledge about that property, but I still have questions to tie things together. These questions may be more personal than you want me to know about, but I must have answers if I am going to serve you best," Kevin finished. He paused for a moment and looked straight at Frank Harley.

"Okay, go ahead and pose your questions," Harley said.

"You may or may not know that someone has been attempting to gain access to records in my computer and backup files I had stored on floppy disks. They have broken into my house twice and attempted to another time. They have kidnapped your branch manager at New Home Mortgage. There are two goons that have been persistent about getting those records, and so far, they haven't been successful. I think someone has been responsible for the death of Kennon Foster and old Jim Hammons. Someone has killed an old black man on the 640-acre farm that adjoins the narrow river channel at Gruntington's Island.

"So that's why she was missing from her job recently. I thought her story was a little weak, but I trust Carol implicitly and accepted her story. Why didn't she just tell me the facts?" Harley questioned.

We were trying to develop more information before we revealed certain things to anyone, and this attempt at the overvalued appraisal was a concern to both of us," Kevin told him.

"Kevin, you have driven straight to one of the main reasons I have hired you. I'll level with you so maybe you can help me on this. I am concerned that I could be accused of murdering Harold Wemberly back in 1986. You know he never was found, and some thought he got lost in the woods, and we just couldn't find him. Some thought he may have drowned or was killed and thrown into the Arkansas River or buried deep in the forest. Of course his body was never found. There are some files that would cast suspicion toward me, but properly construed, could point suspicion to either of two other men, and I'll tell you they have been worried almost sick too. That's probably one reason they wanted to hire you," Harley stated.

"You see, there were four of us on the hunting trip," Harley continued. "We had stayed in the cabin on the north end and had gotten up early the next morning for the hunt. Each of us took his own pickup truck that morning. Harold Wemberly left out first, and the other three of us left soon afterward.

"The day before the hunt, we had signed papers to purchase half of Harold Wemberly's interest in the Wemberly Warehouse Inc. The building was almost complete and we closed the deal. Afterward, our attorney found flaws in the paperwork, and we would need to get Harold to sign the corrections. Harold had walked away with a sizable amount of cash when he disappeared. I understand he took the check and cashed it. No deposit of the funds was ever found. He probably had the money with him in his truck when he died or disappeared."

"Well, Harold didn't survive the hunt. That left half the property in the ownership of Winston Kenwood, Shelton McKinley, and me if the flawed paperwork would hold up and the other half in his heirs. We needed Harold to sign corrected papers unless he didn't show up before seven years. If he didn't show up and seven years passed, he would be declared legally dead, and the flawed papers had a better chance of being valid, but that would be questionable."

"Kevin, I am not sure what happened to Harold Wemberly, but if he were murdered for the benefit of a greater share of that property, it could mean that any or all of we three are vulnerable. I don't know whom to suspect, and frankly, I am always afraid that I am being setup for the hit at times. I have the documents that are necessary for filing to be able to exercise that change in ownership." The other two have asked for copies, but I have refused to let them have copies. They are always worried about the security of the files.

"Now, Kevin, the three of us have heard rumors that Harold Wemberly was alive and was returning to America from wherever he has been, and everyone has been worried about what is going to happen to all these properties. I think Shelton McKinley has been trying to get the upper hand on everyone. I think he has had a low level search for Wemberly going on ever since the disappearance. He is one slick person to be watched."

"All right, Mr. Harley, Carol and I have found that Harold Wemberly had quitclaimed his remaining part of the warehouse to RWR Holding LLC, which in turn has quitclaimed it to GSORWR Holding LLC. I am assuming that is Rufus W. Rudlow and the GSORWR LLC is a corporation for someone. It appears that he has deeded his remaining part to old Rufe or RWR Holding LLC," Kevin told him. "I haven't figured out the GSORWR," Kevin said.

"I'm going to delve into those courthouse papers tonight to read the terms of the quitclaim from Harold Wemberly to the RWR Holding LLC and the quitclaim deed to GSORWR LLC." Kevin said as he was walking away.

"Mr. Harley, I am looking forward to working for you. I'll probably be seeing you tomorrow."

"Very well, Kevin, remember that you can go car shopping tomorrow. You are on payroll tonight. I'll tell Mrs. Harley, and she'll be glad to hear you are going to help us," Harley said.

It was now eight o'clock. The meeting with Frank Harley had gone well and only lasted a couple hours. Of course, there will be some more meetings, Kevin knew. His car phone was ringing. It was Shelton McKinley. "You have thrown in with Frank, haven't you?" he said. "That was a mistake. You apparently don't make wise decisions." He hung up.

How did he know that? Kevin was thinking. "He is either psychic or has ears. He looked in his rearview mirror, and there he was. It was the red Ford F150 pickup truck. They are tailing me," Kevin realized. *They knew I met with Harley. What else do they know? They must be working for McKinley and informed him of my meeting. But he is going all out now and openly coming after me for some reason. The files…it must be the files.* He looked again, and there were two red Ford pickups following. He reached for the Ruger and pushed the loaded cartridge into the butt of the pistol. *They'll have a fight*, he thought. Kevin looked in the rearview mirror again, and they were gone. *What happened? Did McKinley call them off?*

CHAPTER 45

His car phone rang again, and it was Carol. "Hey, Appraiser Man. I have been trying to reach you. I am almost to your house. We need to finish that research work. I think we may have located the documents with the information we need."

"That's great, Carol," Kevin said. "I must tell you though that I have had those goons tailing me, but they have just turned off for now. I don't know what they are after at this time unless they intend to just fight their way in and get what they want. Do you have your Glock pistol with you?"

"You betcha, I do," Carol replied. I am carrying it with me all the time. I'll wait for you. Come on," she said.

The car phone rang again. It was Frank Harley this time. "Kevin, Shelton McKinley called a moment ago and said he was going to make you an offer you couldn't turn down, and he would have the edge on acquiring more percentage of the Gruntington's Island property. I told him he was too late, that you and I had just concluded a deal, and it had nothing to do with the Gruntington's Island. I don't know why he wants controlling interest so badly. We had always wanted to keep it a hunting island. Anyway, I wanted you to know," he said.

"Thank you, new boss," Kevin said and laughed. "He called me just a moment ago and told me I apparently didn't make wise decisions."

Kevin kept watch for the goons, but they never reappeared. He reached his house, and Carol was waiting at the curb. He pulled into the garage and motioned for her to pull into the other space. As soon as she was in he closed the garage door. He entered the house and shut off the alarm system, but after they both were in, he decided to reset the full system. He told Carol to help him close all the blinds and curtains in the house. "I think I want the goons to not know which room we may be in, so I'll leave the lights on in the entire house," Kevin told her. "This is looking more dangerous, and maybe you should get away from here before you get hurt."

"No way, Kevin, I'm with you, and am in it for the long haul. Let them bring it on," she said and laughed.

They pulled the papers from the records they had retrieved from the Secretary of State and found that the principal of GSORWR LLC is a grandson. "Now another mystery," Carol said.

"Kevin, guess who was in today to see about financing," Carol said. "It was Jenny Lafferty. She was asking about getting financing for the 640 acres of land that adjoins the small river channel by the Island. I asked her how much, and she said it might take $1,600,000. I thought she was mad at us, but maybe everyone else turned her down. She offered her house for additional collateral. She said it is valued at a half million dollars and is paid for. I took her application and said this would need to go to the loan committee. I didn't say anything about old Rufe and neither did she. She also alluded to the Gruntington's Island and said she was on a deal for it. I didn't indicate either way if we could possibly finance that. I want to throw that into the mix of all we are looking at."

"Perhaps the urgency for getting my files and or the Jim Hammons files was to get the identity of the principals in those corporations and any other information about them that might show who actually owned what," Kevin said. "I can see that in the Wemberly Warehouse issue and the 640 acres that old Rufe lived on. It appears that Jenny Lafferty wanted to get a clear title ready for the 640 acres. She probably had researched the records also and found the snag with old Rufe. Who killed old Rufe? He was a roadblock for the Wemberly property and the six hundred forty acres."

"Who would benefit at the Wemberly Warehouse if Old Rufe died, Kevin?" Carol asked.

"I have a little more information about the Wemberly Warehouse deal. I made a deal to go to work for Frank Harley today, and he filled me in on some things," Kevin told her. "I want to check some quitclaim deeds in our paperwork we got from the county. Let's pull the quitclaim deed from Harold Wemberly to RWR Holding LLC."

They pulled the deed, and Kevin read through it carefully. "First, I think Harold had these corporation papers made up for old Rufe, because I doubt Rufe was sophisticated enough to have this drawn up, but they appear legal. Also, the deed shows that if the principal, Rufus W. Rudlow, should precede the grantor in death, the property would revert to the grantor. That would be Harold Wemberly, but according to old Rufe, it was some mean guys who beat him up.

The quitclaim deed from Rufus W. Rudlow to his grandson has the contingency that should the grantor precede Harold Wemberly in death, the property would revert to Harold Wemberly. That was a gamble that Harold Wemberly had made," Kevin said.

"Yes, but old Rufe was still alive and Wemberly's disappearance was approaching seven years at which time he could be declared legally dead," Carol concluded.

"The same way as the land," Kevin answered. If Rufe preceded the grandson in death, it wouldn't mean much, but if he preceded Harold Wemberly in death, the property would revert to the owners of the other parts. That would be Frank Harley, Winston Kenwood, Shelton McKinley, and Harold Wemberly if he is alive. Remember? Old Rufe said I *seed* him. That must have been Harold Wemberly that he *seed*. He said *he* was *heah*. But it was *they* who told him he had to go. *They* hit him, took that Harold Wemberly shotgun, and left him for dead. So…we don't know for sure if Harold Wemberly was who he saw, and we don't know who took the body away or why the body was taken away."

The phone rang, and Kevin grabbed it quickly. Who can be calling now, he said a little impatiently. It was Frank Harley. "Kevin, your work has started already," he said. "Shelton McKinley called, and he wants to meet with Winston Kenwood and me tomorrow. He said he is in town and thinks he will have a deal for us. I would like for you to be in that meeting with us. Shelton is wily as a fox, and Winston and I have never trusted him. We have both wondered if he got rid of Harold Weaver and if we could be a target later."

"Okay. I'll be there. Just tell me when," Kevin said.

Carol had gone to Jim Hammons's files again and was reading further into them. She suddenly stopped. "Kevin, come look at this. This may shed a light on something," she said.

They read the pages of notes together. Jim had written: "A well-kept secret was that old man Gruntington, who was a white man, had an affair with old Rufe's wife years ago when she worked as a maid for him and his wife. Old man Gruntington and Rufe's wife had a daughter. She grew up to be a beautiful, young woman, and old Rufe apparently never knew but what she was his. She got through high school and went to work for First Trust Bank of Arkansas. Little known to many people, the daughter and Harold Wemberly saw each other occasionally, and she had a son by Harold. Harold had actually fallen deeply in love with that woman and was supporting her and the boy. Few knew that," Jim Hammons wrote.

"There it is. It's all coming together now. I know who old Rufe *seed* too," Kevin said excitedly.

"*Sh*..." Carol said. "I just heard a sound in the backyard." At that time, there was a sound of glass breaking and a bullet hitting the office wall near them."

"That was from a gun with a silencer," Kevin said. "Get down." They both grabbed their guns they had kept nearby. Kevin crawled over to a back room and turned the light off. He moved over to the window and eased the blind away. He could see two figures crouched about ten yards from the house. As they fired again, he fired four quick shots at the figures, and they both went down. The security alarm went off then and started blaring. It had not gone off at first, apparently because the assailant's bullets had passed above the security beam. One figure was trying to crawl away but the other lay still. Kevin opened the door and yelled toward the two men, but the one figure kept going. He scaled the fence and disappeared across the neighbor's yard.

Kevin told Carol to call the police. "We need to bring them into this now," he said. He moved into the backyard carefully with his gun trained on the figure on the ground. The figure moved slightly, but Kevin could see the gun was out of reach of the outstretched hand. "Hold it, Bud!" he said. "I think you've had enough for tonight. You don't want another bullet. He turned the man over, and it was Fred, Jocko's partner. Your partner deserted you, didn't he, Fred? Now, he'll collect all the money, and you'll go to jail. What a deal, huh? Do you want to tell me who's paying for your efforts?"

"I don't know. Jocko talks to him every day on the phone," he said. "I ain't never talked to him, but I saw him once. He's the big man, but he ain't so big though."

"Where is Jocko headed now?" Kevin asked.

"I need to go to the hospital," Fred whined.

"No, Fred, I think I'll just let you lie here and die. You don't want to cooperate. Where is Jocko going?" Kevin asked. "I think I know. Is it the island?"

"Yeah, you know it."

"Did you and Jocko kill Rufe and then steal his body?" Kevin asked.

"We knocked him in the head, but we ain't stole his body," Fred whimpered. "We ain't no body snatchers," Fred replied a little indignantly.

Kevin felt he was lying. He kept pressing. "If you didn't steal the body, who did, Fred?"

"The little big guy helped. He made us," Fred whined and then he passed out.

The police sirens were whining, and Carol was directing the police to the backyard. Kevin was kneeling by Fred and still had his pistol in his hand. "Put your hands up, mister, and drop that gun!" the policeman commanded.

"This is his house," Carol yelled at the policeman.

Kevin dropped the gun, and the policeman picked it up. "Do you have a permit for this?"

"I don't think I need a permit to have a weapon in my own home," Kevin responded.

"No, I suppose you don't," the policeman said and handed the gun back to him. "What's going on here?" another cop said. "Who's on the ground?"

"This is Fred. His cohort has left. They were using silencers on their guns and trying to shoot their way in. There is his gun on the ground. I don't think they realized that we were armed," Kevin explained. He and Carol told part of the story about some of the things that were going on. "They have been trying to steal some things from the house and this time, they seemed determined to come in regardless of the alarm system." He told them about the other times they had tried to steal some of their important files.

The ambulance came and took Fred to the hospital under police guard, and Kevin and Carol headed out of town. "I think I know where Jocko will head unless he is smarter than I think he is," Kevin said.

He called Sheriff Benefield in Pine Bluff and told him what had happened. "Jocko is wounded and may go to the cabin to hole up unless he's wounded too much. He was moving pretty good when he left."

"I'll take two deputies, and we'll try to catch them at the island," the sheriff said and hung up quickly.

"Carol, I think I know what has been going on. I think there were those who wanted those files for the information and those who wanted them to keep the information from becoming known," Kevin said.

"First, Jenny Lafferty was trying to find the information, that we just found, so she could find out who was the principal in the GSORWL LLC," Kevin said. "She would have wanted that to see who to find to get a clear title. She probably was in cahoots with Shelton McKinley who would buy the land and the part of the warehouse property. Shelton McKinney would do anything to acquire some more property that he wanted."

"And could it be that Harold Wemberly didn't want the secret out," Carol said. "He probably knew that old Jim Hammons knew about the secret interaction with Rufe's daughter from when he was setting up the original financing for the construction of the warehouse. Jim would have found that out in his research and he probably thought you would have that information too because of your consulting with Jim when some refinancing was attempted at your S& L, but why would he be coming back now?" she asked.

"He has been gone six plus years, and after seven years, he could be declared legally dead and the property transfers could take place. That could complicate any return he might be contemplating. If the grandson's mother and the boy are with him, that could really be complicated if the mother should decide to take charge," Kevin explained.

They were driving as fast toward the island cabin as they could safely go. Kevin looked quickly at Carol and marveled at her quick perception. *It's good to have her by my side*, he thought.

They arrived at the cabin as a shootout was going on. It was the sheriff and his three deputies. They had the cabin surrounded, and there was gunfire coming from the cabin. Occasionally, a shotgun burst occurred. "The Remington automatic of Harold Wemberly, I'm guessing," Kevin told Carol. "I wonder if Harold Wemberly is in there."

"Come out with your hands up now." Sheriff Benefield's voice boomed out from the loud speaker. "Throw your weapons out. You're surrounded."

Jocko stuck his arm out with a white rag in his hand. He threw the pistol out first and slowly and carefully eased out of the cabin. Suddenly, a loud boom from the Remington shotgun rang out, and Jocko fell to the ground. The deputies fired into the windows of the cabin, and the shotgun fired several shots.

"Hold your fire, men!" the sheriff ordered. Jocko was crawling over toward the side of the house, out of range of the shotgun. He had been shot twice tonight and was still able to crawl. One of the deputies reached him and picked him up and carried him to the ambulance that had just arrived. They loaded him into the ambulance, and one of the deputies left with him. That left one side not covered, but there was no window there.

"They are coming out," the man on the inside said. "Hold your fire." A woman and young boy came out and ran toward the sheriff's truck. She seemed terrified.

"Please don't kill my husband," she cried. "He's a prisoner."

"Who are you?" Benefield asked her.

"I am Caroline Rudlow Wemberly," she said. "That's Harold Wemberly inside. He is in there with Shelton McKinley.

McKinley has the shotgun. He just shot Jocko for trying to leave. He is desperate. I'm afraid he'll shoot Harold."

"This is our son, Joseph. He is ten years old. He loves his daddy." She appeared extremely frightened and was trembling all over.

Carol jumped out of the Explorer and ran to Caroline and Joseph and embraced them. "I'm so sorry," she said. "You'll be all right. Sheriff, can they go with us, and we'll help them."

"No, no, please. I don't want to go. My husband is in there, and we must get him out alive. I'm afraid of Shelton McKinley. Caroline went on talking. "Fred and Jocko told about beating up my daddy to get him to move. They left him there and came back, saying he will be moving now. They had taken his shotgun that Harold had given him. Harold was so mad that he made Shelton take the men and go get Daddy to bring him here. Harold wanted to stay with Joseph and me or he would have gone. When they came back, they said he was gone."

That's when they threw him in the Arkansas River because he was dead, Kevin thought silently. "So that explains why Shelton McKinley wanted me on his team and sworn to loyalty. He felt I would give him the documents that explained why the property was quitclaimed and maybe find Harold Wemberly."

"Harold was threatening to kill Jocko and Fred then and Shelton McKinley sent them on an errand," Caroline continued.

"That's when they came after us intending to come on us with force and get the files that McKinley wanted," Kevin said. "McKinley was bent on getting what he wanted if it even took killing. All these deaths! What an evil man."

"Shelton McKinley told Harold and me he had listed this property with Jenny Lafferty," Caroline continued. "She had told him where the information was that would explain the quitclaim deeds."

How did Jenny Lafferty have information to send her on the chase about the quitclaim deeds? Kevin wondered. *I think she must have* been trying to undercut McKinley when she was trying to borrow the money at the mortgage company to buy the land.

They knew they should get Caroline and her son away from the gunfire for safety, and they finally convinced her to go with them for the boy's safety. They took Caroline and her son, Joseph, to Carol's house, and Kevin went on home.

CHAPTER 46

Kevin walked into his house, and Frank Harley was calling. "Good evening, Kevin. I heard on the news that there was a shootout going on at the island tonight. Have you heard anything?"

"Yes, Mr. Harley, I think all hell has broken loose out there. We have just returned and brought Harold Wemberly's wife and son back with us. They are at Carol's house."

"Well, of all the surprises of the century!" Harley exclaimed. "Then Harold is alive! I would never have believed it. We all thought he was dead long ago. Frankly, Kevin, I'll tell you now. We all thought that someone in our group had killed Harold. I was afraid that there would be another of us killed at some point by whoever killed Harold. He had taken a fortune from each of us in the high stakes poker game, and I suppose each had wondered if one of us had killed him for that huge amount of cash. Also the agreements we had drawn up was thought to provide for transfer of Harold's share to the survivors of the group if he were to die by natural causes. Harold Wemberly's death was thought to be by accident. If he drowned in the river, that would place his death an accident. The determination had not yet been made, and they had not yet been able to declare him legally dead because there was no body. After seven years, some thought the declaration of death would be considered of natural causes.

"The night before he disappeared," Harley said, "there was a big poker party with the four of us at the cabin. That one was a very high stake party. Harold turned out to be a better gambler than all of us. He wound up cleaning the table and took us for 80,000. He had all that plus another 50,000 that he had gotten from McKinley when he almost went broke and sold McKinley part of his share of the Wemberly Warehouse project. But he was never available for signing the documents and closing the deal formerly. So, Kevin." Farley boomed and laughed real big. "He left there with at least 130,000 dollars cash in his pocket plus whatever he had when he came to the party."

"When Wemberly disappeared, McKinley decided, after the long search, that Harold had gone to Jamaica, because he and his ex-wife would travel down there sometimes. He sent men down there to search. McKinley really didn't want the share of the warehouse project at that time and wanted Harold to buy it back. His men came back without any clues, and McKinley finally decided Harold was dead," Harley said.

"The handwritten bill of sale has been kept in my vault room ever since," Harley continued. "Harold still owns 25 percent after what he sold McKinley. Now McKinley owns that 25 percent he bought from Harold that night, and Winston Kenwood's bank and my bank own 25 percent each by virtue of nonpayment of the loan Harold had taken with our banks. It's pretty complicated now.

"McKinley has been trying to get control of my bank and Winston's bank for several years. We won't let him have any more than what he already has. He managed to get 20 percent stock in my bank and 30 percent in Winston Kenwood's First Trust Bank of Arkansas by some manipulation. He is a pretty sharp cookie and power hungry. I have kept that bill of sale from Harold Wemberly in my vault room to hold McKinley off from some of his efforts. Kevin…this is one reason I need you to help me hold off McKinley in some of his maneuvers. He knows banking rules well and tries various things to grab control of banks and S&Ls," Frank Harley confided.

"Very well, Mr. Harley, I'll do my best to protect you. I am going back to the island to see what happens there. When I left, it was a standoff with Wemberly and McKinley still in that cabin and at least one loaded Remington automatic shotgun in KcKinley's hands, according to his wife."

—⚒—

Kevin drove onto the island and saw the sheriff's and deputies' pickup trucks still there. The sheriff was at the front, and Kevin eased up to them and stopped. Sheriff Benefield told him the two men were still in the cabin. "We have been trying to get them to come out peacefully, and they haven't given in yet. You might be surprised what the issue is now," the sheriff said. One of them states the other has him as a prisoner. The other one states *he* is the prisoner. I don't know who is who, but we are trying to resolve this without anyone else getting hurt. One of them has the shotgun and has already shot one person. You were here then. He was taken to the hospital in Blytheville."

Benefield called out again with the bullhorn for them to come out peacefully. Suddenly, the shotgun was thrown out, and McKinley yelled that they were coming out. He came out with his hands held high. "Don't shoot!" he shouted with his gravelly voice. "He has let me go. Don't shoot! He may still be armed," he said. "He has been holding me prisoner. He killed Jocko," McKinley said. "Watch him. He's a killer."

Harold Wemberly came out then with his hands high in the air. "He's lying, Sheriff. I haven't killed anyone. He's had the shotgun all the while, and he's the one who shot his own man for trying to get out of this cabin. If you handle that shotgun well, you'll find his fingerprints on it and none of mine. Although it was formerly mine, I haven't touched it for nearly seven years. His men have taken that shotgun from old Rufe Rudlow. I'm afraid they have done away with him."

"Sheriff, don't believe this man. He is a liar and will twist the facts. You'll see!" McKinley stated.

"All right, cuff them men and take them in. We'll sort this out after we get them in jail," the sheriff said.

"You can't put me in jail," McKinley said. "I'm Shelton McKinley of Texas, one of the largest bankers in Texas. I have never been arrested. I'll have my lawyers get in contact with you. There is no need to arrest me," McKinley stated emphatically.

"Your lawyers can see you at the jail," Sheriff said. We're taking you in on suspicion of murder—both of you."

McKinley kept grumbling as they handcuffed him. Kevin kept silent but marveled as the exceedingly wealthy man was subdued and arrested like a common criminal.

On the other hand, Harold Wemberly was quiet and went along without much to say.

Kevin told the sheriff what Caroline had said about McKinley and the two thugs. She said McKinley was calling the shots and giving them their orders.

"I think we can get to the bottom of this fairly quick, especially if Jocko is alive. He seemed to be able to get along all right when he rounded the corner of that house," Sheriff Benefield stated. "I want you to be available, and we'll be in touch."

CHAPTER

47

Texas Mogul Arrested! the newspaper headlines stated. The article went on to tell about the shootout that had occurred on Gruntington's Island, and how when it was stopped, Shelton McKinley, well-known Texas financier and property owner in Texas and some property in Arkansas, was arrested and being held on a variety of charges including possible murder.

> Also arrested was longtime missing Harold Wemberly of Little Rock. Wemberly became missing in 1986 after a hunting trip to Gruntington's Island with Shelton McKinley and other notable persons from Little Rock. Well-known bankers, Winston Kenwood and Frank Harley, were along on the trip when Wemberly became missing and a weeklong search failed to find him. It was not known at this writing where he had been. Some rumors were Mexico, some included Brazil, Central America, the Caribbean, and other countries of South America. Harold Wemberly was quoted as saying he had been a prisoner of Shelton McKinley's before and during the shootout with Sheriff Benefield and his deputies. McKinley claimed to have been the prisoner.
>
> Sheriff Benefield stated there was possible evidence to be confirmed that would clarify the prisoner issue and tell who was doing the shooting. Also taken prisoner was Jocko

Condreau who was wounded in the shootout and is now in the local hospital and under arrest with charges of murder. Arrested in Little Rock last evening after an attempted robbery and attempted murder was Whiskers Fred Walker who along with Jocko Landreau had attempted to shoot their way into the home of Kevin Henry, a Little Rock real estate appraiser. Henry shot back at the assailants, wounding Fred Walker who was arrested when police arrived and was taken to the hospital where he was guarded by police. It was stated Jocko Condreau was also wounded at that event, but escaped, to be captured at Gruntington's Island. He was wounded again as he tried to exit the cabin where Wemberly and McKinley remained inside.

Little Rock Police stated that Carol Fleichman, manager of a North Little Rock mortgage company, was at the residence with Kevin Henry doing file research when the assailants attacked, purportedly to take wanted files. Neither Henry nor Fleichman were injured.

A surprise was revealed at last night's startling event and the return of Harold Wemberly. With him was his wife, Caroline, and their son, Joseph. Some may remember Caroline Rudlow, a former employee at First Trust Bank of Arkansas. She and her son disappeared quietly soon after the disappearance of Harold Wemberly, but no connection was made at that time. The whereabouts of her and her son were not known at this writing.

Caroline Wemberly had returned home after years of absence from her father to find that he had just been killed and the body had disappeared. Sheriff Benefield had just discovered the body yesterday, which had been disposed of in the Arkansas River. It had floated down to a bluff at the Gruntington's Island.

—⚬⚬⚬—

Frank Harley called to tell Kevin that he and Winston Kenwood were going to Pine Bluff to see if they could help Harold Wemberly. He said they may need Caroline to testify to the prosecuting attorney about who was holding the gun when she left the cabin. Carol had been told by Frank Harley to take some time to help Caroline and Joseph until things could settle down.

All radio and television stations were milking the story for all it was worth. They had sent crews to the cabin to film it and the area. They found the bluff where it had been said that old Rufe was found. They didn't know yet that Harold Wemberly's pickup was at the bottom of the deep hole in that bend of the river. "Someday, we want to have divers go down and look for the truck," Kevin told Carol on the phone that next day after the shootout.

The phone rang in Kevin's office, and James Carpenter was on. "Kevin, what on earth has been going on? Are you okay over there?" he asked from his place in Oklahoma.

"James, we have been the point of attack for files pertaining to the Wemberly Warehouse. It appears that those two thugs had been hired by Shelton McKinley to get files that I had and also from old Jim Hammons. Jim was killed during their effort to get the files from him. They were going to kill me if it took that to get them a couple nights ago. Fortunately, we were ready," Kevin told James.

"Now, James, it appears that you were involved somehow in leading them to me and New Home Mortgage Company. We think they killed Kennon Foster during their effort to get the files from him. Jim Hammons had files from research he had done about the Wemberly Warehouse years ago. They wanted those files. They couldn't find them there because old Jim had loaned them to me a couple nights before. Then they started at my house with break-ins while I was with you. James, I thought you were my friend," Kevin complained. "How could you do that? Why?"

"Oh man! Kevin!" James gasped and paused. "I *am* your friend, but it does appear I have been inadvertently guilty of helping someone steer those guys to you and the other places. Oh migosh! I think I know how that came about. Please let me tell you. On one of my trips over there, I ran into Jenny Lafferty who said she was trying to find the owner of that 640-acre farm that is adjacent to Gruntington's Island. I told her you had worked on the Wemberly Warehouse loan application once, and it also involved the farmland and the island. I told her she might ask you and someone at New Home Mortgage Company. I told her old Jim Hammons had worked on that after we turned it down. She was supposed to ask someone. I had told her once that I was meeting you for dinner and she could join us and maybe you could help her," James said.

"Yes...that makes sense," Kevin said. "I think I can see what happened. She hated my guts over a low appraisal and would never ask me," Kevin declared. She wanted that information to hand over to Shelton McKinley. She must have had some kind of deal working with him. It must have been Shelton McKinley who sent his thugs to get those files by whatever method it took. They even kidnapped Carol Fleichman once to get me to ransom her with the floppy disks. Jenny must have told McKinley that old Rufe's living on that land would be a problem in getting it ready to sell or transfer. They tried to run him off, wound up killing him, and ultimately throwing him into the Arkansas River. I hope Jenny is proud of her part," Kevin said.

Two weeks later.

SHOOTOUT GUNNER ALLEGED TO BE SHELTON MCKINLEY, the headline of the morning paper read. "The fingerprints, on the shotgun used in the shootout and the attempt to kill Jocko Condreau, are alleged to be those of Shelton McKinley. He has been charged with a variety of things including murder and attempted murder, in an attempt to acquire land in Jefferson County. Jocko is recovering from his wounds in Jefferson County Health Center. He has agreed to testify against McKinley. An unofficial source stated Jocko tags Shelton McKinley as the one who hired Fred and him. Fred Walker is in the hospital in Little Rock and has confessed, saying he and Jocko Condreau were involved in the events when Kennon Foster and Jim Hammons were found dead and in the beating of Rufus Rudlow who was later found dead in the Arkansas River" the news article continued.

A separate article stated that well-known real estate agent Jenny Lafferty's name has surfaced in the parties involved. She did not respond to attempts to reach her. Other deaths suspected to be involved in this case are those of Rufus Rudlow, who lived on the land near the island in Jefferson County, the death of Kennon Foster in Little Rock and the death of appraiser, Jim Hammons in North Little Rock. A full investigation into the affairs of Shelton McKinley has been launched by state officials including banking regulators and by federal authorities.

Harold Wemberly has been released from custody and has joined his wife, Caroline and son, Joseph. Authorities have asked Wemberly to not disappear anymore until they straighten out this mess. A full investigation into the affairs of Shelton McKinley has been launched by federal authorities."

Kevin finished reading the articles in the newspaper and called Carol Fleichman. "Would you reserve your time for a date with me at six o'clock this evening? I have reservations at a different place this time and would like for you to share them with me."

"You mean...a real date, Kevin?" Carol said and he could hear that smile in her voice. "Yes, Appraiser Man, I would be delighted. See you at six," she said.

Kevin picked her up at her house and they drove back to Little Rock and out to Chenal Valley. He turned into the Harley's Estate and straight to the back where a Gazebo was set for eight people. He parked near the Gazebo and walked toward it as other people started coming toward them. "Is this a party?" Carol asked him. She looked over to Cheryl Inmon who was walking toward them with her arm in the arm of James Carpenter. Carol looked at Kevin, who smiled and nodded his head affirmatively. Also coming to join them was Frank Harley and his wife, Penny, and then behind them came Winston Kenwood and his wife, Margaret.

They were seated at appointed seats and served the standing rib roast and the trimmings. The chitchat followed the recent case of the Wemberly Warehouse files until Frank Harley rose and called attention. "My friends, I wanted to take this time with my close friends to announce the addition to our ranks of Kevin Henry as vice president in charge of special assignments.

Winston Kenwood rose then and clinked on his glass a couple times. "Friends of the two banks, I want to announce a new employment to you of someone you all know. I want to announce that James Carpenter is moving back to Little Rock and will be coming to work with First Trust Bank of Arkansas as vice president in charge of mortgage lending."

The usual applause followed, and Harley said, "Kevin, the floor is now yours."

Kevin rose and asked Carol if she would stand. "This lady has worked with me through some dangerous and harrowing but rewarding experiences. She has been a lifesaver for me and a vital helper in working through this Wemberly Warehouse case. I have grown to love her dearly. Carol, I have decided I am a very lucky person and don't want that luck to run out." He knelt to one knee and was looking up at her as he pulled a small black velvet box from his pocket. "Will you be my wife and the mother of my children?" he asked.